too good to be true

too good to be true

PRAJAKTA KOLI

HARPER FICTION

An Imprint of HarperCollins *Publishers*

First published in India by Harper Fiction 2024
An imprint of HarperCollins *Publishers* India
4th Floor, Tower A, Building No. 10, DLF Cyber City,
DLF Phase II, Gurugram, Haryana – 122002
www.harpercollins.co.in

2 4 6 8 10 9 7 5 3

Copyright © Prajakta Koli 2024

P-ISBN: 978-93-6569-339-3
E-ISBN: 978-93-6569-204-4

This is a work of fiction and all characters and incidents described in this book are the product of the author's imagination. Any resemblance to actual persons, living or dead, is entirely coincidental.

Prajakta Koli asserts the moral right
to be identified as the author of this work.

All rights reserved. No part of this publication may be reproduced, stored in a retrieval system, or transmitted, in any form or by any means, electronic, mechanical, photocopying, recording or otherwise, without the prior permission of the publishers.

Typeset in 11/15 Adobe Caslon Pro at
HarperCollins *Publishers* India

Printed and bound at
Thomson Press (India) Ltd

MIX
Paper | Supporting
responsible forestry
FSC® C010615

This book is produced from independently certified FSC® paper
to ensure responsible forest management.

To the imaginary people in my head who dragged me through every chapter. Next time, write it yourselves.

*I hope this book sets the romantic bar in your life so high that
everyone you meet brings a ladder to the first date.
Don't settle for less, cutie.
Love you.
Enjoy :)*

27 MARCH 2023

AVANI

So, I met this guy.

It's been an interesting Monday.

At 7.30 a.m., when I shuddered awake to the doorbell and sleep-walked to the door, I should have known that Raghu Kaka, our milkman, would have forgotten to leave the milk packet in the basket I'd suspended from the top of the door and left it on the floor instead. Again. And that our neighbour Mhatre Kaka's cat would have torn into the packet and licked the milk sloppily off the floor. AGAIN.

Clearly Shanta Tai was running late, or it was usually her shrill '*Didi, uth jaoooo*' sharp at 7.20 a.m. that worked as my morning alarm.

I slammed the door shut and headed into the shower. Slightly refreshed, I made chai (black, just like I hate it), decided to have breakfast at work, snatched up my book from the bedside table and tote off the wardrobe knob, and dashed out the door.

Traffic was crazier than usual as I flagged down a reluctant taxi. An unexpected off-season shower the night before had turned the city to mush and citizens were now left to deal with it. I loved how surprised and underprepared Mumbai always was for the rains. It was like, every year when the first rain clouds threw their dark shadows over the terrain, the government responded with, 'Waterlogging? Oh, but that *never* happens here. Let's decide on MAP (Monsoon Action Plan) 10000.0.' This was followed by lousy attempts to remedy the situation by digging the city inside out and hastily filling it back, only so that the rainwater could find new ways to clog it up good and proper the next time around. Every year the city struggled with floods, potholes and waterlogging, and yet we romanticized the first rains the following year like nothing better ever existed.

I don't know if you can tell, but I've never been a fan of the rains. Especially untimely ones, the ones I don't have the chance to mentally prepare for—or have my gumboots ready for. *Deep breaths, Avani. Everything gets better when you get to your favourite place in the whole world. The bookstore.* I paid the taxi driver and stepped out.

I remember Rhea laughing in my face when, a little over a year ago, I'd offered to work at the billing counter at her family's age-old bookstore, gloriously named Bombay Bound, in the heart of south Mumbai. Part-time, I'd told her, before my classes began at uni in the afternoons.

'You're studying to be a lawyer, Ani. You already don't have a life. Why would you want to spend five hours every day selling books and counting cash when you could do literally anything else in that time? Or *anyone* else. Go have a life. Be free,' she'd said, waving her hands around in front of my face in her usual animated self.

But I'd fallen in love with the bookstore and the building that housed it from the day I walked in for the first time. It was like walking into 1903 (that's when it was constructed, as its founding stone claimed). Rhea's family had bought it right after Independence, but had not changed much about it since. It wasn't very big or very vintage-y in the fancy south Bombay way of things. If you ask me, it was humble and had a beautiful personality—which is more than I can say about a lot of people I know.

The bookstore was my safe space. I loved every bit of it. It had a rattly metal gate that opened on to a small veranda facing the street. One could leave a drenched umbrella there or wait for a cab if it was too sunny outside. A wooden twin door served as the entrance to the store. The wall on the left served as a gift shop of sorts. It had everything you'd get in a gift shop but hung on the wall on tiny pinheads—keychains, pens, stickers and other knick-knacks. My workstation was on the right, at the billing counter, directly opposite the gift-shop wall, and could be accessed through a swinging wooden door. I loved how perfectly placed the counter was. It had a view of almost every aisle in the store, it was right next to a window that opened out to the street outside and was just four steps away from the store's café, where Martin made the world's best cappuccinos.

I got to the bookstore just in time to greet a regular customer, Meera Aunty, who'd been bingeing on romance novels ever since I had nagged her into picking up her first one about a year ago. Twenty-three books later, Meera Aunty was the perfect companion to discuss all my favourite romance-novel tropes with. As she saw me, she told me in her sing-song voice how she hadn't thought she'd like the alpha-male billionaire in the book we were both reading, but in the end had succumbed to his charms, and there was no going back now. We chatted for a few minutes while I printed out the bill for her, and then packed the sequel neatly in a paper bag and handed it to her.

Most Mondays at the store were slow, which suited me fine. I caught up on my e-mails and assignments, worked out a schedule for the rest of the week and made my way to the café to grab a coffee and a croissant. Martin was surprisingly chirpy that day about the freshly baked eclairs (not a morning person, he's not), but I stuck to my demand for a croissant, just to piss him off.

Martin had moved to the city from Goa a couple of years ago and landed a job at the bookstore when Rhea had put out an inquiry on the store's Instagram page about wanting to start a small café there. He came for his first meeting dressed in a muscle tee and harem pants, with a box full of the flakiest croissants he'd baked as his résumé, and regaled Rhea with stories about his training as a pastry chef and his dreams of becoming a bartender someday. About ten minutes into the conversation, Rhea had decided he was it. Just as well, since the other two applicants didn't show up.

After lord knows how many croissants, Martin and I had become tight. I loved walking into work and seeing his scowling face every morning.

This morning, though, along with his 'perfectly baked eclairs'–induced effusiveness, it was clear he wanted to thrill me with details of his extravagant weekend adventures. But the enemies in the book I was reading were just about to become lovers and, as much as I found Martin's stories entertaining, I decided I wanted to be loyal to my book boyfriend instead. So I picked up my coffee and walked back to my desk after minimal chatter.

Apart from Meera Aunty, who had left, the store hadn't seen a single customer yet. Clearly this Monday was crawling at a snail's pace for everyone. I picked up my book, pencil ready in my hand to highlight my favourite lines as I read. Aaji—my grandmother—hated it when I did that in her books. She called it vandalism. That's one of the reasons I needed a job in the first place, so I could buy my own books to vandalize. What better luck than to land one at a bookstore?

I lost track of time as I followed the lives of the enemies-turned-lovers in the book, and next I looked at my watch, it was past 2 p.m. Almost time for Rhea to arrive. She'd been driving me to uni for my classes, and although she insisted she was doing it to practise her driving, I knew she really just wanted to meet Dhruv, my classmate—quite the cutie. Dhruv, too, pretended to forget her name every time she left after dropping me, but that look in his eyes when he saw her—yup, I knew that one. A full year, and he still hadn't mustered up the courage to ask Rhea out, and I knew she was waiting for him to do just that. But I got free rides to uni, so I had no complaints.

I was about to walk over to Martin for another coffee when the quaint bell hung at the entrance dinged. Someone had entered the store.

Now, when I tell you to sit down for this, sit your ass down. When I tell you that I'm about to describe to you what could literally be a page out of a book titled 'Avani's Wet Dreams about Hot Boys', shut your mouth and listen. Pay. Attention.

He was tall, about 6'2 or 6'3. Not sure—I'm not a ruler—but tall enough for me to know that if I hugged him, I could listen to his heartbeat. He wore a navy blue suit. The kind men on the covers of spicy romance novels wear. Not a crease to be seen—crisp, clean and tailored to fit his broad shoulders and long legs. He wore leather shoes that didn't have a speck of dust on them. My first thought: Did he get airdropped into the store? Because, I'm sorry, you can't be living in Mumbai and be walking in from the street with no dust on your shoes. But I digress ...

As he walked towards the aisles and started browsing the Non-Fiction section, my eyes panned up to his face. His hair was dark and styled neatly away from his face, and he had a slight stubble along his cheeks and chin. He couldn't have brown eyes, could he, because if he did, I would have to surgically cut my heart out, pack it in a red box and hand it to him. But there it was.

Brown, like the cover of my favourite leather-bound notebook. Brown, like the colour of that singular dusty ray of light coming in through the top window just touching his hair and shining on to the floor. Brown, like the wooden shelves and floors of the bookstore. Brown, like the coffee in the mug I was holding. Brown, like the sand on Chowpatty at twilight. Brown, like the colour of my skin.

I stared for an alarmingly long time, waiting. What was I waiting for? I should look away before he ...

Fuck. Before I could avert my eyes, he did the one thing that I knew was going to be the death of me. He locked eyes with me and smiled, and—you've got to be kidding—DIMPLES.

And then I did what every girl would when a hot guy looked at her and smiled. I ducked. I ducked like I had something to hide. I ducked like I was in a water-balloon fight with him on Holi. I ducked like if he so much as looked in my direction I would self-combust into a heap of Avani ashes. It took me a minute to tell myself: *Hello, you're twenty-three, almost a lawyer and you WORK at the bookstore. If there's anyone who has a reason to be there, it's you!*

I slowly stood back up. Thankfully he was browsing the opposite aisle, with his back to me. I straightened my kurta, quickly rubbed on some lip balm (my lips were chapped—no other reason whatsoever), slowly settled into my seat and went back to reading my book. From the corner of my eye, I tracked every step he took until he disappeared somewhere near the Self-Help aisle, one of the only places I couldn't see from my seat at the billing counter. Minutes ticked by. After reading the same line eight times, I finally moved to the next one. And caught a whiff of aftershave. I looked up to see God's favourite child looking straight at me, holding out a book.

'Hey, how much is this one?'

'I'm fine, thank you. How are you?'

Silence.

Wow, Avani.

Blood throbbed in my ears. I was the captain of my college moot court group. I'd won every elocution competition since I was ten. I'd toured the world and represented my school and country at international debating championships. Hell, I was also the only student in the history of Vasant Vihar

High School to have spoken back to Mistry Sir, who was the strictest, most impossible teacher any student had ever had. And this ... *this* ... was when my brain decided to glitch?

I cleared my throat and put on a brave face. 'Sorry. I misheard you. That'll be 599. Would you like to donate a rupee for our girl education project?'

'Sure.'

'Please fill in your details at our customer register so you get a Gratitude Discount Coupon for your next purchase.'

'Sure.'

'Interesting choice, I have to say. Do you like cars?' I said as I looked up to give him his change, but ... The doorbell dinged and he was gone. He'd left. Without the change for the 2,000-rupee note he'd given me. I hurried to the door to see if I could catch him, but he had vanished.

I walked back to the counter, my head in a whirl.

Rude. Didn't even say bye.

You're not friends, Avani.

Yeah, but still. Greetings are courteous.

Why do you care?

I don't care.

You have a crush.

Balls.

You're thinking about him.

Yuck.

You can't stop thinking about his eyes.

Oh, what do you know? You're just a stupid voice in my head.

Do you think he'll come back to take his change?

Bye.

4 APRIL 2023

AVANI

What should I wear?

I've been alive for over twenty-three years now. Let's say that till I was about five, Mamma decided the clothes I wore. Most days, after school, I stayed home with my books, so till I was sixteen I was mainly in my school uniform, or in shorts and a T-shirt. Weekends were for tennis and swimming, so I would be in tracksuits and swimming gear. All through high school and undergrad law school, I was in the I-don't-care-how-I-look-I-am-more-than-my-looks phase, which, in hindsight, wasn't the greatest stand to take, because … umm … in all the group photos from college I look like a homeless child that my friends had adopted and sponsored.

The point is, I never once cared about what I wore to any place. Ever. Not once.

Why then, since the past one week, had I had just one thought: *Where's my black chikankari kurta?*

There are two things you should know about my black chikankari kurta:

1. It's the most expensive piece of clothing I own. I gifted it to myself when I took a trip to Lucknow with Aaji last year. Rs 3,499 for a kurta? That's worth

at least ten books, if not more. But it was totally worth every penny because …
2. Nobody, I repeat, NOBODY, looks hotter than Avani in her Black Chikankari Kurta.

A week had passed since Rude Hot Guy had walked into the bookstore and changed the face of every romance-novel hero I had ever imagined. Every day of this past week I'd tried searching for my Black Chikankari Kurta and failed. Today, I'd decided, I was going to look for it one last time and then let it go. Because I wasn't the girl who dressed up for hot strangers who might or might not walk into the bookstore I worked in. I wasn't the girl who spent a week hoping that said hot stranger would take time out of his obviously busy life to return for the change to their purchase. And I definitely *wasn't* the girl who spent twenty-five minutes in front of the mirror, unable to decide which shade of lipstick to wear.

I looked one last time in the customary places, hoping the Black Chikankari Kurta would magically appear in one of them, and gave up. I reached for my oversized Guns N' Roses tee, leggings and trusted Kolhapuri slippers, swung my tote bag over my shoulder, grabbed my water bottle and locked the door behind me as I stepped out. Since I didn't have classes to attend that day, I'd promised Rhea I'd stay a couple of extra hours at the bookstore while she went with Dhruv to look for which new car to buy. Lol.

I got to the bookstore just in time to get a cup of coffee with Rhea before she left for her date.

'It's not a date, Ani!' she yelled over her shoulder as she walked out. 'And don't forget to tally the stocklist.'

I groaned. Inventory was my least favourite part of this job. (Yes, I know I am studying to be a lawyer. Shut up.) I leafed lazily through the pages of the inventory register for a few minutes until the lines and numbers blurred into nothingness. I slapped it shut and threw it inside the drawer for next-week Avani to deal with, and headed over to two giggling young girls huddled over a book in the Romance aisle. It was H.D. Carlton's latest dark romance. Needless to say, I'd already read it and knew exactly what the pair was giggling about. I smiled and started talking to them about other romance books that might be a bit more suited to young reading. The girls seemed bewildered but warmed up to my suggestions after a bit. This must have gone on for about half an hour when I heard the doorbell ding. A familiar whiff of aftershave hit me.

'Hello …' the voice called out.

I ducked.

Again?! WTF! He can't even see you from where he's standing! But the girls now staring at you sure can.

'Is anyone at the counter?'

Stand back up. Words. Use your words.

'Excuse me? Is anyone …'

'She'll be right with you, sir,' I heard Martin's voice. 'Sorry, she's a little shy and awkward. Avani! Someone is looking for youuuuu …'

Fucking Martin. Remind me to buy eclairs from the neighbouring bakery tomorrow and tell him they were better than his.

Use. Legs. Walk. Now.

'Sorry, I was at the back. Didn't hear you. Hi!' I said cheerily. Maybe a little too cheerily.

Why were the words coming out all squeaky?

'Hi.' He was smiling.

'How can I help you?'

'I'm looking for a present for my niece.'

'Oh, how sweet. How old is she?'

'She's about to be four and already loves books. I'm worried that when she grows up, she's going to turn into a nerd who works at a bookstore or something.'

Wow. This man is suddenly five per cent less hot.

'I mean ... not like that's a bad thing ...' His face changed. He cleared his throat.

Was he nervous? I forced a smile and directed him to the Children's section.

'Lemme know if you need help.'

I walked back to the register. What an ass. Speaking of ... No, I hadn't checked him out. Broad shoulders. Sharp nose. Clean shave this time, no stubble. Whatever. I don't mind being The Nerd Who Works at a Bookstore. That's going to be the title of my autobiography, where a certain hot man mysteriously trips and falls and breaks his perfect nose in chapter twelve.

It was his tone. He had said it like it was a joke. Like it wasn't enough. Not good enough anyway, because you can't wear expensive suits and shoes and fancy watches to go to work at a bookstore.

I took my seat at the counter, opened the drawer and took out the inventory register. Might as well ruin my mood all the way since it was already halfway there.

A few minutes later, I caught a whiff of his aftershave again.

'Do you like rock music?' Rude Hot Guy was making small talk as he stood at the counter with the books he'd picked up.

'You don't have to make small talk to cover up the opinion you've already formed of me. I'm a nerd who works at a bookstore. There obviously can't be more to me than just that. And that will be 1,499 total. You can add an extra picture book on my behalf. Happy birthday to your niece.'

'That's not what I meant. You're—'

'Is that all?' I cut him off mid-sentence.

'Er ... I'm sorry. I didn't mean to be rude.'

He waited for me to respond.

I glared at him.

'I just like your—'

'Here's your change. Unless you want to walk away without collecting it this time too.'

Mid-sentence again. Boom. And I didn't stop there. I left the change on the counter and walked to the café.

Fuck inventory, I raged within. *And I'm so glad I didn't waste my Black Chikankari Kurta on this guy. He barely even deserved the Guns N' Roses tee ...*

Oh ... My tee ... That's what ...

'Don't worry, I won't tell anyone.' I jumped as Martin leaned over the coffee counter and whispered conspiratorially into my ear.

'Tell anyone what, Martin?' I asked sharply.

'That you're working very hard to make sure the store makes zero sales and people never come back.'

'Shut up. He's bought books both times he's walked in.'

'I see we're tracking someone's visits. Have a li'l crush on the hot suited guy, do we?'

'Nonsense.' I looked around the store, but Rude Hot Guy had left. I turned towards Martin and said, 'I'm just hoping he comes back so I can apologize to him for being an ass today.'

'My, my … Look at Avani feeling remorse for snapping. You're mean to me all the time, bitch.'

'Takes one to know one.'

Rarely did Martin laugh the way he did just then. The foundation of our friendship was built on uninhibitedly roasting each other—and I wouldn't have it any other way. I spoilt him with Shanta Tai's famous puran polis and he spoilt me with the world's best croissants and cappuccinos. If I was being honest, everything baked and roasted and brewed by Martin was the best in the world. And snapping—that was my love language for *my* people. The people I loved.

As to why I was skulking around the store wrapped in my Guns N' Roses tee and guilt? Because I might not be the friendliest face in most rooms, but I generally wasn't mean to people I didn't know either. Especially to customers.

Now, how was I to find this guy and apologize to him? Was it that big a deal? Why did I even care?

7 APRIL 2023

AVANI

My professor broke her hip bone.

Now I know it's sad, but hear me out. Being a law student was tough and tedious, and as much as I loved it, I didn't like it as much on some days. I had swum through my bachelor's degree in law like a fish in the calmest pond. Easy. But my post-graduation dreams sometimes got me feeling like I was in a seafood restaurant's live fish tank. You know, the one everyone stares at before choosing the creature they want on their plate, cooked in butter garlic sauce? Exposed, nervous, strangely naked and constantly in fear of being picked up and put in boiling water.

Which is why when I woke up this morning and found our uni group chat had been renamed 'Ipsita broke her Hipsita', I chuckled, apologized to the universe for my instinctive response to our Intellectual Property professor's distress and then rejoiced at the thought that there would be no classes *and* that it was a Friday.

I loved Fridays at the bookstore. They were the designated days for a book club meet in the evenings and, though it almost always got cancelled every week, most of our regulars stopped by. The store buzzed with familiar faces and new ones.

The café did great business from Friday through the weekend because we got many young college couples looking for a quiet corner to meet in. On these days, Martin brought out his big guns. Eclairs, croissants, home-made mustard and ham sandwiches, and Friday faloodas. The whole show. And then, once we downed the shutters, there commenced a secret happy hour that nobody knew about. Not even Rhea's dad. Martin transitioned from baker to bartender and served up delicious cocktails named 'Bloody Mary Poppins' and 'Rudyard Tripling'. Maya, our friend who joined us at the bookstore whenever she got a break from her design studio, usually spent the Friday happy hour with us, and we rung the weekend in with music, crappy dancing and several drunken rounds of Cards against Humanity, the Hogwarts pack.

Utterly content at being gifted an extra free day, I decided to sleep in and get to work a little late that day. I took a longer shower, finished reading the novel I'd picked up earlier in the week, fantasized a little about the hero and called for breakfast from Anna's tapri downstairs. Shanta Tai and I worked on my compost pit and spent some time gardening and bitching about her sister-in-law. I'd never met her, but by the end of the conversation I was positive I hated her. And after *all* of this, I still had thirty minutes before I left for the bookstore. The store was a twenty-minute walk but a thirty-minute taxi ride from home. If that isn't Mumbai traffic in a nutshell, I don't know what is.

A happy morning came to a standstill when I found myself lounging on my balcony swing chair with Instagram open on my phone and my finger hovering over the search bar.

Hmm. How do you stalk people when you don't know their name? Hadn't my phone heard me talking to him? Why hadn't it suggested his Instagram account to me yet? Where was that creepy feature when you needed it?

Why are you trying to find him on Instagram, Avani?

I ... I want to apologize.

An Instagram apology? That's just lousy.

So should I apologize in person?

Yes. That way you get to sniff ... umm ... meet him again.

Isn't that too much?

I mean, you could invite him to tonight's happy hour at the bookstore.

I don't know his name, remember? How do I find him?

I have two words for you. CUSTOMER. REGISTER.

I hate how I make a convincing argument. I should be a lawyer.

About an hour later, I walked into the bookstore with a spring in my step and the voice in my head screaming, '*Stalker!*'

Martin sat at the billing counter while Rhea animatedly chatted with him with a croissant in her hand.

'No crumbs on the counter, friends!' I yelled.

'Mom's here!' they yelled back in unison.

I went over to hug Rhea and paused when I noticed that she was wearing make-up.

'Looks like we're *accidentally* going to run into Dhruv at the happy hour later tonight.' I puckered up my lips and kissed the air dramatically as Rhea made a face.

I threw my bag over the counter and headed to the coffee machine for a cappuccino. Martin was usually very strict about anyone touching the machine, but on Fridays he let us make our own coffees.

I was waiting for the mug to fill when …

'Hi.'

DON'T DUCK.

I turned around like I'd heard someone cock a gun behind my back. Slow and careful, taking in every inch of the café as my eyes panned across it to finally lock into a pair of gorgeous brown ones. Blue shirt, casual blazer and trousers, spotless shoes and a leather laptop case in one hand.

'Oh, hey! It's you. Who's the poor customer?' he said.

'Excuse me?'

'Whose coffee did you just poison?'

I pursed my lips to hide a smile. So did he.

Hi, dimples.

'I'm Avani.' I held out my hand.

He took it. 'Hi, Avani.'

Strong handshake. Long fingers. Warm hands. Soft palm. Skins touching. Still didn't have a name …

'So you're a barista too?' he asked.

'No. I just handle the billing counter. But I'll get Martin for you. You can place your order with him.' I felt a strange warmth on my cheeks.

'Martin!' I yelled, louder than I needed to, startling myself and cracking my voice a little.

Martin dragged himself over like his feet were chained to concrete blocks. After a hundred years, when he finally completed his long journey of five steps and arrived at the café counter, he stood playing eyeball tennis between Rude Hot Guy (I really need a name here) and me.

I cleared my throat and broke the silence.

'So, coffee? What name should Martin write on your cup?'

Look at you being James Bond, Avani.

'We're not Starbucks. Calm down. And there is literally no other customer at the café.'

And look at Martin being annoying.

I turned to give Martin the most sinister I-will-remember-that smile, made a mental note to step on his new white Converse shoes the first chance I got and started walking towards my seat at the billing counter.

'Aman.'

I stopped and turned. Again, slowly. *What's with the theatrics?*

'Sorry?'

'I'm Aman.' He smiled.

'Aman …'

'Aman Raina.'

'Nice to meet you, Aman Raina. See you around.' I smiled, showing more teeth than I have in my mouth, turned around and continued walking.

Aman Raina.

Let the stalking begin.

AMAN

I'm an idiot.

Did I have to go to the bookstore three times in two weeks? No.

Did I have to try to be funny and piss her off? No.

Did I have a four-year-old niece who loved books? No.

Did I have to bunk my weekly evaluation meeting by faking a headache so I could sit in this café pretending to work? No.

But here I was. At 1 p.m. on a Friday afternoon. If any of my friends had spotted me sitting in that corner by myself sipping coffee, I'd have a lot of explaining to do.

Sometime over these past two weeks, my life seemed to have changed. I was driving down the street when I saw her walk into the bookstore close to my apartment. White kurta, blue jeans, silver jhumkas. She had a round face, bushy brows and brown hair that swung across her back every time she jerked her head to get the rogue strands out of her face. She had smiled at someone as she had stepped into the bookstore, and it was the most gorgeous smile I'd seen on any woman in a long time.

The fact that I remembered, or even noticed, these little things after just a glimpse of her baffled me. Most of my days were filled with looking at tailored suits and computer screens, sitting in boardrooms and attending formal lunches. Only the occasional birthday celebration or human resources' team-building offsite trips exposed me to colours beyond grey and navy blue. Don't get me wrong, I love my job. I've spent most of the thirty-one years of my life watching my father build and run a successful textile business, and from the time I was ten—or eight, I forget—I've wanted nothing more than to grow into his shoes and have a corner office like his. Well, I am there now. Not bragging. I was raised to be proud of anything my hard work produced and I've been taught never to forget that.

I had turned up at office every day at 10 a.m. sharp since I had turned eighteen. I'd been Papa's intern for the first year and then his third assistant for three years. On multiple occasions my parents had sat me down to ask if I wanted to explore something else—another workplace, a different career. They had told me repeatedly that I didn't have to get into the family business if I didn't want to. And as much as I appreciated being given the choice, I never once thought of doing anything else with my life. I grew up watching my parents love each day of building the company with dignity and pride, and I honestly couldn't wait to take on that responsibility.

When Papa turned fifty-five a year ago, he decided to take voluntary retirement and move with Ma to our home in Mussoorie. Since then, I'd loved every day of being CEO of Raina Textiles. In fact, I would've said I had been quite content with my life until just a few days ago, when I'd first seen Avani.

I always had things to do, places to be, people to meet. And when I didn't, I stayed home. But not over the past two weeks.

Now sitting in the bookstore with my second cup of coffee and laptop open to a random office e-mail, the clock's hands seemed to be crawling and I couldn't help but notice that Avani hadn't moved in about an hour. She was sitting on a stool by the window near the billing counter and had her back to me. She seemed glued to her phone. I wondered whether I should walk over and initiate a conversation, or continue to pretend-type and wait for her to look in my direction …

'So, you like?' The guy from the café, Martin, asked me from across the coffee counter. He must have seen me stealing glances in her direction over the past several minutes.

'Excuse me?' I feigned surprise.

'The coffee. You like? I roast the beans myself, every day.'

'It's great. Thanks.' I gave him a thumbs-up and went back to looking intently at my laptop.

'Your office is in the neighbourhood, no?'

I looked up to see him watching me curiously.

'I googled you. It's not every day that we have a billionaire CEO stopping by for coffee, and, ah, views.' He didn't look in Avani's direction, but his shoulders panned towards her, while his eyes stayed on me.

'I was looking for some quiet close to office. Financial year end. I work better in silence. And the views aren't unhelpful.' I grinned.

A hint of a smile touched his face and he nodded faintly. 'Can I get you anything else?'

'I'll take two more coffees.'

Martin raised his eyebrows and tilted his head in a knowing manner. 'Coming right up, boss.'

I had a high-pressure job. Everyone around me was always waiting for me to falter so they could throw my father's struggles in my face. Nepotism was a touchy topic with most people these days. I got up every day and brought my point to bear at every table I sat at. I'd stood up to people twice my age without batting an eyelid. I was relentless when it came to business. And yet, the idea of having a cup of coffee with a girl was making my chest tighter. This was new.

I shut my laptop, pocketed my phone, picked up the two mugs of coffee Martin set down on the table and made my way to the window by the billing counter. Avani must have sensed me approaching in whatever voodoo-telepathic way that women know and sense things, because she put her phone down on the windowsill and turned to face me.

'Hey.'

'Hi.' She smiled and looked at the extra mug in my hand. 'Martin didn't tell me he had a new waiter.'

I chuckled and placed the mug on the windowsill. 'Yes, I start today. He's offered to pay me in unlimited eclairs and the chance to share one coffee with any employee of my choice. Given he's busy, you were my next best option.'

'Oh, I don't have to be,' she said, and before I could ask her what she meant, she yelled in the direction of the café, 'Shambhu Kaka!'

I turned to see a man in a grey kurta and white pants walking out of the pantry behind the café, nodding gravely in her direction.

'*Sir tumchya sathi coffee gheun aale aahet. Ya. Basaa.*' Sir has got some coffee for you. Come, sit.

She gave me a fake smile, mischief brimming in her eyes, picked up her phone and her book, and skipped towards the coffee counter, looking back only when she got to the table I was seated at. She pulled out the chair I'd slid into place, sat down and called out to Martin.

'Martin, I'll have what he's having.' She bit her bottom lip to hide a smile as she seemed to turn her attention to the book.

This girl was going to be the death of me.

AVANI

This guy is fucking perfect.

It took a couple of minutes for my heartbeat to return to normal after I left Aman standing at the window with Shambhu Kaka while I took his seat at the café.

When did you become the female model in a men's deodorant commercial, Avani? Since when do your eyes involuntarily shut halfway and your head tilt backwards at the scent of a man's aftershave? Thank god you had your back to him.

I stole a peek in his direction and saw him standing with Shambhu Kaka, his face slightly turned away from me. His eyes caught the afternoon light and were now a lighter brown, and his dark brown hair shone in loose waves. Friday hair, a little more casual than the first time he'd walked in.

How did I know these details without looking at him directly, you ask? Well, the bookstore was filled with mirrors. Great for making a small space open up and just as useful for staring at hot strangers whom you could later stalk on Instagram. Speaking of Instagram, the man played a strong engagement game for someone with only thirty-odd posts on his feed.

Let's see what we've got to know so far ...

He was the CEO of a family-owned textile company. He travelled often to Mussoorie, where his parents lived with six adorable dogs, and he had a regular social life. A couple of photos with three other guys about his age, seemingly on some sort of vacation. There were also two girls who seemed consistently present in his party and vacation pictures. They weren't related to him. I'd checked. No signs of a romantic involvement with either of them, although one of the girls had commented 'cutie' on every photo; the other had a private profile.

The rest of his page was pretty regular. Exotic vacation pictures (in some of which he was shirtless and which I might or might not have scrolled past slightly slower than the other posts), smart formal pictures of handshakes with important-looking people. And sunsets.

I was about to click on his LinkedIn profile next when I heard loud laughter from the direction of the window and looked up to see Aman and Shambhu Kaka throwing their heads back, guffawing over something while they sipped on their coffees. Now, I'd worked at the bookstore for almost a year, cracked innumerable jokes and *not once* had I got this reaction from Shambhu Kaka. Martin and I turned to each other in sync and mouthed 'wow' in tandem, eyebrows raised. Shambhu Kaka could single-handedly bring gloom to any room by simply walking into it. Don't get me wrong, he was sweet, but lord knows the man was as dull as a hairpin. We'd hardly ever heard him speak a word, let alone laugh out loud. Most days we didn't even know if he'd come in to work until we found the books brushed dust-free and our lunchboxes cleaned spotless and drying upside down on the pantry counter.

What was so funny, I felt like asking out loud. Care to share with the class?

'There's something about that seat, it seems.' Martin had walked up to me and was now sitting on the chair opposite mine.

'Huh?'

'Whoever sits there,' he said, pointing to the chair I was sitting on, 'keeps staring in the direction of the window.' His smile told me I would soon be bombarded with questions I wouldn't have answers to.

'Was he staring at me?'

'Don't act like you don't know. I saw you looking at him through the mirror, you creep!'

Right. It was silly trying to hide anything from Martin. Maya, Rhea and I might be BFFs, but Martin got me in ways the girls didn't. There was something that tied us together in situations such as this one, where he saw right through me.

'You have to see his Instagram,' I said in a hushed tone, pushing my phone towards him. 'This guy is fucking perfect. Textbook son, dog lover, successful, social, hot in a suit, hot in swimming trunks, hot in a T-shirt, hot without a T-shirt.' I whispered the last two lines almost out of breath. Why was it so hot in here?

Martin snatched up my phone and scrolled through the profile while I kept an eye on Aman to make sure he couldn't see what we were huddling over.

I had almost forgotten I was at work with all this teenage fun time I was allowing myself to have, when Meera Aunty walked in.

'Who are you?' she demanded when she spotted Aman, who had moved to the billing counter by now, reading the back cover of a book I had left on the counter. 'This is Avani's seat ... although you do look immensely better than she does on that stool. So I won't complain. You can call me Meera.'

Classic Meera Aunty.

'Hi, Meera,' I heard him saying. 'I should've taken this seat much earlier today if I'd known you would walk through that door. You have a very beautiful smile. All the women I've met lately scowl at most things I say.'

Idiot.

Shambhu Kaka nodded in greeting at Meera Aunty, took the empty coffee mugs and walked past me into the pantry. *Traitor. I'll deal with you later.*

I walked up to the counter and smiled at Meera Aunty as she wiggled her brows at me and walked away to the Romance section.

I turned to Aman. 'Could I get my seat back, Aman? We don't usually let customers go behind the counter, so playtime's over. Some of us have jobs.'

'Of course.' He threw his hands up in submission and hopped off the stool. The swing door that gave us access to the counter was narrow and allowed only one person at a time to pass through. Aman waited for me to go in before he sidled past me on tiptoe. His arms brushed against my hips as he took one slow step after another until he was out. I felt the hair on my arms stand up.

He turned to me and winked as he walked over to the café. He winked. The guy *winked*. At *me*. My stomach flipped and my cheeks turned hot as a sudden urge to duck and crawl under the counter arose from deep within. Thankfully, my limbs protested and instead of the habitual duck, I stood there looking at him like a doe caught in the headlights. Then, before my brain and heart could form a well-discussed way forward, my tongue went rogue and blurted out, 'Do you like happy hours?'

He looked at me as he reached the table he'd left his laptop on. 'I just had a happy hour and I don't hate it.'

'No …' I shook my head, unable to stop chuckling. 'Do you like cocktails? We have happy hour here at the bookstore later this evening … if you're interested.'

'I don't drink.'

Of course he didn't. This guy was the template that got lost when God did Her laundry without checking the pockets. Hence, the one and only piece.

'Oh. Never mind, then. See you soon.' I forced a smile.

'What time?'

'Sorry?'

'What time is "soon"? 8 p.m.?'

'You said you didn't drink.'

'I'm fun even without any alcohol in me.'

I'm sure you're more fun with alcohol in ME.

'We'll see about that,' I said as I made a show of getting busy with the cash register.

'We will. See you at 8.' He packed up his laptop, paid and walked out the door without looking back.

'See you,' I whispered as the door closed behind him. Then, finally, after what felt like hours, I breathed.

Who *was* this guy and what in the name of god was happening here?

Did I tell you Martin is freakishly strong?

Yeah, Martin is freakishly strong.

He simply walked over to me, scooped me up from behind the billing counter, carried me over to the café counter and set me down on it.

'Talk, bitch.'

I know God has a sense of humour, because just then, like clockwork, the doorbell dinged and in came Rhea. 'About what?' she asked, taking off her jacket and skipping over to the interrogation zone.

Fuck my life.

'About Avani's new hot rod.' Martin has a way with words, as you would have noticed.

I opened my mouth to protest, but no words came out.

'Boy toy?'

I cringed.

'Man muffin? Dick stick?'

'Eww ... shut up!' Rhea and I whined together.

'*You* shut up! I saw you undressing him with your eyes. Now spill,' Martin said.

'You are SO extra.' I ignored Rhea's dancing eyebrows and drawn-out 'Ooooooh, Avaneeee' and continued in a monotone. 'There was no undressing. He's sweet. And I was feeling bad about snapping at him the other day, so I invited him to our happy hour. I'll buy him a drink and say sorry and that'll be it. Let's not overreact here. And let's please behave ourselves when he gets here in hopefully four hours and thirty ... three minutes.' I glanced at the antique clock that hung on the gift shop wall.

Silence. I could feel Rhea muffling a snigger. My ears felt hot again.

'Okay, fine,' Martin said after a few beats, bobbing his head gently. 'Won't say a word. I agree, actually. Let's not overreact. I like that you're keeping it all under control by counting every minute down since he left, by the way. Good plan.' He disappeared into the pantry.

Jerk.

Meera Aunty emerged from somewhere near the Romance aisle with a telling smile. 'Okay, kids. I have to be off ... have a taash party to go to. Enjoy your raging hormones!' she said, giving me a mischievous look. She had obviously heard our entire conversation.

'Enjoy your trash party, Meera!' Martin called out.

She rolled her eyes at Martin's words, hugged me goodbye and walked out of the bookstore.

I used this welcome distraction to get off the coffee counter and was walking to the billing area when I was yanked back like a coat on a hanger and dragged off to the staff bathroom.

'So? What did I miss?' Rhea asked with a twinkle in her eye. The kind of twinkle a child has in a candy store, a parent has at the gates of a daycare centre when they are dropping their kids off for the day—or the kind a crackhead has at a music festival.

I took my time replying, acutely aware that I had to choose my words carefully. Why? Because this was Rhea, the group leader of 'Romantics Anonymous'. Everything was a sign for her. Everything was dreamy. She would see this situation as so much more than it actually was and I wasn't ready for that. I wasn't ready to be told that the universe had sent Aman to be exactly where he should be so our paths would cross.

'Maybe the universe sent him—'

'NO.' I cut her off. 'Rhea. No. Please don't read more into the situation than needed. I would like to believe that the universe has more important things to take care of than making Aman appear out of the blue in my life. Like world peace or whatever else the girls on beauty-pageant stages talk about. Hell, I'll be pissed off if the universe had *anything* to do with this, because I've been praying for my skin to clear up for way too long now, and if this got prioritized over that, I'm done with writing my morning affirmations. It's just one drink and an apology. I don't want you to freak out about this, okay?'

'Mm-hmm.'

It must have seemed like a ramble to her, because for the first time in forever Rhea replied with a nod. No counter argument, no alternative explanation, no looking for the silver lining … nothing. Just a nod. She hugged me, kissed me on my cheek and walked out. I looked at myself in the mirror, told myself to get it together and followed her out.

It was still only around 4 p.m., which meant I had four whole hours to get my heart to beat normally and my armpits to stop sweating. Martin was busy at the café with two new customers who had walked in and Shambhu Kaka was hovering gravely around the two tables of college kids working on some project who had ordered nothing more than a coffee close to ninety minutes ago.

I walked over to the Bestsellers section. I'd been meaning to buy Dhruv a present for his birthday (which I'd missed three months ago). I knew he loved murder mysteries. Since I had no clue about what was hot among the mass murderers' fan clubs, I figured the Bestsellers section would be my best bet. After a brief confusion between an anthology of serial-killer stories and a contract killer's journal, I picked the journal. I mean, at least the killer in this one was guaranteed to have a great self-help routine going if he was journalling, right?

The next forty minutes were spent in wrapping up the book in purple crepe paper, decorating it with white ribbons and writing out an elaborate note wishing him the best for the year to come. I wasn't even that close to Dhruv. I hung out with him because, one, he was the only student in class who could talk about things other than law, and two, because Rhea had become so immensely interested in him.

Gift wrapped, accounts tallied, book finished, work schedule for the next week sorted, hair brushed, lip and cheek stain fixed, perfume heavily sprayed ... and I still had time to kill before the clock struck 8. Why were the clock's hands moving so slowly? Was it never going to be 8 p.m.?

AMAN

She's something else.

I don't remember the last time I walked on the streets of this city that I love so much.

Growing up, Papa would take Gagan, my elder brother, and me on walks along Marine Drive every weekend. He bought us cotton candy and pizza at the pizzeria by the sea. Every Saturday, when we left the house, Ma would warn us not to eat while we were out, and when we came home we'd lie to her about the pizza and settle in for a second dinner. It was the perfect crime—or so we thought. Once Gagan flew off to London for college when he turned seventeen—I was fourteen then—I slowly got busy with friends over the weekends and the walks were reduced to just framed photographs of the three of us on my nightstand.

Until today.

I knew I would reach home from the bookstore in about seven minutes if I took the car. But a walk sounded right today. I needed a few minutes to myself to play back in my mind every second I'd spent breathing the same air as

Avani. I wanted to hit pause every time she smiled to reveal the faintest dimples right below the curve of her lips, every time she tucked her hair behind her ear to buy a second to think about what she wanted to say next, every time she bit her lip to hide a smile when she knew I was looking at her, every time she rolled her neck back to stretch and revealed a mole near her left earlobe and every time she looked in my direction with those big, beautiful eyes.

I laughed a little when I caught sight of myself in the reflective door of a store I walked past. I'd never seen that smile on my face. Shy and slightly wonky. Like I was thinking about something I didn't want anyone to know about. Which was true.

I picked up the pace. As much as I was enjoying this lazy walk, I also had to get some important work out of the way before the happy hour at the bookstore. Martin was right when he had said my office was in the neighbourhood, but he didn't know that my home was also just a couple of minutes away.

Soon I was waiting for the private elevator in the lobby of our building. I entered and smiled at the liftman who'd worked for us for the past nine years. My parents had bought and renovated this building a few years back and it had been our home ever since. And now that Ma and Papa were in Mussoorie and Gagan was working in London, the top three floors were all mine.

I nodded at the liftman as I exited the elevator and stepped into the lobby that led to my penthouse apartment, taking my jacket off and placing it on the marble console table in the entryway of my living room. My phone hadn't stopped buzzing since I had left office earlier that morning. I needed to get to it before I could leave for the bookstore again. I took my laptop and walked into my home office. The next few hours zoomed by on endless calls and e-mails.

And the next time I checked my watch it was forty minutes past 8 p.m.

Goddammit.

AVANI

Veins porn.

Nobody is an hour late to a party unless it has to do with:
1. Being (or trying to be) fashionable.
2. Mumbai traffic. (In Aman's case this would be an unacceptable excuse, since he lived and worked somewhere in the neighbourhood. I stalked him, so I know. No reason for judgement here, please.)
3. Another party. (He didn't want to leave it to come to a humble bookstore happy hour with nine people and limited alcohol, which is irrelevant because he doesn't drink.)

'Maybe his date is late,' Martin drawled. I flipped him the finger and rolled my eyes.

'Why are you getting so worked up, Ani?' Rhea said. 'It's not even a date. You can just text him your apology. Or DM him on Instagram. You've stalked him already.'

Martin and Rhea high-fived on that.

I rolled my eyes. Who even high-fives any more? It's not 2002.

I walked over to the makeshift bar to join Maya, pausing on the way to steal a glance at the road outside to see if I could catch sight of Aman. What if he saw the 'Closed' sign outside the main entrance and thought he'd been pranked? Should have told him the secret party had a back-door entry, right? Right.

Maya was sitting on a stool, looking at her phone. She was the least dramatic among the present company. Especially in matters of the head and heart. She had started her design studio all on her own when she was just nineteen and was now considered one of the city's top graphic designers. She spent her days being the boss bitch at her studio and her nights being a recluse, tucked away in her swanky four-bedroom apartment on Carter Road, painting canvases that sold like hot cakes at high-profile exhibitions. She was the wise elder in our little group of three strange women. The first time I'd met her at a pottery class I was struggling to get my clay to not wobble off the wheel. She was sitting next to me, already having finished moulding two plates and one pot, and offered to help. She didn't speak much but there was something so warm and calming about her that I found myself wanting to spend more time by her side. By the end of the class we had exchanged Instagram handles. And now, a year later, Maya was not just a close friend, but also one of my biggest inspirations.

'He'll come if he wants to,' she said in her calm voice without looking up from her phone. 'Stop acting like he's the first guy you've ever seen.'

'I'm not,' I snapped. 'I came over to spend time with you.'

Her eyes met mine as she picked up her drink and squeezed my arm. 'Desperate is a horrible look on you, Ani. You're gorgeous. Now finish your cocktail and say that to yourself.' She slipped her elbow through mine. We downed our Pina Colabas (Martin really needs to name his cocktails as well as he makes them) and had just begun to raise our empty glasses to each other when a familiar scent hit me in the face like a saucepan.

Aftershave. I turned on cue.

There he was. Looking different from when I had seen him earlier in the day. His hair was wet, which meant he had just showered, which meant he had come from home, so ten points. He'd shaved for tonight, which counts as effort, so another ten points. And he wasn't dressed in his usual suit and tie. Instead, he had on impeccable dark blue jeans that hugged everything the way they deserved to be hugged, a pair of black Vans sneakers and … wait for it … a black button-down shirt that fitted him like it was stitched after he had worn it. It had floppy collars that fell neatly on each side; the fabric stretched across his broad shoulders and slid down his biceps, wrinkling ever so slightly when his arms moved.

He located Martin first and shook hands with him. He'd casually folded the sleeves right above his elbow, showing just enough forearm for me to let out a quick breath before allowing my eyes to track the veins on the back of his palm when he lifted his hand to lightly touch his collar. But my gaze automatically stopped en route at the slit of his shirt on his chest where the second button lay casually open, revealing rogue strands of hair.

Aren't we easy? What does it take, really? Just some forearm and chest hair? Spicy.

'Ani!' Maya interrupted the distinctly illegal turn my thoughts had begun to take. 'Go on!'

She nudged me in his direction and then pulled me back by my shirt sleeve to say, 'Behave, okay? Be nice.'

AMAN

Avani and her Virgin.

'Look who's finally here! We weren't worried at all that you'd ditched us!' Martin yelled over the music when he caught my eye.

I laughed. 'Looks like I'm late,' I said, walking over to the coffee bar, which had transformed into a regular bar for the happy hour and at which Martin was mixing cocktails.

'It's a bookstore happy hour, dude. All you missed were painfully nerdy discussions about these bookworms' favourite editions. What can I get you?'

'How about a watch?' I heard a familiar voice say, and turned.

There she was.

'Hey,' I said.

'You're late.' She tilted her head to one side.

'I know. I apologize, sincerely. Got caught up with work and lost track of time. Let me make it up to you. What are you drinking?'

'Oh, we don't get to decide what we drink here,' she said, taking a step towards me. 'Fridays are for Martin to practise his cocktail-making skills. And we are his guinea pigs. The menu tonight has his newest concoction. The Pina Colaba.'

'What!' I laughed, shaking my head.

As I leaned in to give her a hug, she stood on tiptoe and said softly into my ear, 'You must try one. And feel free to leave whatever tip you think appropriate if you like it. We're saving up for Martin's bartending school.'

I nodded and called out to Martin, 'I'll have two Pina Colabas. One without alcohol, please.'

I scanned the room as we waited for Martin to make our drinks. There were two girls and a guy standing at the other end of the billing counter, who I assumed were friends of Avani's, because they were checking me out in a way only a girl's closest friends can. Like they knew about me. Had Avani asked them to size me up and share their opinions about me later? I smiled and waved to them. One of the girls turned away immediately, like she'd been caught stealing, and the other waved back. The guy didn't do either. He just stood there staring in no particular direction. Looked like Martin had made his drink slightly stronger than everyone else's.

'Here we go. One Pina Colaba for Avani and one for her Virgin,' Martin announced.

She swatted his arm and I pursed my lips to hide a smile.

'I mean a virgin Pina Colaba for Aman. Enjoy!' Martin chimed and walked away towards the group at the billing counter.

I took the two glasses and dropped two 2,000-rupee notes into the tip jar. 'Cheers!' I said as I clinked my glass with hers and took a sip.

'You like?' she asked.

'I love,' I replied.

She paused, then looked up at me. 'Listen,' she said, 'I wanted to apologize. For the other day.'

'What day?' The music seemed to have been turned up and I found myself practically shouting into her ear.

'What?' she said loudly, leaning towards me.

'What day?' I repeated.

'The day I snapped at you.'

'You snapped at me?'

We were now bellowing at each other.

'Yeah, when you asked me about my favourite rock band.'

'Oh ... That's okay. I deserved it. That nerd comment wasn't very nice either.'

'I'm sorry!' she yelled.

'I'm sorry too!' I yelled back.

'IT'S OKAY. THANKS FOR COMING TODAY.'

Whoever had plugged their phone into the boxy speakers of the store really needed to calm it down.

'WHAT?'
'THANKS FOR COMING!'
'ONLY YOU COULD MAKE ME COME—'

Someone chose that very moment to turn down the music. And I froze.

Martin stopped mixing drinks.

The group at the billing counter stopped talking.

All eyes turned to me.

From the corner of my eye I saw Avani staring straight ahead in stunned silence.

Goddammit.

'I meant ... I had no plans of stepping out this weekend, but I couldn't not come and see you tonight,' I managed to blurt out. 'That's how I was planning to end that sentence,' I added to the room at large.

Avani seemed to relax. She batted her eyelids at me dramatically, a smile dancing on the corner of her lips, and waited for me to say something more.

'My my. Look at you kids taking this conversation to third base. Very hot.' Martin broke the silence. '*Come*, Aman,' he said, stressing on the word for effect. 'You should meet the rest of the gang.'

Avani picked up her drink and started walking away, but stopped mid-step, turned around to look at me and said, 'I can't make you come if you don't move when I move, you know.'

I laughed and followed her.

She really was something else.

AVANI

The glaciers are melting.

'It's getting late. I'm going to make a move. Are you staying?'

It was annoying how time had seemed to crawl when I was waiting for Aman to get to the party, but now it seemed to be zooming by.

He smirked. 'Are you asking me to come home with you, Avani?'

'What? No, that's not what I meant.'

'Pity. I wish you had.'

I swatted his arm and hopped off the bar stool. I picked up my tote from behind the counter and turned to realize he was on his feet too. He looked even taller now that we were both standing, or was I just a little bittle tipsy?

'Are you staying?' I asked him again.

'Nope. I'm walking you home.'

'My home is a twenty-minute walk from here,' I said.

'Perfect.'

'You don't have to …'

'I know.'

'I-I'm sure you have an early day at work tomorrow.' I could hear my voice sounding as awkward as I felt.

'I do.'

'Then you should go home.'

'I can't, sorry.'

'Why not?'

'Because I'm walking you home. If you'd like me to, that is.'

I bit my lip and nodded.

He smiled. 'Well, shall we?' He waited for me to start walking towards the back door.

It was a little after midnight, so it wasn't completely quiet and deserted, but it wasn't buzzing with activity either. A few cars and pedestrians passed by occasionally.

We walked side by side in silence for a while. Every few metres he slowed down to match my pace, and I picked up mine to match his whenever I felt the warmth of his company moving away from me.

After a while, he broke the silence. 'I feel like one of us should start talking about the stars.'

I chuckled, but looked up at him and asked innocently, 'Why?'

'Because that's what they do in movies in such situations. They talk about the stars.'

'I don't see any stars,' I said as I looked up at the sky. 'We can talk about the pollution, though.'

'Or the depleting ozone layer.'

'Or the melting of the glaciers.'

'Or the importance of waste segregation to reduce carbon.'

'Ooh, dirty talk this early in the relationship? I'm a lady, Aman.' I shook my head, grinning, and looked away.

He let slip a light laugh. It was a half laugh, more like just a hum, but I could feel goosebumps on my arm.

We didn't speak for the rest of the stretch. No asking about each other's lives, what we did when we were not working, where we liked to hang out, what our favourite food was.

None of it. Every now and then his hand would brush against mine, or I would feel his breath on my hair when we accidently came closer to each other while walking, when he looked at me thinking I wouldn't notice. Beyond that, it was silence.

It surprised me that not a single second of that silence felt awkward. I didn't once feel the need to say something inconsequential to make conversation, not one stupid joke pushed past my lips to fill in any gap. Strangely, I felt calm, comfortable. I drew in a long breath to fill my lungs, maybe for the first time in years.

When we reached the gate of my apartment complex, he asked, 'May I call you?'

I took a step towards the gate, then turned around to face him. 'Yes, you may.' I looked into his gorgeous brown eyes, not wanting to move away even an inch more. I could just station myself there for the night and take a nap while I stood before him. Like a horse.

Nap like a horse, you mean. Not stare like a horse. Because horses nap standing up ...

Oh, just shut up. Let me enjoy this.

'Maybe I will,' he said, tilting his chin down slightly.

'Maybe I'll pick up when you do,' I said, grinning. Not trusting myself to stand there any longer while those brown eyes bore into mine, I turned and started walking towards the building.

'You didn't give me a number,' he called out after me.

'I know.' I paused, half-turning towards him. He was standing at the gate looking as gorgeous as anyone possibly could in that black button-down shirt.

He shrugged and waved. 'Goodnight.'

'Goodnight.' I entered the elevator with a broad smile on my face.

I know you're cute, Aman Raina. But if you want my number, you're going to have to do a lot better than simply ask for it.

―

8 APRIL 2023

AMAN

How soon was too soon?

I woke up to my phone ringing on the nightstand. Every Saturday, 8.30 a.m. Like clockwork. My weekend catch-up call with Ma.

'Did we wake you up?' I heard Ma's voice on the other end of the line.

'You say that every Saturday, Ma. And then you call me at exactly the same time the next week. Yes, of course you woke me up.' I smiled into my pillow.

'Okay, good. Now that you're up, talk to me. What are your plans for the weekend?'

I sat up in bed with the phone to my ear, propped up the pillow against the headboard and leaned back. The city, with no regard for the weekend, was already up and running. I could faintly hear cars honking, and soft music and chatter from the terrace café next to my apartment building. Sunlight filtered into my room through the sheer curtains Ma had so thoughtfully picked out for the French windows, the plants on the balcony soaked in the day and my mind wandered to the previous evening.

'Ma, I met someone ...'

I guess this is where I tell you a bit about my parents. Ayesha and Anil Raina met when they were first-year postgrad students in business school in Mumbai in 1986. Ma had just got her law degree and Papa had finished his degree in commerce and administration. They fell in love over the first few months of spending time together as friends and project partners, and got married in their mid-twenties, right out of business school. When Ma got through a course in London to specialize in company law, Papa went with her. Gagan was born there that very year and when he was two years old our parents returned to Bombay and set up Raina Textiles. They started in Papa's elder brother's garage and together grew the business to what it is today. A huge, framed photograph of the first makeshift office set up around a few rugged desks and chairs, with Gagan sitting in Papa's chair and a six-month-old me in Ma's lap, was displayed in the lobby of our apartment. I used to be embarrassed by that picture through my teens but had grown to be very proud of our journey.

My parents had raised Gagan and me to be what we wanted to be. Gagan had chosen to work in London for a luxury retail brand and I had never wanted anything other than to be like Papa. And now I was in the city all by myself while my parents grew organic vegetables in the hills for fun.

I missed living with them. When all my friends were getting their own places I never gave the idea a second thought. And it wasn't like I was looking for a pad to indulge in nefarious activities—I don't engage in any. The occasional sneaking in of a female friend or two in the penthouse had been easy enough. And more often than not I would wake up to my parents having breakfast with said female friends. So you see how I never felt the need to move out.

My parents had been with me through every rough day, every heartbreak and every roadblock I had faced growing up, and slowly but surely, my parent-son relationship with them had changed to one of friendship. And it remained the same now, even though they were not in the same city any longer. And so, when I saw Ma's name flashing on my phone this morning, I knew I had to tell her about Avani.

'Hold on,' she said. 'Anil! Come here now!'

I smiled sleepily. Of course she had to.

I heard Papa enter the room and come to the phone, which was probably kept on their coffee table on speaker mode. It was an audio call, but I was pretty sure they were crouching over the phone like Gagan and I used to over our transistor when we would secretly listen to cricket commentary in our bedroom during exam week.

'Say again, beta, what you were saying,' Ma said encouragingly.

'I met someone. It's not a big deal. I've only—'

'Oh, good. You finally met the guy for a quotation? Send it to me before you confirm anything. These cleaning services loot you when you give them work in bulk.'

That was my father for you.

'Anil!' came my mother's stern voice. 'Let him finish!'

'What? What did I say? Wait, Aman, have you hired them already?'

'Anil!'

'That's okay, beta. We trust your decision. If you think they—'

'Beta, we'll call you right back,' Ma said, exasperated, and hung up.

I closed my eyes and chuckled to myself. I unplugged the phone from the charger and made my way to the kitchen, one floor down.

None of our home staff worked on Saturdays, so it was just my morning coffee and me. As I put a pot on to brew, my phone vibrated on the kitchen counter. I put it on loudspeaker.

'Who is she? Have we met her before? Do we know her? Do you have a picture?' Ma's pitch was getting higher with every question she breathlessly posed.

I rubbed the back of my head and smiled at the phone.

'Her name's Avani and she works at a bookstore close by. That's all I know about her right now. But I just wanted to tell you that I met her,' I said.

'Okay ...' Ma sounded unconvinced. A short pause later, she said, 'Wear your black shirt when you go to meet her next, okay? You look very handsome in it.'

I laughed. 'Yes, okay, Ma. I'll do that. Got to go now. Breakfast, and then I have some errands to run. Love you. Have fun.'

'Love you, beta. Take care,' she sang as she hung up.

I didn't have much planned for the day other than the one assignment that had been on my mind since the previous night. I needed to get Avani's number, and I had to do it without looking like a complete creep.

The one great thing about being the CEO of a company was I couldn't remember the last time I'd had to look someone up. I had inherited from my father the super-efficient Sheryl (or should I say she inherited me, since she was a hundred years young and had known me since I was a child), who could dig people out of the woodwork if need be, should I even mention I wished to talk to them. As tempted as I was to call Sheryl, because I knew she would get me Avani's number, e-mail and Aadhaar card number in less than fifteen minutes, I kind of liked the challenge of getting hold of it myself.

My first stop, naturally, was Instagram. But after twenty minutes of typing and scrolling and searching, I came to the conclusion that Avani wasn't on Instagram—not as 'Avani', at least. Googling didn't help either, because it wasn't 2010 and, presumably, Avani didn't have a history of crime or publicity stunts. I thought of looking for Martin or Rhea or Maya, or even Bombay Bound, and getting through to Avani via them, but something told me that would be way too easy. So I did what every mature man would—I sat on the couch and sulked with my espresso in hand.

What was it about my time with her last evening that made me want to question everything I'd ever felt for anyone before this?

There was something about the way she looked at me. Like she wanted me to know what she wanted me to do, but then immediately changed her mind about it. Like last evening, I knew for certain that she wanted me to ask her out, but she'd refused to give me her number when I'd asked for it. I could almost see her sitting at her bookstore counter, with her head buried in a book and a smug smile on her face, occasionally glancing at the door because she knew she'd teased me enough last night to get me to come back to the only place I knew for sure she would be.

The phone rang, with Sheryl's name flashing on the screen, interrupting my thoughts.

'Good morning! Apologies for calling on the weekend, but I need you to come down to the office to look at some final details for our presentation on Monday. Only if you don't have any prior commitments, of course. Or I can see what I—'

'Good morning to you too, Sheryl. You really should breathe between sentences. You'll find it helpful,' I said, smiling.

'Right. I'd not even had my chai when that witch from your marketing team called asking for your personal number. I'm telling you she's looking to take you home to her parents.'

I laughed. 'Preet is happily married with a kid, Sheryl. I think she just wants the presentation to go well.'

'Men,' sighed Sheryl, 'so clueless ... Should I schedule the meeting for 1 p.m., then? I'll get you some home-made fish curry I've made for lunch. For making you work on the weekend.'

'You're the best, Sheryl. I'd love that,' I said and hung up.

The office was a fifteen-minute drive away, and I usually used that time to go over my prep notes for everything I had lined up for the day. Since today was just a quick review meeting and a lunch date with Sheryl later, I gazed out of my car window, hoping to catch a glimpse of that gorgeous face as we crossed Avani's bookstore. But we zoomed past the store double quick that day. Where was the Mumbai traffic when you needed it? What business did the streets have being so empty on a Saturday morning?

The meeting went well. Nothing much had changed from the last time we had reviewed the presentation. But this was a big one for us and I was glad the team was looking to be extra prepared. Sheryl won my heart again with the tastiest fish-curry-rice lunch I'd had in a while. Ever since Ma and Papa had moved to Mussoorie, Sheryl had been feeding me home-cooked meals every other day. She sighed and tutted every time I spoke about Ma. The two had been friends for years, and it was possible she thought that I missed Ma's cooking, but one of the few things she didn't know about Ma in all their years of friendship was that the woman hadn't cooked even once in her life, at least not for us. So averse was she to spending time in the kitchen that she had even taken our cook Gopal and his family with her when they moved to Mussoorie.

Meeting done and lunch devoured, I found myself thinking of coffee and croissants ... No, I told myself. It's too soon. I was sure I was close to being labelled a creep after

I had turned up at the bookstore yesterday and spent almost the entire time staring at Avani from across the room—and then of course there was my mid-sentence fiasco from last night.

Going back so soon would make me look desperate and hopeless.

But when would it be a good time to ask her out to dinner? When would it not be 'too soon'?

12 APRIL 2023
AVANI

Did he die?

I don't particularly like Wednesdays. They are like unnecessary stoppers jammed into the centre of the week. You can't look forward to anything, because you already did that on Monday. You're exhausted but somehow pat yourself on the back for getting halfway through the week. And it's too early to celebrate because you have two more days of classes to sit through before it's Friday evening. It's a strange day.

So Wednesdays were strange—but this one was stranger. I had woken up feeling strange, gone to work strangely moody and sat at the billing counter thinking strange things.

Four days were a lot of days. Did I need to worry that he hadn't turned up at the bookstore or at my home, forget spending time figuring out how to get my number and then calling me?

Had I played too hard to get? Or maybe he had faced some sort of a problem? What problems did rich people face? Maybe he had a business emergency and had to fly abroad? Maybe he had got arrested for being too hot and was being held hostage by the police in a dimly lit junkyard in nothing but his boxers? Maybe he had amnesia and was roaming the streets unaware of who he was and that he'd ever met me ...?

No. No. No. Avani. No. You're not doing this. You're not sitting here acting like the women in those old romance novels, thinking you aren't enough because a man (A. Man. Aman. Yes, very punny, ha ha) *isn't giving you attention.*

'Are you in love with him or something?'

Martin, as always. A champion at shattering my chain of self-affirming thoughts.

'What?' I snapped.

'What's with the mopey look? Hot-boy-steel-buns hasn't called yet?'

'Don't call him that. Yuck.'

'Like you don't agree.' He laughed and slapped my arm.

'Ow. Shut up.' I glared at him. 'I wasn't even thinking of him.'

I wasn't in a Martin mood today. I got off the stool and walked to the water cooler. I don't know why they call it that, I huffed to myself—the water is always lukewarm at best.

Martin must have picked up on my weird mood, because he followed me, and like the irritating person he is, just stood there next to me. Not looking at me. Not asking questions. Just staring at the fucking water cooler.

Seconds later, I blurted out the thought that had been eating at me. 'Do you think he died?'

'What the fuck?' Martin laughed. 'Have you lost it?'

'He hasn't called, or texted. Or found me on Instagram. He hasn't even added me on LinkedIn,' I whined.

'You're not *on* LinkedIn.' Martin narrowed his eyes and I knew the exact moment he realized what I'd done, because his face changed from confusion to surprise in a nanosecond.

'You made a LinkedIn profile so he could add you on it? You fucking loser! Ha ha ha ha!'

Laughing out loud *at* someone was so disrespectful. Honestly.

Also, it wasn't *that* funny. Or was it?

'Aaaargh. I'm pathetic. I know.' I buried my face in my hands.

'Aww, baby, you're not pathetic,' Martin half-said, half-laughed as he pulled me into a hug. 'You're just a li'l dorky. I'm sure he's into that.'

This was why I loved Martin. He was annoying, but it was easy to be around him, and somehow he always knew the right things to say.

'It's been four full days, Martin. He clearly isn't interested,' I said as my face dug into his shoulder.

'Are *you* interested?' Martin leaned back and held my chin up.

'I mean … I want to be friends …'

'Oh fuck off. Why do you always do this?' Martin held me by my shoulders and shook me.

'She did what now?'

Rhea. How did that girl always manage to walk in when I was having one of my meltdowns? And I hated repeating stuff.

'Avani is being Avani,' Martin explained. Swinging me around by my shoulders, he walked me towards the café.

'Brown-eyed babe cutlet hasn't called yet?' Rhea asked.

'Okay, what the fuck are these nicknames?' I said. 'And to answer your question, no.'

'Shocking,' she said animatedly, 'given you refused to give him your number. Why don't you just call him? You have his number in the customer register.'

I'd be lying if I said I hadn't contemplated doing that. I would also be lying if I said I hadn't opened the register and fed his number into my phone. And an even bigger lie would be declaring that I hadn't specifically excluded him from the DND mode. Come on, I didn't want to miss his call!

But of course I was not admitting to any of this to these two.

'Can everyone just calm down?' I said. 'I'm fine, okay? I had a good time with him, but that's that. I wanted to apologize, and I did. My life was just fine before all of this happened and it will continue to be fine without him.'

'Without whom?'

OMG. How many times was I going to have to repeat this whole situation?

I turned to see Maya walking into the store towing a suitcase of unusual dimensions. She preferred to hand-deliver her artwork to buyers and today was delivery day for a regular client who lived near the bookstore.

'Don't ask.' Rhea rolled her eyes.

'Stud-guy-sexpot is still MIA?' Maya asked.

'All right. No more nicknames!'

'That's not even the problem,' Martin explained cheerfully. 'The real problem is that our friend here is running away.'

'Avani ...' Maya took a step towards me but I cut her off mid-sentence.

'Guys. I don't know how this has turned into such an intense discussion. But I'm checking out. I have classes. I will see everybody tomorrow. Okay?'

I gave Martin a stern look, swung my bag over my shoulder and walked out the door. I loved my friends, but sometimes I liked to marinate in my thoughts for a while before I opened the floor for discussion.

I wasn't particularly liking how my own heart was being a stranger to me. So, having barely taken three steps on the street outside the store, I pulled my phone out and typed: *The glaciers are melting.* And hit send.

There. Now, instead of worrying about why he hadn't messaged, I could spend the rest of my day worrying about why he hadn't replied. Fan-fucking-tastic.

Seriously, though, I just hoped he was okay.

14 APRIL 2023

AVANI

Somebody make me stop.

On most days I am a reasonable, mature, level-headed woman who thinks before she acts, who is prepared for consequences, who prioritizes logic over stomach flutters. But it had been two days since I had sent Aman that stupid message and I had still not heard back from him. By the time I had reached uni that day, my snap decision to send Aman that message hit me on the head like Newton's proverbial apple.

Clearly, in my brain-fogged state, a few important factors had escaped my attention.

1. The point of being coy and not giving my number to Aman in the first place had been to keep a safe distance and to measure effort. Which was a great plan for assessing potential partners—except that I had ignored the fact that he hadn't put in *any* effort to stay in touch with me, and had, instead, texted him first.
2. I wasn't yet sure what I wanted from him. I wasn't looking for a relationship, but I had hinted that he should call me and had then acted crazy because he hadn't.

3. After that ridiculous slow-motion walk I had done for effect that night from my apartment gate to the building, texting him first showed desperation.
4. Especially since he had not given me his number. I had snuck it out from the customer register, which showed effort on MY part.

The noise I made at this renewed realization must have been something between a gasp and a hyena's mating call because everyone in class turned to look at me with curious expressions.

Right. Class. Yes, I was in class.

The professor stopped professoring, the students stopped studenting and my brain stopped braining.

'Is everything all right, Avani?' Mr Ghoshal asked.

'Uhh … yes. I … uhh …'

Speak, you idiot.

'I'm just …'

Words. Get them out.

'Toilet.'

Toilet? What was I, two? This was getting worse.

'You wish to use the facilities, you mean?' Mr Ghoshal said sternly.

'Facilities. Yes, sir. Please.'

'Sure.' He turned to face the presentation on the screen. A few of my classmates sniggered. I could feel Dhruv's eyes piercing into me from across the row.

'You okay?' he mouthed when I looked at him.

I gave him a thumbs-up and left the room.

What's that Olympic sport in which athletes do something that looks like a cross between walking really fast and running really slow? Yeah, you could well think I was a gold medallist in that if you saw me trying to dash from the classroom to the women's washroom without drawing too much attention to myself.

As soon as I got into a stall, I pulled out my phone. No notifications. Not one. Not even the ones asking me if I wanted a home loan.

What was going on with me? I might not be Beauty Queen 2023, but I had nice eyes and a great butt. I loved myself and had more self-respect than to text a guy I barely even knew and then allow myself to be distracted in class by it.

I'd met men before. I'd been on dates before. I needed to get a grip.

It's those dimples.

They are nothing great.

It's those brown eyes.

Many people have brown eyes.

It's the forearm vei—

Ding. My phone vibrated in my hands.

It was Rhea.

Dude. Come to the bookstore after class. Moody-eyes-man-candy just walked in!!

My heart skipped a beat, but for once my brain stepped in sternly. Okay. Here was a rare opportunity to save face.

I knew I'd sounded too desperate in that text I'd sent, but now I could hold my ground by not rushing to the bookstore midway through class.

He was at the bookstore? That was fine. If he had been too busy to get in touch for one whole week, I was too busy with classes now. I wasn't going to run to him the minute he showed up. I wasn't a girl at anyone's beck and call. No, sir. Studying to be a lawyer wasn't any less tough than running a multibillion-dollar business. I would go back and finish my classes for the day and head home like I always did. I didn't have to be at the bookstore till tomorrow morning, and that's the way it was going to stay. If he didn't get to see me today, too bad—that was just something he would have to live with.

'Mr Ghoshal, sir? I don't feel all right. May I please be excused from classes today?'

Really? You were so close, Avani.

Oh, shut up!

I stood outside the bookstore for a good five minutes trying to get my breathing back to normal and not look too excited. There had been absolutely no reason for me to run like my house was on fire once I had left the university premises. I was sweaty, my hair was a mess and I was breathing like an asthma patient in space.

Way to make an entry, Avani.

I chugged down all the water from my sipper in one go, shoved it into my tote bag and opened the door.

There it was. Aftershave.

I took a very deep breath before walking towards the café, where Rhea and Martin were talking to Aman across the counter. I focused on the empty stool next to him and headed towards it.

'You're here!' Rhea exclaimed.

'You're early. You never get done with classes'—Martin turned around to check the store clock—'by 6.30 p.m. You usually get home by 9. Everything all right?' He turned back around with an infuriatingly innocent look on his face.

'Classes ended early today,' I shot back. 'Mr Ghoshal wasn't feeling well.'

'How come Dhruv didn't come with you?' It was Rhea this time. 'We were supposed to hang out at the bookstore tonight.'

'I don't know, Rhea. Maybe he had a date.'

Rhea made a face and mouthed 'low blow'. I flicked one eyebrow and took the seat next to Aman. I threw my bag on the countertop and turned to face him.

'How have—'

'How are yo—'

I unwittingly smiled, and gestured for him to continue.

'How are you?' he asked. He was smiling too.

'I'm good. You?'

'Good.'

'How's everything else?'

'I've … uh …'

He was interrupted by Martin, who announced, 'Okay, that's enough third-degree torture. Watching you two make small talk is the single-most boring thing I've witnessed today. Ani, Aman hasn't called you or attempted to get in touch because one of his dogs fell sick and he had to fly to Mussoorie to take care of her. He landed earlier today and got caught up with work, but has come to see you the first chance he got. Aman, Avani has been quite the sourpuss these past few days while she waited to hear from you. So, please, kids ... go talk, eat, fuck, do whatever you like, but stop being emotional teenagers who clearly want to know each other better but are too silly to tell each other that.'

Aman and I stared at him, our mouths open.

'Also, while you're at it, Aman, please ask Avani about her LinkedIn page, will you?' He looked at me wickedly, latched his hand into Rhea's and walked away from the coffee counter.

Both of us were too stunned to say anything for a minute or so. Then Aman broke the silence.

'You hungry?'

'Starving.'

Quietly, we gathered our things and hopped off our stools. Aman waited by the end of the counter for me while I turned to wave goodbye to Rhea and Martin, who were pretending to rearrange the bookshelves.

I looked at Aman as he put his phone to his ear and asked his driver to bring the car to the front of the store. How could I miss someone I'd never really been with? Why was my heart filled with such relief now that he was next to me? And why couldn't I stop smiling?

Somebody, please, make me stop.

I waited on the kerb, making mental notes of conversation starters that could come in handy for the rest of the evening while we waited for his car to arrive.

You should ask about his dogs.

Dog. Singular. He didn't know I'd stalked him enough to know exactly how many dogs he had (six) in his Mussoorie home, what their names were (Sheeba, Coco, Dodo, Billu, Gappu and Momo) and how long they'd been around on earth (three, four, four, two and eight years, and the youngest one four months) and what they looked like (all very cute).

'My dog's okay, by the way.' He looked at me over his shoulder with a smile.

My head jerked up with almost mechanical force. My ponytail slapped me in the face and my neck made a strange crackling sound. My eyebrows threatened to flex beyond my hairline and my eyes were wide. 'Sorry?' I tried to sound as casual as I could. Had I thought out loud again?

'My dog? Sheeba? Whom I had to visit in Mussoorie? Yeah, she's fine now. She got stung by a bee in our garden and had the worst allergic reaction. She had to be rushed to the hospital, but she's doing much better now.' He said it like he had been rehearsing this piece in his mind for a while.

'Oh. Good. I'm glad.' I smiled. 'Can I see a picture? Of Sheeba?'

'Sure.'

He pulled his phone out of his pocket. 'Here.' He held it out so I could see the picture of an adorably furry black-and-white mountain dog that looked like a bear.

I was about to comment on how cute Sheeba was and ask how he had known she'd had an allergic reaction because under all that fur I couldn't tell her head from her tail, when a car glided to a halt in front of us. Aman stepped forward and opened the back door for me.

Good timing, I guess. That would have been a stupid thing to say.

'Thank you.' I smiled and slid into the seat while Aman shut the door and came around to sit next to me.

'Ashok, Sapore Italiano jaayenge,' he said. Then turning to me, asked, 'I hope you like Italian food.'

'Oh, love it,' I responded, sounding slightly fake enthusiastic.

We must have spent a total of three minutes in the car but the silence was pounding in my ears. I could see the GPS display on the dashboard telling us that the restaurant was another thirty minutes' drive from there. All I could hear were muffled traffic sounds, the rustling of Aman's shirt every time he moved his palms over his thighs and the sound of my quick, nervous breaths.

If I'd known he was going to take me to dinner, I would have worn my expensive perfume. Instead, I was in my maroon kurta and jeans, with my hair in a lazy ponytail and small silver jhumkis in my ears. Thank god I'd worn my Kolhapuris instead of my regular slippers. I was contemplating touching up my lipstick before we got to the restaurant when …

'You look pretty today,' Aman said. A shiver went up my spine and I fisted my hands into balls. Seriously, was this man psychic? Or was I that predictable?

'I'm a mess.' I laughed nervously.

'Yes, you are.'

'Excuse me?' I dropped my jaw for effect.

'What?'

'Your line is supposed to be, "No, Avani, you're not a mess. You look perfect."' I sat up in my seat and turned to my right so I was facing him directly.

Calmly, he replied, 'I thought my line was, "I could get used to this mess." But sure, we can do yours too.' He leaned a little towards me and tilted his chin so he could look into my eyes as he said, 'No, Avani, you're not a mess. You look perfect.'

Let's be honest. It was a mediocre line. It wasn't poetry. It wasn't groundbreaking. It was a semi-impressive line at best. But it was the way he said it that was anything but regular. The corners of my lips tugged at a smile and I bit down to hold back.

'I could have done much better, no?' He squeezed his left eye shut and sat back in his seat with a pouty face. 'That was such a mediocre line. I swear to you, I can do much better.' He laughed.

What on earth is this mind-reading sorcery? My armpits were getting sweaty again and my heart was beating fast. I tried to will every thought in my mind to disappear.

'Are you okay?' he asked and gently placed his hand on mine.

In a regular cute-boy-touches-my-hand situation, I would have turned my hand over so I could intertwine my fingers with his. In my strange freaking-out-but-blushing-but-also-wanting-to-hold-his-hand-but-worried-about-my-sweaty-palms situation, I just stared at his hand holding mine for what must have been an uncomfortable amount of time, because I was jolted out of my dumbfounded trance by Aman's laughter.

'Stop overthinking! I can practically hear your thoughts.'

Yeah, no shit.

'Sorry.' I finally breathed out. 'I've just really waited to hear from you. I was …'

Okay, what exactly was I going to say just then? I wasn't sure, but all these words were coming out and forming sentences that I wasn't prepared for.

'What?' he asked softly.

'Never mind … You'll think I'm silly.' I shook my head and looked out the window.

'You should hear my thoughts if you think anything you say will sound silly to me.'

'I …'

'Avani?' He leaned in again. 'It's okay.'

'I was worried you had died or something,' I blurted out.

Words, as usual, said before thinking. I regretted them the minute I heard them myself. My guardian angel must have banged her head on the wall yet again and all the gods must have collectively slapped their foreheads in disappointment.

Wow.

I was expecting Aman to either burst into a fit of laughter or judge me for being so dramatic. He did neither. Instead, he sat up in his seat, turned his body towards me, held my right hand in both his palms and brought it to his lips. Gently placing a kiss on my knuckles, he said, 'I would have if I didn't get to see you tonight.'

I swallowed the lump in my throat.

He can't be real. Can he?

AMAN

Not soon enough.

'You're staring,' Avani interrupted my thoughts.

We were in the private dining area of my favourite restaurant in the city, having pulled up at its entrance just minutes earlier. By the time I'd walked around the car to open the door for Avani, she was already stepping out. I watched her straighten her kurta, fix her bag on her shoulder and look up at me … I swear I would give every last rupee of my inheritance to live that moment over and over. Even if it were just one more time.

'You're breathtaking,' I said.

That earned me a chuckle and her cheeks flushed pink again.

'Do you have connections with the underworld?' she asked with what I hoped wasn't genuine concern.

I laughed.

'Why are we sitting away from everyone else? Like you're some ganglord who has the police looking for him?'

'I thought we'd want some privacy.'

'Ouu. Is there more knuckle-kissing on the cards? I hope you have protection,' she teased.

I grinned and pressed the little button on the side of the table, and moments later a server walked in.

'*Buonasera, Signor Raina. Sono lieto che possiate cenare con noi stasera. Qualcun altro si unirà a lei?* Good evening, Mr Raina. Glad you could dine with us tonight. Will anybody else be joining you?' the server asked.

'No, Marco. *Tutti coloro di cui ho bisogno stasera sono qui con me nella stanza.* Everyone I need tonight is right here in the room with me.'

I didn't look up from the menu as I said this, but I could feel Avani's eyes on me.

'*Mi piacerebbe avere una insalata di burrata con pesto e pomodori e un contorno di pane di segale come antipasto,*' I said. A burrata salad with pesto and tomatoes, and a side of sourdough bread.

'*Sì, signore. Desidera qualcosa da bere?* Would you like something to drink?' the server asked.

'*Sì, una bottiglia del vostro miglior vino bianco, per favore. Grazie.*' Only the finest wine will do this evening.

I shut the menu and placed it on the table. 'I took the liberty of ordering the starters and some nice wine. I come here all the time. I hope you like it.'

'OMG. I'm getting murdered here tonight. Take whatever you want, just let me go, Mr Ganglord.'

'Ha ha. Funny.'

'So you speak Italian.' She sounded impressed.

'*Si*,' I replied with a smile.

'Where did you learn to speak it so well?'

'How do you know I speak it well?'

'I mean, unless the waiter sucks at Italian too, from what I heard, I would say you speak it well. You didn't fumble. You sounded confident. It's … it's hot!' she said with a grin.

'You find Italian-speaking men hot?'

'*Si*.'

'Wow, thanks.' I grinned.

'No need to thank me. Just get me that Italian waiter's number and we'll be even. You think he's single?' she said, smiling mischievously.

Slowly she took the menu from my side of the table and started flipping through it.

'Funny,' I said. 'Speaking of numbers …'

Suddenly she stiffened. Her face changed. That wicked smile vanished and the pink on her cheeks was back. What had I said?

'Yeah, about that …' She shifted uncomfortably in her seat. 'Umm … look …'

'It's okay,' I said before she could finish. 'It's all good. Don't worry about it.'

'Really? You didn't think it was creepy?'

Creepy? Did she know I had almost asked Sheryl to get me her information?

'Er … I don't understand,' I said cautiously. 'What was … creepy?'

'My text.'

Text?

'Your text?' I asked, confused.

'Yeah, I ... I'm just so sorry!'

Okay. Now I was really lost. 'I have no clue what you're talking about, Avani.'

'I know it was stupid, okay? You don't have to tease me about it. Drop it, please.' She threw the menu at me.

'Okay,' I said, catching it before it could crash into my plate.

'Okay?' She widened her eyes. 'That's all you're going to say? Okay?'

'I ... er ... I don't know what you're talking about, so ... I guess okay would be the only appropriate response,' I replied, my face probably mirroring the completely baffled expression on her face.

'So, if you text me something that only the two of us know about, should I reply with "okay" too? That's acceptable?' She sounded offended.

I reached across the table, took both her hands in mine and gently squeezed. That seemed to do the trick, because whatever was churning in her mind seemed to calm and she looked into my eyes.

'You want to tell me what you're talking about, crazy lady?' I said with a smile.

She sighed and gently freed her right hand from my grip, leaving the left one still between my palms, and picked up her phone. She scrolled till she found what she was looking for and turned the screen towards me.

It was a chat window with one message sent by her to an unknown number.

The glaciers are melting.

What was I missing here? This was a reference to the conversation we'd had when I'd walked her home after the happy hour at the bookstore. I stared at her phone in confusion, and then my eyes went to the number at the top of her screen. Suddenly everything made sense.

'Baby, that's not my number,' I said softly. 'This is Ashok's number. I usually pass it off as mine when I don't want to share my actual number. Like at malls or ... in bookstore registers.'

Her mouth fell open. I couldn't help but grin. Nobody had ever before done anything like this to connect with me. I wanted to hold her face and kiss her, hold her in my arms and laugh till she laughed with me.

But she seemed mortified. 'Shut up,' she whispered, dropping her head on the table, trying to hide her face from me.

I stayed still until I saw her shoulders moving up and down and then heard muffled laughter come through. I joined in.

She looked up and freed her hand from mine to hide her face with both hands. 'Oh god. I'm *such* an idiot,' she said, half laughing and half exasperated.

'No. You're a mess, and I can't wait to get used to it,' I said, smiling.

I didn't care if it was too soon. I was pissed off at destiny for not making me walk into that bookstore earlier. How had I lived all these years without knowing her?

AVANI

Dessert.

Clearly, God has a wicked sense of humour. Because of all the ways She could tell me to chill and not overthink that text, She chose the one that embarrassed me the most. When I tell you how my insides were squealing even as I laughed at my total stupidity, just take my word for it.

'Wine?' the server interrupted my thoughts.

Really, dude ... Now?

'*Si, grazie.*' Aman took the wine bottle and a glass of diet soda, and gestured to the server to leave. He then poured the wine for me and raised his glass. 'To Ashok?' he asked, flashing me a gorgeous smile.

'To Ashok,' I said, raising mine, laughing. I took a much larger sip than I normally would have and shook my head in disbelief. Of all the ways I had imagined our first date to go, this wasn't even close.

'So ... what's Mussoorie like?' I asked.

'You've never been?' He looked surprised.

'Not once.'

'We must change that.'

A part of my heart fluttered as I imagined travelling out of the city with Aman and getting to know more about him and his life in his place of comfort.

'Mussoorie is where one part of my heart lives,' he continued. 'See ...' He pulled his phone out of his pocket and opened the photos app. 'My parents and my six dogs.'

I nodded, pretending I didn't know about them already, like this photo wasn't sitting in my phone gallery and three different chat windows.

'This is home,' he said, scrolling to a photo of a beautiful mid-century mansion surrounded by sprawling lawns. It seemed to be located at the centre of a vast estate in the midst of rolling, forested hills. 'Here's one of my parents …' I saw an elegant couple sitting comfortably on the porch of the mansion. It was like a postcard from the bookstore's gift-shop wall.

'It's beautiful … They're beautiful.' My heart was filled with a warmth I couldn't explain. My parents and I hadn't taken many photos together, not at home, not on vacation. The only pictures I had of them were at their respective work events, and there was one of the three of us from the time I had broken my leg and they'd come to visit me at Aaji's house.

We spent the rest of the evening chatting about each other's childhood dreams—his had been to be a doorman at a fancy hotel because he loved the uniforms, and mine had been to become a writer, because I liked how pretty my handwriting was and I thought that was what made great writers: their handwriting. We also discussed our common dislike of horror films. ('Why would I voluntarily give myself nightmares?' he exclaimed. My thoughts exactly.)

Kind of full from the salad and bread from our starters, and after Aman tried to get me to order half the menu, we eventually decided to share a plate of pasta for the main course. The bottle of wine was apt company. It did a rather good job of keeping my nerves from getting to me.

A couple of hours later, the wine now coursing comfortably through my veins, Aman gestured at the menu again and asked, 'Dessert?'

'I have a name. It's Avani.' I winked.

He let out a breathy laugh. 'Okay then.'

He got up, gesturing to the server that we were done, and walked over to hold my chair as I tried to stand up, immediately feeling the three glasses of wine talking back to me. Whew! Thankfully, Aman had turned away to call Ashok, and saw none of the wobble in my knees as I bent down to pick up my bag and slowly raised myself out of the chair.

'Shall we?'

I smiled and walked ahead of him. He gently placed his hand on the small of my back as we passed the server by the door.

'*Gracias*,' I said proudly.

'That's Spanish,' Aman whispered from behind me.

Damn it.

I was just about to step into the car when my heart skipped a beat. I gasped as I turned around to face Aman.

'We forgot to pay the bill!'

'It's okay,' he replied calmly.

'I'm not sure what you mean. It's not okay, Aman.'

'Avani …'

'How did they not follow us out with the credit card machine? They follow me all the time.' I started moving back towards the entrance.

'So you've fled from restaurants without paying bills before?' he teased, holding me back by my elbow.

'Shut up. Come, let's pay.' I tugged at my arm.

'Avani ...'

I paused and looked up at him. Finally reading his face, I said slowly, 'You own the place, don't you?' Of course he owned the busiest, most expensive restaurant in the city. Of course.

'Let me at least go back and fill out my feedback for this lovely evening,' I said.

'Plus,' I added, looking mischievously back at him while I headed in, 'I might just get that waiter's number.'

He laughed and shook his head.

When I returned, Aman was waiting by the kerb. He gently led me back to the car and opened the door. I got in. The drive to my apartment complex was quiet, calm and everything else the wine was making me feel.

It was the wine, right? It had to be. I mean, I'd met the guy properly, like, twice. I'd had dinner with him ONCE. You can't say much about anything in such little time. That's not how it worked. Right?

Ashok parked the car by the pavement outside my complex gate. I opened the door and stepped out, and Aman did the same. He took a step towards me and held out his hand.

'Give me your phone before you start blank-calling my cook.'

I smiled like a goof and handed him my phone without protest. He fed in his number and hit the call button, disconnecting just as his phone started to ring. He then saved his number on the contact card, grinning, and showed me the screen. He'd saved himself as Hot Italian-Speaking Guy.

I held out my hand for his phone. He handed it to me and I clicked on the latest missed call on his log and hit 'save'. There, now he had Bookstore Nerd's number. I smiled at his sheepish expression as he saw the name. He took his phone out of my hand, and without breaking eye contact, locked my phone, took a step closer to me and dropped it into my tote.

My heart started doing that thing where it stopped listening to any logic or reasoning my brain was desperately trying to communicate to it. The hair on my neck and arms prickled, my breaths came shorter and faster. I could smell his aftershave like it was the only scent in the air. And I was suddenly aware of how close he was standing to me.

His eyes slowly moved to my lips and I parted them without so much as a thought.

Was this happening?

He tucked a strand of hair behind my ear. I took a soft step back and rested against the car's door. He took a step closer and placed his left hand on the car, by my neck. With his right he cupped my face.

He leaned in and I could feel his lips brush my ear as he said, 'Goodnight, gorgeous.' And then a soft caress on my cheek.

I let out a shaky breath and managed to say, 'Goodnight. Thanks. Dinner.'

Almost a whole sentence.

His thumb swiped gently across my jawline before he rocked back on his feet and tucked his hands into his pockets.

'Don't thank me,' he said. 'Meet me tomorrow?'

'Try tomorrow?' I asked softly.

'Can't wait.' He smiled and stepped away.

I used all the strength and willpower left in me to move my limbs. I placed one foot after another and walked towards the complex gate, not daring to turn around, because something told me that if I did, I wouldn't want to go home that night. At least not by myself.

I kept walking and didn't turn around even as I reached the elevator in my building and pressed the button. I stepped in and pulled the grill gate shut behind me.

It was too soon. Why was I taking all of this so seriously? Why was my body betraying my mind? I'd been reading too many romance novels.

But what was I supposed to do about this stupid smile that I couldn't wipe off my stupid face?

AMAN

Goodnight, gorgeous.

The city lights blurred into streaks as Ashok drove me back to my apartment. I leaned back, one hand running over my jaw, trying to process the last few minutes. She'd looked up at me, wide-eyed and startled, when I'd cupped her face. Her skin was soft, her scent warm and floral, and when I leaned in close, I swear I could feel her heart racing as fast as mine.

And then I had said it. Goodnight, gorgeous.

I meant to pull back immediately—keep it smooth, like every other interaction—but my thumb had lingered a second too long on her cheek. My entire body was tense, every instinct fighting the urge to close that tiny gap between us and kiss her.

But I didn't.

Why didn't I?

I exhaled as Ashok slowed at a traffic light. I tapped my fingers against my knee and replayed the moment in my mind for the hundredth time. She'd smiled at me when I'd pulled away. Not her usual mischievous grin, but something softer. Warmer.

She'd liked it.

A car honked nearby, jolting me out of my thoughts. The light turned green, and Ashok smoothly guided us forward.

I hadn't even turned on the music. That was unlike me. The quiet felt louder tonight, the weight of what had just happened filling every corner of the car.

I couldn't shake the look in her eyes when I'd said goodnight. Like she'd been waiting for something, unsure if I'd give it to her. And maybe I didn't—at least, not fully.

You're playing it safe, Raina. Too safe.

――

15 APRIL 2023

AVANI

Cute chaddis.

I woke up to the sound of my phone buzzing on the bedside table. Even in that half-sleep state, I hoped it was a text from Aman, but it was better than that—it was a call.

'I haven't stopped thinking about you,' were the first words I heard.

Hmmm. Not a bad way to start the day.

I was about to tell him I had that effect on people, hoping to get a laugh out of him so his dimples would make a comeback—in my mind if not before my eyes—but he continued with, 'Have lunch with me today.'

My eyebrows crawled closer to each other even as my lips pressed together in a smile. 'We had dinner last night …'

'I have dinner every night. Don't you?'

'I do.'

'Eat with me this afternoon.'

'You're asking me out on a date within twelve hours of our last date?'

'Yes.'

What could one say to something like that? He was honest and straightforward, and he did not beat around the bush. In fact, there was no bush. It was tall, scanty grass at best, well mowed and smelling like summer.

Avani!

I'm thinking of a meadow, not pubes, you pervert.

'Is that a no?' he said, bringing me back to the conversation.

'Let's have coffee first?' I replied instinctively.

I had no reason to turn down Aman's offer, to be honest. But I couldn't find an excuse to agree immediately. I mean two dates in twelve hours was ... quick, no?

I pictured Martin, Rhea and Maya collectively rolling their eyes even as I had the thought. I have to admit my guard was always up around new people, no matter who they were. Perhaps it was because I'd grown up with no siblings and dysfunctional parents, and I'd had to look out for myself all along. It's not like my parents fought or made home unpleasant for me, but the fact that they were incompatible was obvious. On most days, they were well-rounded individuals, a perfect couple. That was perhaps what stayed with me the most, years after I'd moved out of their home and into my grandmother's after their separation. I sometimes wondered if I would have handled my parents' marriage falling apart better had they fought and screamed like other unhappy couples. Instead, they went through life looking tranquil and content until one day Mamma packed her bags and left. I was with Aaji then, in Pune for a vacation, and was told about her leaving over a casual phone call from Baba. I couldn't remember now what my immediate response had been. I'd thought it best to push the news into the deep recesses of my mind and treat it like a film I'd once vaguely watched.

I switched Aman's call to speakerphone as I swung my feet over the side of the bed and made my way to the kitchen. My brain was screaming for coffee. Setting the phone down on the counter, I put some water on the gas to boil.

'Tell me about your friends,' I said, nonchalantly changing the topic. He hadn't responded to my counter-proposition for a coffee date.

'Well, I don't seem to be very good at making them,' he replied, his tone quieter now.

'What's that mean?' I said sleepily.

'I mean, I can't get them to have a meal with me, so having them console me when I'm crying over a bad day seems quite a distant scenario.'

'I see … So do you call all your friends "baby"? That must get exhausting. Yo, baby! Wanna grab a few beers?' I barked in a fake gruff voice, trying to imitate a man's. 'Wanna watch the game at mine, baby? We can call all our other babies. Yo! My babies and I are going to Goa, wanna join us?'

A hearty laugh came from the other end of the line. I was getting used to the sound of that. 'Yeah, something like that,' he said. 'However, your idea of what boys do when they hang out isn't stereotypical at all, I see.'

'What do you mean? It's accurate,' I replied, sensing sarcasm in his tone.

'It's as accurate as you getting into pillow fights with your girlfriends every time they stay over and then painting each other's nails pink.' He chuckled.

'That's exactly what we do. And then we give each other orgasms with our favourite vibrators,' I replied plainly, stirring my coffee in and moving to the sofa to settle in there.

'Fuck my friends, I want to know more about yours now.'

'Shut up.' I laughed. 'Now tell me about them.'

'Come over ... meet them.'

'There's a party, is it, and they'll all be there? What's the occasion?'

'Oh ... er ... one of them is moving to London later next week, so there's a farewell party at my place ... tonight. It's not many people. Just a few special ones. And one that's very special.'

'Do I finally get to meet the wife you've been hiding all this time?' I teased.

'Nope.'

'Then?' I asked playfully.

'*They* do.'

I wish I'd taken a sip of my coffee right before he said that so I would have something to choke on for effect. This guy didn't hold back on anything, did he? It was almost like a conveyor belt transported his thoughts from his mind straight to his mouth without going through any sort of filter in between. It was refreshing, but also nerve-wracking. I could never tell what was going on in that gorgeous head of his, but then every time I started to wonder, he told me what it was, voluntarily.

I was silent for a while, as was he. Then I asked, 'So, then, instead of lunch or coffee, we have a party! Great! What time?'

'Tonight, 9 p.m., my place. I'll text you the address. And bring the others along too. It'll be fun for everyone to meet.'

'I'll see you then.' I smiled into the phone.

'See you, baby.'

Click.

I immediately opened our group chat and texted the gang about the party they were invited to.

Me: He either really likes me or really hates me if he's making our second date a meet-the-friends situation.

Rhea's response popped up almost immediately.

Rhea: How does that mean he hates you?
Me: Maybe he's setting up his friends to scare me off ... that way he won't have to do it himself.
Maya: Wow, we didn't wake up cynical at all this morning.
Martin: Did he finally realize that the ONE in your name stands for the number of meetings it takes to realize that you're boring? A-one-eee.
Me: Sooo clever.
Martin: Maybe he just wants to see you again without making it awkward.
Me: In his house. With his friends. And mine.
Martin: It's a party. Not an orgy. Unless it is. Then I'm in for sure.

Me: *Shut up. And yes. You're all going to be there.*
Maya: *Can't, babe. Got dinner with the fam tonight.*
Rhea: *Yeah, me neither. I have movie plans.*
Me: *Get Dhruv!!*
Rhea: *Who said anything about him?*
Martin: *It's cute how sly you think you are.*
Me: *Fine, whatever. Martin, I'll see you in the lobby of Aman's building at 8.50?*
Martin: *Not unless you want to go arrange the silverware. Meet me at 10.*
Me: *Party is at 9.*
Martin: *Exactly. Text me the address. Wear cute chaddis.*
Me: *Yuck.*
Rhea: *Yuck.*

AMAN

What am I, twelve?

Right, so now I have a party to plan.

The last time I'd lied about a party was to my parents when I was thirteen. I told them Gagan and I were going to watch a classical music performance with Gagan's then girlfriend's parents, but we went straight to a club with our other friends. That was the night I had my first drink and decided that alcohol wasn't for me. Now, eighteen years later,

I'm a full-grown adult who's just lied to the girl he likes about another fake party, for no reason whatsoever. And now I'd have to call my friends—some of whose messages about previous parties I'd chosen to ignore—and get them to come over to my place *tonight* and pretend that one of them was leaving the country for good.

Great going, Raina. Great going.

I checked the clock. I had about ten hours to put this thing together. First things first, I opened my boys' group chat.

Wolfpack
(Lame? I know ... We made this group when we were in junior college would be my excuse.)
Me: *Guys, drinks and dinner, my place, tonight. Tell me you're all in town.*
Jogi: *What's the occasion?*
Me: *You're moving to London later next week and I'm throwing you a farewell gig.*
Jogi: *Lol. Who's she?*
Mahi: *Our man's met a girl? Spill, dude.*
Me: *Just help me get this party together and I'll tell you everything when we see each other.*
Mahi: *I'm in Delhi, bhai. But I need details.*
Jogi: *I can make it. How many people do you need?*
Me: *Enough so it looks like a legit party, but not so many that it gets out of hand.*
Jogi: *Consider it done. See you in a bit.*
Nikhil: *Wohoooo! Count me in. Getting my girl along.*
Jogi: *Dude, ask your girl to get her girl along too. The short-haired one.*

Nikhil: *She has a name, asshole. Mishti. Yeah, fine, I'll check.*
Me: *Guys, I need this girl to like me, okay? Behave.*
Mahi: *Chick's got him all wound up and shit. Too bad I'm missing this. Have fun, fuckers!*

I knew I could always count on this lot. We'd attended junior college together and then Jogi and I had gone to the same university for our postgrads in marketing and business studies, respectively. Jogi's family owned a hotel chain with branches across Himachal and Punjab, but, unlike me, he had no intention of taking over the family business. He'd spent most of his free time after college with my parents and me at our Mussoorie home. Even today, Jogi visits my parents there more often than I do. And they love him.

By the time I was ready to leave for a meeting at a hotel close by, I had made a call to Sheryl to inform her about the party, and rattled off a list of to-dos while I was away—get the house cleaned, order enough food to feed anywhere between four and forty people, and arrange for a bartender and waiting staff. On a whim, I called our company's event manager, Meghna, and asked her to spruce up my balcony with sofas and mist fans so it could be used as an outdoor lounge. She fell silent for a moment when I said I would have guests walking in within hours, but recovered quickly and promised it would all be done in time.

I made one final call to an old college friend who had an acoustic band to check if he was in the city. He was, and free to perform live that evening. I had no idea what kind of music Avani liked, but I was hoping I couldn't go wrong with acoustic covers.

Checklist ticked off, for the moment at least, I slipped on my shoes, adjusted my jacket, called Ashok to bring the car to the entrance and stepped out of my apartment. The day ahead was packed with work.

AVANI

Let's not read too much into this.

If there's one thing I've learnt from the hundreds of romance novels I've read over the past few years, it's how to romanticize and build up regular situations in my head and then freak out when things don't happen that way in real life.

For instance, I remember the day I moved into my apartment and thought, 'Can't wait to have a cute guy for a neighbour who'll come knocking on my door asking for milk, and then fall in love with me.' Consequently, I spent the first four days of my life in the building stressing over what to wear and how much make-up to apply so I didn't look like I had an Only Fans account, only to find that my neighbour was Mhatre Kaka, who spent most of his day on his balcony—right next to mine—in his vest and blue striped pyjamas, talking loudly to his cat.

Or when I took that trip to Mahabaleshwar with members of a book club I rarely participated in and packed everything cute I owned in anticipation of spending time with a boy I'd spotted at the last meet—only to have to borrow and wear said boy's sister's oversized tee and shorts because my conditioner bottle exploded in my backpack and turned all my clothes into lookalikes of papier-mâché artefacts.

Or the time I had just finished thanking the gods for having a dashing co-passenger seated next to me on a flight from Pune to Delhi for an intercollegiate moot court competition, only to discover he had the strongest opinions on how plant protein had become more popular than whey protein because everyone in Los Angeles was turning vegan after meditation had gone viral on TikTok—which he continued to share with me incessantly in a squeaky undertone. I swear his biceps deflated an inch with every stupid, judgy comment that came out of his mouth.

Anyway, point being ... I didn't want to work myself up too much after my phone call with Aman. The anticipation of meeting him later that evening did give me mini butterflies, but I decided I wouldn't let that dominate my entire day.

I had a life.

AMAN

Set and go.

I'd hardly walked into my apartment and put my laptop bag down when the doorbell rang for the first of many, many times that evening.

First it was Sheryl and the waiting staff. Then it was Jogi and his driver with crates and crates of beer and champagne. Then it was the decorators. While Sheryl instructed the staff and dispatched Ashok to pick up food from our restaurant, the decorators got started moving the furniture around on the balcony. Jogi walked up to me as I settled on the living room couch with a cup of coffee. He popped open a bottle of beer and sat down.

'Why are you sending me to London next week, dude? What the fuck?' Both of us laughed.

'Don't know, man, just kinda slipped out,' I replied, scratching my jawline.

'Who is she?'

'Avani,' I said, biting the inside of my cheek to stop myself from smiling at the mention of her name.

'Avani ... Hmm.'

He held up his beer bottle and tilted it in my direction before taking another swig.

This is why Jogi and I had stayed friends. He was a little bit of both of us. He liked his parties and road trips as much as he liked staying home and beating every FIFA score of mine on PlayStation. On some days, if I needed to unwind after hectic work hours, Jogi and I could sit in the same room and not utter a word to each other. We'd either be gaming furiously or he'd be reading a book and drinking his beer while I'd be mindlessly strumming on my guitar. But every time he sensed that I had had a tough day, he would turn up and be at my side.

I sat back on the couch and checked my phone for missed messages or calls, mentally making a note of everyone who had promised to turn up. I hadn't expected so many of my friends, and their friends, to be so quick to respond. But I guess everyone loves a party.

By 8 p.m., my apartment had been cleaned spotless, the food had been delivered and was ready to be served, the waiting staff was being re-briefed by Sheryl, the bartender had set up his station at my bar counter and was getting lectured by Jogi on making the perfect whisky sour, and the band was setting up its instruments in the corner of my living room just by the balcony, which had been transformed into a phenomenal boho backyard by Meghna and team, complete with carpets, lamps, a canopy of fairy lights and floor cushions and couches. I looked around, satisfied, and decided to hit the shower.

I let the cold water run over my body. And as my nerves calmed, my thoughts turned from the party to an image of Avani in the shower with me. I shook my head and opened my eyes wide to push the image out of my mind. It had clearly been too long. I turned the shower off and stepped out, a towel wrapped around my waist as I walked to the closet. Without much thought I picked out the black button-down half-sleeve silk shirt and baggy grey dress pants. I quickly brushed my hair and put on my white sneakers before stepping out. I walked back almost immediately to pat on some aftershave. I hadn't shaved today, but I'd gathered she loved the smell.

In the time that I was away, a few people had already arrived. Jogi was chilling with Nikhil and his girlfriend (who'd got her short-haired friend along, so I was sure I wasn't going to see much of Jogi around later). Meghna and her team were chatting with Sheryl, and a few others, who I guessed were Jogi's friends, sat by the lamps outside, smoking. Avani hadn't arrived yet. I looked at the clock: 8.40 p.m. I headed towards Sheryl with a flute of champagne that I picked up from one of the many trays that were circulating.

I sneaked up on her from behind and whispered, 'Hi, sexy!' She jumped and slapped my arm in mock anger.

'Thank you, baba,' she said as she took the champagne from me and took a sip. 'What are you celebrating? Why this fancy party suddenly?' Her tone seemed a bit too casual.

'And how come you stayed back? You hate parties. How come you're hanging around for this one?' I countered, narrowing my eyes.

'What? I love parties …' she replied quickly.

'Ma asked you to check Avani out, didn't she?'

'I need to send her one picture of your girl and I'm out. This is too loud already.' She rolled her eyes and took a sip from the flute, not even attempting to fib. I laughed and shook my head while she linked her arm into mine.

'Is she here yet? Which one is she? I hope none of those squeaky ones there …' she said, eyeing the group on the balcony with a disappointed look.

'She's not …' I began, and then the doorbell rang.

AVANI

Don't get drunk.

The doorman let me through a set of giant glass doors into a fancy lobby, and I gave the receptionist my name. She ticked it off a list on her desk and nodded. I perched nervously on a sprawling velvet sofa, waiting for Martin and tapping my foot nervously on the shiny marble floor. A couple walked in and went straight into the elevator. The girl wore expensive golden heels. The guy had on a velvet dinner jacket that matched the sofa I was sitting on. When they opened their mouths to speak, all the suspicions I had were confirmed. They were Gujarati.

'Sorrysorrysorrysorry! My Uber cancelled and I had to walk from the store,' Martin rushed in, huffing.

'It's fine. I just got here. I'm glad you came.' We started walking to the elevator.

'Madam?' The doorman called out to me. 'The one on the right.'

Martin and I exchanged confused glances, then, thanking the doorman, walked to the elevator on the far right of the lobby. Entering, I turned to press 19, only to find that there was no 19. Or any other number, for that matter. There were no buttons at all. What kind of lift was this?

The liftman, who had clearly anticipated our predicament and was hovering around, peered in and said, 'Apologies, Madam. Raina residence?'

'Yes, please,' I said, glancing at Martin.

'So fancy,' he mouthed while fanning himself with his fingers.

I looked down and chuckled as the liftman stepped in and pressed no button at all. The lift doors shut and then opened in what seemed like half a second. We'd reached the nineteenth floor. Thanking the kind liftman, we stepped out into what looked like a lavish lobby before we encountered a massive wooden door with the name plate: RAINA'S. I stood in front of the door, listening to the faint laughter and music coming from inside.

'They'll like you, Ani. If they don't, there's something wrong with them,' Martin said, nudging my shoulder with his.

I let out a big breath, rolled back my shoulders, straightened my kurta and rang the doorbell.

You know how I had crushed on his black button-down shirt on the night of the happy hour? Yeah, scratch that. Because there was a new button-down shirt tonight and this one won hands down. Shorter sleeves, more biceps, draping the broad shoulders and the rest of his frame to even more perfection, if that were at all possible.

Let's pan up from the bottom now, like they do in the movies. Chunky white sneakers that looked super comfy and super casual. Very different from his usual leather dress shoes. Baggy dark-grey pants that hung casually on his waist. His left hand was still on the knob on the inside of the door, his body leaning on it, while his right hand held the frame of the doorway. And, to top it all, he had a day-old stubble, and … what was this now … loose, curly hair on his head! It was always so well brushed and never out of place, I hadn't imagined his hair to be curly.

'You came.' He flashed his dimples and locked his brown eyes with mine.

'I'm glad I came too, Aman. Thanks, man!' Martin announced, and walked right past Aman, leaving me standing alone in the doorway. I could hear his voice fading to a 'Wow!' as he moved further into the apartment.

Aman laughed, and called over his shoulder without breaking eye contact with me, 'Thanks for coming, man!' He nodded in the direction of the living room.

I took a step in and, as was my habit by now when I visited people's homes, scanned everyone's feet. Rich people wore shoes inside their houses too … Right. So I kept mine on and followed Aman. He led me to the bar, where Martin had already begun chatting animatedly with a tall, rather handsome-looking guy.

'What can I get you?' Aman asked, standing next to me, quite close. The music wasn't loud, but I didn't mind the proximity.

'Gin and tonic?'

'One gin and tonic, please,' he told the bartender.

'Jogi, you seem to have met Martin already. This is Avani.' He pulled me closer to his side and rested his elbow on the bar. 'Meet Jogi,' he said, turning to me.

'Hi.' I waved, not sure why I was feeling so shy. This wasn't an arranged-marriage-please-ensure-everybody-approves kind of meeting.

'Hi, Avani. It's very nice to meet you. I'm so glad you could make it.'

Jogi, a close friend judging by the sense of comfort he had around the space, looked like he was always on the road. His skin was tanned, he wore a white linen shirt with beige pants that were also linen, his hair was long and loosely tied in a bun and on his wrists were many, many bead bracelets. Didn't look much like a Swiftie, so I assumed he was into meditation and organic teas.

Aman handed me my drink and took a glass of water for himself, and while he and Jogi chit-chatted with the bartender, I turned to face the rest of the party and took in the space. The living room was huge and the balcony equally large and beautifully done up. There were multiple seating areas across both spaces, and expensive art and framed photographs, of family, vacations and dogs, hung on the walls. A live band of three guys was playing in a corner of the room while some people chilled on the balcony. I liked how casually there was a band here. No massive speaker connected to someone's phone that was being reel-scrolled even when they went to the loo. No fighting over aux wires, no ads in the middle of playlists. A real live band. Two entryways on opposite sides of the living room led to long, dimly lit corridors, and a third in the left corner led to a spiral staircase. Phew.

'Are you planning a heist? All the family jewels are in the treasure box buried under the second-floor bathroom tiling.' Aman's voice brought me out of my trance.

'I thought the family jewels were in your pants. But I must be mistaken,' I said casually with a shrug, taking another sip and looking up at him.

He closed his eyes and drew in a breath. 'Walked right into that one, didn't I?'

'Yes, you did.' After a pause I said, 'Aman, you have a beautiful home.'

'Thanks, it's all my parents. This'—he waved his hands at the decor pieces and artwork—'is all Ma.'

'It's lovely, really. She has exquisite taste. I want to see what's outside too.' I took a step towards the balcony.

'Sure. Allow me ...' I felt Aman's hand on the small of my back as he led me to the balcony, which had a gorgeous view of the sea on three sides. It was warm outside, and humid, but the view was so breathtaking that it didn't matter.

He nodded to a group of people standing in one corner of the balcony and settled on one of the two couches that were empty, patting the seat next to him. I smiled and sat down, taking in the heavenly scent of his aftershave that had been lingering ever since I'd walked in. He turned to face me and stretched his right hand over the back of the couch behind me. When I turned to him, I saw he was smiling.

'What?' I asked.

'Nothing.'

'You're creepy,' I said.

'And you're gorgeous.'

I rolled my eyes in mock annoyance, acutely aware that he was sitting closer than I had imagined.

'So, tell me about everyone,' I said.

'You've met Jogi. He and I went to junior college and business school together. He is one of my best friends and sometimes my parents' third—and favourite—child.'

'You have siblings?'

'Yes, an older brother, Gagan. And that right there'—he nodded towards a group of one corporate-looking guy and two smartly dressed girls—'are Gagan's college friends who also work with us. Akash, Meghna and Mona. They own an event management company.'

'Who are the two girls and that guy smoking there?' I asked, motioning towards the group that had now moved from the dining area to the opposite side of the balcony.

'That's Nikhil—we also went to junior college together—and that's his girlfriend Khushi. And the short-haired girl is Mishti, Khushi's best friend.' He waved at them.

The short-haired girl started walking towards us the minute she saw us looking in her direction, and took a seat on the couch next to ours. 'You must be Avani,' she said.

Nikhil and his girlfriend had followed but preferred to stand at a distance.

'Hi, yes. I am. It's nice to meet you,' I said with a smile.

'Same here ... What do you do?'

'I'm studying to be a lawyer.'

'Oh. I heard someone say that you were a receptionist at a bookstore or something,' she said with a condescending air.

'Yeah, I work part-time at Bombay Bound. It's not too far from here.'

'So how did you meet bachelor of the year here?' she queried, winking at Aman.

I could feel Aman shift closer to me on the couch, moving his hand towards my shoulder from behind.

'I actually saw her outside the bookstore when I was driving by and decided to walk in more than once, pretending to buy books for my niece,' Aman answered for me.

'But you don't have a niece,' Nikhil said.

'Exactly,' Aman said, looking at me.

I blinked in shock. 'What?'

'Guilty.' He threw his left hand up in submission, smiling.

I shook my head in disbelief. 'Whom did you give those books to, then?' I asked.

'My liftman Madhav's daughter. She's about the age the books are appropriate for.'

I could feel my heart bursting into a thousand tiny hearts. He had fake-bought books because I worked at the store? I leaned into him, nudging his chest with my shoulder.

'Wow! Classic Aman, huh? He always does these cute things when he likes people. I remember how he insisted on dropping me home after every party when we first met.' Ah, that's why Short-Haired Girl was so bitchy. An ex-girlfriend?

'Yeah, only that Avani was completely sober, fully dressed and not vomiting when I met her at the bookstore,' Aman said with a forced smile, his tone uncharacteristically sarcastic.

I wanted to spit my drink out, but Nikhil did that for me. Which earned him a glare from Khushi before she followed her livid friend out to the living room.

'Babyyyy!' Nikhil called after Khushi as he stubbed out his cigarette, laughing.

'It's nice to finally meet you, Avani. I'll be right back,' he said. 'You'll get used to the drama now that you're here.' He winked at Aman and went in to find his girlfriend.

Finally meet me? Had Aman been talking to his friends about me?

'And that's why I don't go out much,' Aman said with his eyebrows raised, looking towards the living room.

I nodded.

We looked away from each other, simultaneously let out a big sigh and immediately broke into a fit of laughter.

'I'm really glad you came,' he said, looking at me.

'I am too.' I shrugged lightly and downed my drink.

'Come, I have to show you something.' He held his hand out as he rose from the couch.

I took it, saying, 'Can we get another drink first, though?'

'Of course. The same?'

I nodded, and we walked to the bar, where Jogi and Martin were still chatting.

I sidled up to Martin and whispered in his ear, 'He said he wants to show me something.'

'Must be those family jewels,' he replied, looking at me sideways. He had heard that! 'I hope you wore cute chaddis like I asked you to,' Martin continued in his usual drawl.

'Shut up.'

I could feel a slight ball of excitement in my stomach. I knew better than to expect Aman to want to hook up with me tonight, but the thought of being alone with him, away from everyone else, still made me nervous. The good kind of nervous.

'Shall we?' asked Aman as he handed me my second drink.

'We shall.' I took a large sip and slipped my hand into his.

Don't. Get. Drunk. I told myself as I followed him up the spiral staircase.

And took another large sip.

16 APRIL 2023

AVANI

Why am I like this?

I heard my phone vibrating on the bedside table. My mouth was dry and my head hurt as though someone was pushing it through a shredder. I opened one eye to check the wall clock. It was a little past 7 a.m. I groaned and managed a half turn to reach for my phone. My head whirled wildly for a bit, but I forced myself to open my eyes. I was in my bed. Dressed from head to toe in the outfit I had worn the previous night to Aman's party. I saw one earring on the pillow. The other I hoped was still in my ear, but I didn't have the energy to find out. Right next to the earring was a red drool stain.

Wow, what had happened last night?

I reached out, picked up my phone and promptly switched it to silent mode. Even the sound of it vibrating against the wooden table was hurting my ears. I managed to sit up and leaned against my headboard.

Breathe. Let's start there.

I reached out instinctively for my water bottle, always perched next to me, drank a few glugs and breathed some more.

I scanned the room. Nothing was out of place. My laundry was still lying on my reading chair, unfolded, the book I was reading sat on my desk just the way I'd left it and my plants were chilling in the sunlight by the window, as they always did.

Okay. Memory. Needed. Come back. Breathe.

I could now remember taking my second drink and walking up the staircase with Aman to the second floor of his gorgeous penthouse. Must have been quite a few stairs, because I'd downed my second drink by the time I'd stepped foot on the hardwood floors as I followed him to a big wooden door. I remembered I'd been nervous, the alcohol making my brain form dirty images and my inhibitions melting away.

Aman had opened the door and ushered me into a room that was the most beautiful home library I had seen in my life. Wall-to-wall shelves of vintage dark wood on every side, with books organized alphabetically to make every reader orgasm on sight; the floor covered in a gorgeous maroon and bottle green handcrafted rug; two big armchairs arranged in the centre of the room with a wooden coffee table between them that had more books piled on it and a chessboard neatly placed on one side.

Wow, and wow.

'I knew you'd love this room.' Aman smiled at me as I took two steps into the library with my mouth wide open.

'This is your library?' I think I yelled this bit out.

He chuckled and took a step towards me. 'Ha ha! Yes. My father's, originally. But also mine.'

'Fuck off,' I gasped. 'This is the most beautiful library I've ever seen. Is that a first-edition set of Dickens's best?' I may have been screaming at this point.

He laughed and walked towards the shelf I was squinting at (the books were placed higher than my line of sight and I was a teensy bit tipsy, as I explained). He pulled out a wheeled ladder from a hidden duct and rolled it to the shelf.

'You have a ladder on wheels?' I squealed, pressing both my palms together near my chest. 'Can I ride? Please!'

He raised one eyebrow and the sexy smirk was back on his face. 'You don't have to ask me twice.' He winked.

I pursed my lips and tilted my head, nodding slightly. 'And I walked right into *that* one.'

He smirked and climbed two steps of the ladder, giving me the perfect view of his perfect ass. Eye-level. Right there. Up for grabs. One-arm distance away. Yum.

I must have looked at his butt for a moment too long, because when I finally snapped out of my daze and looked at him, he was looking down at me, amused.

'If you are done checking out my ass, do you want to take this book home?' he asked, smirking.

I could feel my cheeks flush red. I took the book from him, put my empty glass down on the coffee table and flipped the book open to take a big whiff.

Ahh. Heaven.

'I don't believe I'm holding a first-edition copy of *The Pickwick Papers*! This is a gold mine. I can live here!'

Aman stepped off the ladder and wheeled it back to its storage space.

'My father loves the classics. He's quite the collector.' He walked towards a glass cabinet.

'Did you spend a lot of time here too?' I asked.

'I did, but for a very different reason,' he said with a glint of mischief in his eyes.

He swung the cabinet doors open to reveal a fully stocked bar, with bottles and glasses of all sizes, colours and labels neatly arranged on the shelves. 'Gagan—my brother—and I would sneak here often when things got overwhelming. He would make himself a drink and we would chat for hours. I have good memories of this room.'

I smiled at him as he picked up my glass and fixed me another gin and tonic.

'Do you bring all your dates to this room? Is that your move?' I asked, taking a sip of my third drink.

'Oh no, I have a secret sex dungeon for most dates. The library is for nerdy bookstore staff only,' he said with a straight face.

I let out a loud snort and started browsing through the shelves.

… And that's all I could remember now, sitting on my bed, head being hammered from the inside.

At some point I had memories of him saying something on the lines of, 'Are you sure you want to switch to Scotch after drinking gin all night?'

I had visions of the inside of an elevator and a car, but nothing beyond that. Everything was a blur. So I picked up my phone and opened the group chat with Rhea and Maya. Martin would have told them something. But before I could type in a question, I gasped. I had about forty unread messages. About thirty of them were pictures.

Fuck my life.

I opened the first one. I was sitting on the bar with a bottle of gin in my left hand, my right hand wrapped around Martin's neck—goofy-faced, all teeth showing.

The second one was of me behind the bar, making drinks. *Very much the pro, Avani. Well done.*

The third one was of me, again, engaged in what looked like drunken ballroom-dancing with a girl I didn't remember meeting at the party.

The fourth one was of me again—this time on the balcony. Was I singing?

There were more pictures, mostly of me, trying to dance with Aman's liftman and a few other people on the street.

I closed my eyes in shock.

I let out a loud groan. Why did I have no memory of this? And, most importantly, why was Aman not in any of these pictures?

Triple-decker
Me: *WTF did I do?*
Rhea: *She's awake! Hahahaha! Morning, sunshine.*
Maya: *Ahh. The dreaded morning after.*
Me: *Shut the fuck up. Calling you both.*

I hit the video call button on the top right corner of my screen and waited for my BFFs to laugh at me on video. Rhea answered first with a wide grin on her face. Maya joined after, looking as calm and composed as she always did.

'Soooo? How was your night?' Rhea sang.

I let out a long sigh. 'Stop being annoying and tell me what happened,' I snapped.

'Calm down. Nothing happened. You had a great night. Clearly. Did you see the pic of you riding the duck in the children's park?' she said, not even attempting to hold back her laughter any longer.

'Yeah, we weren't there. We just heard about it this morning. You looked hot in the kurta, though,' Maya said.

'Oh god. How do you have these pictures? I'm going to kill Martin. I took him along specifically for this reason. I knew I would try to drink my nerves away around Aman,' I said, rubbing my face with my free hand.

'Bitch, I didn't do shit,' I heard Martin's voice. But he wasn't in this group. What was going on?

'Martin is with you guys?' I asked the girls.

'Nope,' Maya replied. 'I'm in the car on my way to work.'

'Nope,' came Rhea's reply.

What the hell? Was I hearing things now? I slowly got off the bed, still trying to get my limbs under control, and walked out to my living room.

Martin was sprawled like a blanket on my couch. The living room was a mess. There were board games strewn around—and were those knitting needles? Okay, someone needed to speak the fuck up.

'Girls, I just found a Martin on my couch. Lemme call you back,' I said and hung up.

'Wake up!' I picked up Martin's legs that were dangling off the couch and put them on my lap as I sank into the couch. 'Speak. What happened last night?'

He opened one eye and peered at me. I shook his legs vigorously to wake him up. He lazily sat up, stretching like a cat who'd slept for a year, and said, 'Good morning, beautiful.' And without answering my question, he got up and ambled towards the kitchen.

One thing about me, I'm as much an uninhibited person on alcohol as I'm a guarded one when I am sober. And I've not had one of these blackout nights in months, maybe years. I decided that if Martin didn't start speaking right now, he was never going to speak again. I followed him to the kitchen and glared at him as he made coffee.

'What?' he asked casually. 'I miss the Avani I met last night. She's so much more fun than the grinch who sits at the bookstore every day.'

'Oh my god, Martin. Just speak. What *happened?*'

'Nothing happened, bitch. You finally let your hair down and acted like the twenty-three-year-old you are. You had fun. That's what happened. And if you're asking if something happened with Aman ... no, it didn't. He just got to see the Avani who's fun and carefree. For all you know, it was a good thing to get drunk so early on in your little whatever-ship this is. Now he knows what he's signing up for.' He winked.

I hid my face in my hands. 'Did I say anything stupid?' I asked sheepishly. Because I knew I must have. With that many drinks in me, I was just surprised I hadn't woken up with Aman's name tattooed on my butt.

'Not so much what you said, but what you did,' he said.

'Martin ... WHAT did I do?' I could feel the heat rising up my neck and to my face, and a slight numbness taking over my arms.

'What you did was lick Aman's biceps,' he said plainly, bursting into laughter even as he moved away, out of my immediate reach.

I closed my eyes and sank to the floor.

The doorbell rang, and I felt my head start to hurt again. Martin ignored it and continued to laugh like a hyena, so I got to my feet and dragged myself to the door, making a mental note to tear off the bell box and burn it for being so loud and annoying, and yanked it open.

'Good morning, gorgeous. Coffee?'

AMAN

If you didn't know it already, I'm in love.

'You're up early,' I said, walking into Avani's apartment.

'Barely,' she whispered as she settled into a chair and reached for the cup of strong Americano I'd set down on her dining table. 'I'm so sorry about last night.'

Here she was, my girl, with her morning hair and sleepy eyes, looking exactly like I'd left her in her bed the night before. Gorgeous.

I grinned as I tucked a loose strand of hair behind her ear. 'You don't have to apologize. It was fun.'

'It's not fun now ... for me! I don't remember much after we left your library, and my friends are really unhelpful in these situations. I did something stupid, didn't I?'

'Define stupid.' I raised my eyebrows for effect.

'Ohhhh god,' she lowered her face into her palms and whined.

'It's fine, really,' I said. 'You were drinking and having a great time. It's normal. Everyone does it.'

'Not everyone ... *You* don't do it!'

'Yeah, well, but I get to do something better!' I bent down and whispered in her ear, 'I get to watch you do it.'

'Amannnn!' she cried, looking at me now, half-smiling.

'Hey!' I held her face in my hands till her eyes met mine. 'Stop overthinking it. You were being really cute.'

'Yeah? Was I cute before or after I licked your biceps?' Her smile had disappeared again.

I pursed my lips to hold back my laughter and looked into her eyes. I didn't think she would remember that, honestly.

'During.' I nodded and narrowed my eyes.

She folded her arms on the table and buried her face in them. I laughed and placed a soft kiss in her hair.

'Drink the coffee and lots of water. And there are donuts in the box. Eat them. You need the carbs.'

'You're leaving?' She looked up at me. Was that sadness in her eyes?

For a second, I thought of pulling my phone out to call Sheryl and ask her to move my meetings by an hour, but we had a big day at work and Papa was joining us on a call in exactly forty minutes. 'Got to get to work, baby,' I said softly. 'But I'll call you after?'

I gave her one last look and started walking towards the door when I saw something moving in the kitchen. I stopped in my tracks and peered in that direction. 'Avani, don't freak out, but I think there's something in the kitchen,' I said, taking a cautious step towards it.

'It's just Martin. He stayed over,' she said, without looking up from her coffee cup.

That was strange ... He'd been here all this time? I'd dropped him off last night at Jogi's apartment for their after-party. When had he got here?

'Martin!' she called out. 'Aman's here with donuts!'

'Hey, man.' Martin walked lazily out of the kitchen in his boxers. 'Thanks for the donuts. We needed them.'

'No worries, man. I hope you guys feel better soon. See you later.'

I began to walk out, then looked over my shoulder from the doorway. 'And Avani?'

'Hmm?' She looked up.

'You can lick my biceps anytime you like.'

She smiled coyly and bit her lower lip. 'Be careful what you ask for, Raina.'

I chuckled and pulled the door shut behind me as I left her apartment.

I looked back at the door as I waited for the elevator, thinking about the night before, when I'd last stood in front of it. The door was made of dark wood and had a hand-painted plank hanging at the centre with her name on it. A colourful decorative hanging with little bells at its ends hung along the top of the door frame. It looked like it was handmade. Large planters with tall plants flanked the door on both sides, and a wooden shoe cabinet placed along the left wall had smaller plants on it. Last night, when I'd practically had her hoisted on my shoulder while I dug into that bottomless bag of hers for her keys, she'd told me what each one of those plants was called.

I entered the lift as it arrived and met Ashok in the car, unable to stop smiling as I remembered the conversation.

'You want to know what they're called?' she'd slurred, waving her hand loosely at the plants.

'Yes, I do.'

'This one is Pintu. That one is Chhotu and this one is Ramesh,' she had introduced, her voice brimming with pride.

Right. 'What about the others?' I'd asked.

'I don't know. You and I left the party, silly ...'

I'd let out a small laugh as my fingers finally found her keys. I unlocked the door and almost keeled over as a sleepy Avani put her full weight on me as I carried her inside. I had never really asked her if she lived alone or with parents or a roommate. But I knew I couldn't let her go home alone in this state.

Her living room was warm, comfortable. More plants, colourful rugs, a navy blue couch piled with cushions and larger cushions strewn on the floor, and a large, framed painting of a mountain range hung above the couch. Beyond the room was a balcony with more plants and what looked like a swing chair.

'If you're planning a heist, jewels are on the fatroom boor,' Avani said, wiggling her eyebrows at me.

'Nice to know that the alcohol hasn't affected your memory as much as it has your speech,' I replied, grinning. 'Come on, let's get you to bed.' I tried to pull her off the floor, where she had settled right after we'd entered her home.

'Oh, Aman, how do you always know the right things to say?'

I shook my head and bent down to put her arm around my shoulder. She looked into my eyes and put both her arms around my neck instead.

'Now would be a nice time to read my mind, Raina.' She'd looked at me with half-open eyes and a gorgeous smile.

How I'd wished I could hold her face in my hands and kiss her, but I'd much rather she remembered every detail about our first kiss. So I bent lower, put my arm under her thighs, lifted her up and threw her over my shoulder in one swift motion. I liked how easily her body fit on mine.

'Okay. World is spinning,' she said. 'Loving the view, though.'

'Oiii!' I reacted when she slapped my ass with both her hands. 'Behave!'

She giggled and held on to my waist.

I entered her bedroom, turned the lights on and slowly lowered her on the bed. She threw her shoes off and got comfortable under the covers. She looked at me with mischief in her eyes and as much as I was tempted to get in next to her so I could hold her as she drifted off to sleep, I knew it would be too soon—and she was very drunk. I kneeled on the floor next to her bed and ran my fingers through her hair.

'You're okay?' I asked softly.

'I am now ...' She shut her eyes almost immediately. I stayed there looking at her for a couple of minutes, then I stood up, flicked the lights off and walked out of her apartment.

'Good morning, sexy.' My customary morning greeting always got Sheryl smiling. I picked up the folder she'd kept ready on her desk, and entered my cabin. Sheryl followed.

'How was your night?' she asked casually.

'It was great. How was yours?' I asked.

'Not much happened after I left your party.'

'So, you and Ma didn't spend an hour discussing Avani last night?'

'She told you? We had decided not to tell you that we think you two make a cute pair.'

'She didn't, actually … *You* just did.' I laughed. 'Shall we?' I asked, holding the folder up.

'Yes, please. The boardroom has been set up. Everyone should be there in the next five minutes.'

The rest of the day was one meeting after another. I barely got time to breathe. Finally, at 3 p.m., when I took off my jacket and sank into my office chair, exhausted, I noticed my breakfast sitting on my desk, next to my lunch and afternoon smoothie.

I loved days like this at the office. Full and productive. Strategizing, brainstorming, closing loops, filling gaps, learning more about each aspect of the business just by watching Papa do his thing. I used to be messy about planning my day until Sheryl took over my professional life, and now everything was arranged in colour-coded order on my calendar.

I'd just taken a sip of the smoothie and opened my laptop to check my e-mails when my phone pinged.

Avani: *YOU clicked all those pictures of me and sent them to my friends?! The deceit! No wonder you weren't in any of them.*
Me: *Haha. We needed proof. Because there was no way anyone would've believed the things you did if there weren't any pictures.*

Avani: *Okay ... I'm going to stop asking about your party now because I'm not enjoying a single thing I'm being told! How's your day been?*
Me: *Busy. Yours?*
Avani: *Will head to the bookstore now. Head's not spinning so much any more. Thanks for the coffee and the donuts this morning.*
Me: *Any time. Happy reading. :)*
Avani: *You too!*
Avani: *I mean, happy working.*

I smiled and put my phone down to go back to my e-mails. A minute had passed before my phone pinged again.

Avani has sent a photo.

I opened my chat box and downloaded it. It was a picture of me with a huge wet stain on my crotch from the time at the party when someone had run into me and spilt their drink all over me. I looked disgusted, but also like I'd peed my pants.

Me: *Touché. :D*
Avani: *You've met your match, Raina. ;)*

She was right about that.

20 APRIL 2023

AVANI

This can't be real.

After the very happening alcohol overdose, I was grateful for a slow Thursday at home. Exams were upon us, so classes had become more infrequent from this week and we were expected to have our noses buried in our textbooks. The last few days had been rather mundane. Just the regular home-bookstore-classes-home routine, peppered with flirty message exchanges with Aman. In between telling me I was gorgeous at least three times a day, he'd tried to explain to me in detail what he did in office—I understood the CEO part but my mind wandered when it came to the financial nitty-gritty of his work. Instead, I imagined how perfect he would look when he was sitting at his desk discussing important stuff and the company's future with his colleagues, and unbuttoning and rebuttoning his jacket between meetings.

I'd called Martin early this morning, right after rescuing my milk packet before it became Mhatre Kaka's cat's post-breakfast snack, and let him know that I was taking the day off from the bookstore. He'd whined about it for a bit, but then shut up when I told him I needed some time to study for the exams—and be on my own for a bit. I also messaged Rhea to ask if she could cover my shift for the day. Luckily, she was free and agreed. From the time I'd been a child, alone time had been important to me, especially when I needed a breather from the world to clear my head. At one point, dealing with my dysfunctional relationship with my parents had got so overwhelming that it had started affecting my schoolwork and my relationship with my friends. With gentle nudges from Aaji, I'd realized I needed to realign myself to make my own well-being my priority. The last few weeks had been a lot. University had been tough, I was slightly behind on my classes, I'd let someone new enter quite deeply into my life, and I missed home. This morning, I'd woken up tired and decided I needed to disengage for a bit.

It was 8 a.m. and I was still in bed, scrolling through my social media feed, when my phone buzzed and Aaji's name flashed on the screen. I answered immediately.

'Hi, Aaji! Good morning!'

'Good morning, my dove. How are you?'

Listening to Aaji's voice always put a smile on my face. I missed her every day since I'd moved to Mumbai from her home in Pune. When my parents had separated, Aaji had taken me in when I refused to stay with either of them. Not that I didn't want to live with Mamma or Baba—they had tried really hard to convince me I should be with one of them—but I never felt as close to them as I did to Aaji.

'I'm okay. Took the day off from work. How's your back?'

'Good enough to get back to my plants. You should see the garden, Avani. It's abloom! I'm glad you're taking time off for yourself. How are your classes going?'

'Classes are good. It's a slow semester and I have to catch up a bit. And work at the store has been good too.'

'Good, good. I'm so proud of you for working at such an early age.' I could tell she was smiling.

'I'm twenty-three, Aaji. People start working as early as seventeen these days. Besides, I'm just working because I can't get enough of the bookstore.'

'Avani, love, never do that. Never make yourself believe less about what you do. You work there because you like being independent and want to support yourself while you live in that big, scary city. Also, don't take my bragging rights away, please! All my friends cry about how their grandchildren are milking them for international trips, and I show off all the gifts you send me. Thank you for the smoothie-maker, dove. I love it. I use it every day.'

'Don't thank me, Aaji! I miss you. I'll come see you next weekend ... or maybe the one after that.'

'Come any day you want. Let me know a day before so I can shop for all the things you like to eat,' she said. 'Okay, listen, I am going to hang up now. Have to go to yoga class with my friends. Did you know they have puppies now at the classes? They are so cute. *Accha, chalo* ... Love you, my dove.'

'Ha ha ha! Send me photos! Love you, Aaji. Bye.'

I hung up, my heart quite full.

It was a bright, clear day and the Mumbai sun wasn't being the worst. So I jumped out from under the covers, made my bed, put my phone on charge, brushed my teeth and made my way to the kitchen for a cup of tea. I placed the cup and the new book I was reading on a tray and took it to the balcony, dragging along a floor cushion behind me. I settled in next to my beautiful potted palm, the sun shining just enough for me to enjoy it on my legs while the blue-and-white extendable canvas shade shielded the rest of me from it.

You know what I love about a good romance novel, especially a deliciously written dark romance, like the one in my hands now? That everything wrong and toxic in the real world seems so legit and obvious in the fictional one it creates. Of course the male protagonist killed the server who'd dared to look down his captive fake girlfriend's blouse while pouring her wine. Of course he burnt the server's body in the restaurant's oven but only after he'd plucked out his victim's eyes to keep them as souvenirs. And of course the girl loved him all the more because of how protective and possessive he was being about her. Fuck the girl, *I* had begun to love how protective and possessive he was being. Just the thought of how much I was enjoying the book suddenly put things in perspective for me. As much as I loved a good romance novel, sometimes a little more than the next person, it was scary how a well-written one could toy with your brain and make you feel things that were not real. Which didn't mean I wasn't going to get right back to the book and finish it ...

A good hour later, my mind properly shaken by what I'd been reading, I staggered to the kitchen for another cup of tea. While the water boiled, I heard furious mewing from outside the main door and felt generous enough to give Mhatre Kaka's perpetually hungry cat a bowl of milk in the hope that she would spare the pack left at my door at least once that week. I took the steaming cup of tea to the bedroom and picked up my phone from the bedside table. There was a message from Rhea telling me she was at the bookstore, along with a photo of a new shipment that had just arrived. I had been waiting to unbox and shelve a carton of books for over a week, so I made her text-promise me that she would leave this one for me to do as well. I also had a message from a certain broody sex bomb whom I hadn't stopped thinking about.

Aman: Good morning, gorgeous. :)
Me: Good morning, you.
Aman: Reached the bookstore?
Me: Took the day off.
Aman: Is everything okay? Are you okay?

I smiled at the screen, twirled on my toes and lay down on my bed. Everything else could wait.

Me: I'm fine. Just taking the day off. It's been a long few weeks. I just wanted to stay in and read and eat and then read some more.
Aman: Hmm. What are you reading?
Me: This mafia romance in which the main guy kidnaps the girl he likes and forces her to marry him, or he will kill her brother. And then they fall in love.
Aman: Okay. It was nice knowing you. Have a great life.
Me: Hahaha, shut up! It's a fun read. It's called fiction for a reason, you know?
Aman: Wow. Dark.

Me: *What are your plans for the day?*
Aman: *Nothing much. Standing in my kitchen waiting for the coffee pot to fill as I text you. Might make some breakfast and stay in. Not going to the office today. Will work from home, I think.*

Did he just hint that he's almost free today? Should I suggest we meet?

If he wanted to meet, he would've asked you. He wouldn't go about dropping hints.

I could invite him over …

You don't want it to look like you're hinting at something else.

I just don't want to leave home today … And why are you making this so difficult?

Aman: *Where did you go?*
Me: *I'm here … sorry. So, not much happening with you today then?*
Aman: *Nope.*
Me: *Just staying home and drinking coffee?*
Aman: *Yep.*
Me: *Fun fun.*

Fun fun? WTF? My small-talk abilities were clearly non-existent.

Aman: *Avani?*
Me: *Yes?*
Aman: *Yes, I would like to hang out today. Do you feel like it?*

I tapped my phone to my forehead and laughed to myself. How did I not expect this guy to see right through me? He'd been doing it ever since we'd first met.

Me: I don't want to leave the house.
Aman: Okay, coming over with supplies.
Me: Supplies?
Aman: I'm making you breakfast. :)
Me: Careful, Raina, you're going to ruin all the other guys for me.
Aman: Baby, there will be no guys left when I kill them one by one for looking in your general direction.
Me: Welcome to the dark side. :)
Aman: See you in a bit. ;)

This guy does NOT cease to surprise me. He was kidding with that line, quoting a classic dark romance hero, right? He had to be. He wasn't the type to be into dark romances. Either way, just the fact that he'd said the words made him a hundred times hotter. I re-read his message a few million times and made a mental note to listen more and picture him naked less when he got here. I'd be chill.

Forty minutes later, when my doorbell rang, I held myself back from leaping out of my couch and letting him in.

Glad you have the 'chill' thing going well, Avani.

I opened the door to see a dimpled face grinning at me from behind paper bags full of food supplies. Oversized white tee, black shorts, the coolest Birkenstocks, wet hair, the smell of aftershave.

'You showered?' I said with my mouth half open.

'Hello to you too.' He placed a soft kiss on my cheek and walked past me into the house, strode straight to the kitchen and deposited the bags on the counter. I locked the door and followed him.

'I'm not allowed to shower?' he asked, taking things out of the bags and placing them on the counter.

'It's no-work-no-classes day for me. I don't shower on days off. I feel filthy standing here when you smell like a god,' I said, perhaps a little irritably.

He gave me a hearty laugh. 'I worked out this morning, baby. I had to shower. Also, you look adorable. Morning bed hair might just be my favourite look on you. Can't wait to see it more often.'

'I'm going for a shower.' I rolled my eyes and turned to leave the kitchen when he gripped my wrist and pulled me towards him, swivelling me around. I gently hit his hard-as-fuck torso and my hands landed on his chest. He let go of my wrists and placed his hands on my waist.

I hadn't even brushed my teeth, I thought in panic. Or had I? He leaned in and my eyes closed on cue.

This is it. This is how it happens.

I could smell his aftershave as his warm breath hit the column of my neck. I tilted my neck back slightly so I could line my lips with his and took in a short breath. Electric currents channelled from my chest to my knees. If Aman hadn't had his hands on my waist, I would've fallen to my knees, and—

Fuck, Avani, not now.

I swallowed the lump in my throat to bring myself back to sanity and give in to whatever was about to happen, when I was swiftly scooped off the floor and placed on the kitchen counter. My eyes opened to see Aman's face inches away from mine, his hands placed on the counter on either side of me.

'You're gorgeous, you know that?' he whispered.

'I might've heard that every now and then, yes,' I teased.

'You'll hear it more often now.' He stayed as he was, studying my face while I explored his. His curls fell loosely on his forehead. His dreamy brown eyes stayed locked with mine. I wondered what it would be like to run my fingers along his jawline. And his hairline. And his shoulders. And …

'Okay!' He straightened up without warning. 'Eggs and French toast sound good?'

I swallowed and nodded.

'Coming right up.' He started opening the cabinet drawers and the fridge, and arranging the eggs, milk, cheese and bread, among other things.

Help him, Avani!

Maybe I should have jumped off the counter and helped him chop and prep. But my limbs didn't respond. I had a hot, dreamy guy in my kitchen cooking breakfast for me on a lazy Thursday morning.

This could not be real.

'So ... what's your thing?' I asked in the general direction of the kitchen.

'Huh?' Aman asked, peeking out from behind the fridge's half-open door, from where he was taking out a bottle of water.

We had just finished one of the best breakfasts I'd ever had. French toast *and* masala omelette, both perfect. I'd devoured massive portions of both in silent admiration, groaning like ... never mind what ... and had now finally arrived at putting into words the questions swirling in my mind for a few weeks.

'Do you have a huge toe? Or a chalk-eating obsession? Or are you a murderer?' I asked.

'What are you asking, exactly?' He laughed, drying his hands on the kitchen towel. He settled in on the sofa and patted the seat next to him, inviting me to his side.

I padded over and sat down facing him, with my legs tucked under my butt.

'Am I a murderer?' He pretended to ponder, mischief in his eyes. 'Why? Are you into that?'

'Depends. What do you prefer? Halal or jhatka?'

He laughed loudly. 'Wow, I can't ever predict what's going to come out of that mouth of yours.' He continued laughing.

'It's a valid question, you know. How do you kill your victims? Quickly?'

'I'm very much a poison-your-victims-by-cooking-them-breakfast kinda guy ... How are you feeling? A little dizzy?'

'Maybe,' I sniggered.

'Good, then. I must be really good at what I do.' He tugged at my chin as I kept looking at him. 'I need to know, though. Why do you ask?' His face turned serious.

'Just waiting for the other shoe to drop.'

'I don't follow.' He creased his brows.

'I don't know how to explain it.'

'Please try.'

'Being with you is like being in a public washroom.'

'Wow, baby. That wasn't what I had in mind when I asked you to talk dirty to me,' he mused.

'No! I mean, it's like when you're in a public washroom and you've latched the door shut but the minute you're butt-naked, squatting over the toilet, you fear someone's going to barge in and see you. Like, I know I've locked the door, I've double-checked, but I still worry about flashing an unsuspecting aunty. You know?'

'I really, REALLY don't.'

'What I mean is …' I said slowly, 'nobody is this perfect. There's got to be something wrong with you.'

'There are many things wrong with me.'

'Tell me one thing that you don't like about yourself. Anything.'

'Let's see … For one, I don't like that I don't take time out often enough to visit my parents in Mussoorie.'

I was going to exclaim that that hardly cut it, but the expression on his face made me pause. Gently, I asked, 'You miss them?'

'Every day.'

He looked at his fingers caressing mine. Slowly, he brought mine to his lips. 'Don't you miss home?'

'I do. Every day, like you. I might visit my Aaji next weekend in Pune.'

'Oh, tell me about her.'

Growing up, I was always confused while talking about my family life with friends, peers, colleagues or just about anybody. I didn't know how to put my life into words. My parents had separated, but they remained cordial and shared responsibilities when it came to me. I lived with my grandmother, away from both my parents. And now I lived by myself. It was the 'whys' that I never had answers to. Why did my parents separate? Why hadn't I chosen to live with either of them?

'She's everything to me. She raised me in her home in Pune till I decided to move to Mumbai for further studies. I miss her ... a lot ...'

'And what about your parents? Are they in Pune too?'

'No, they aren't.'

I knew he wasn't satisfied with the answer, but he didn't push further. From what little I knew of Aman, he had picked up on my refusal to answer the question.

The rest of the afternoon went by lazily. We watered the plants. I introduced him to Shanta Tai, who winked at me and gave me a (very uncharacteristic) thumbs-up in approval as soon as Aman had turned away. We went through the naughty covers of various kinds of romance novels and a gazillion photos of Aman's dogs on his phone.

This was not how I'd expected my Thursday to go. My plan was to eat the previous night's leftover Chinese takeout from the fridge and spend the day reading in bed. When I told Aman I had to catch up on a couple of missed classes from the week gone by, I was half-expecting him to get up and leave. But he surprised me by saying, 'Oh you should do that. Do you mind if I hang around and read this dirty novel of yours, meanwhile?'

'Sure, knock yourself out.' I smiled and went off to get my laptop from the bedroom.

My brain was nowhere near paying attention to the notes on my screen and I stole frequent glimpses at Aman lazing on the floor cushion on my right, reading. He looked relaxed. I saw his brows shooting up occasionally at what I'm guessing were some of the early non-veg parts, but other than that he seemed at peace by himself. Even till a few days ago, the most attractive thing in my living room was a perfect croissant Martin had baked. I got it home so I could click pictures of it during the golden hour. And now this beautiful man was lounging in my room, one hand holding his head up, flexing those yummy biceps, and the other holding one of my favourite books.

The more I looked, the more this strange new feeling kept grabbing at my chest. I didn't quite recognize it. I had been in a couple of relationships before, but if I were being honest none of them really drew me in. They were short. Like I was watching the screening of a film and then I just abruptly got up and left. Like I was looking at them through translucent glass. I could see most things in detail, but I knew if I reached out to touch them, I would touch nothing. Just the cold glass. I knew that for things outside my realm of comfort, I built my walls high enough. They were lowered for very few in my life. Aaji, Rhea, Maya, Martin. In them, I had everything and everyone I needed.

Was there room for one more person? How did Aman fit in so easily? I knew practically nothing about this guy who was making me feel all sorts of things. I wished I could say he was everything I was looking for. But I also knew that I didn't know what I was looking for. I was in alien territory, and every minute I spent with him was equal parts beautiful and terrifying. It occurred to me that it was like I was living in a romance novel, but without the option of flipping a few chapters ahead to know how it ended. It seemed to be playing out fine as of now, but I didn't know what the title was and I couldn't look up the reviews to see if it was worth it.

'I can hear you thinking,' Aman interrupted my chaotic train of thought.

He must have caught me zoning out with my mouth half open and eyes out of focus.

'Aha! What did you hear?' I asked, shutting my laptop and turning in my chair.

'Everything that you wanted to do to my naked body.' He sat up with a smirk and wiggled his eyebrows.

'Okay! That's enough with romance novels for today,' I said and walked over to him. I bent down to pluck the book out of his hands, and before my brain could make an informed decision, I took the book, turned around and sat down on his lap.

On. His. Lap.

What in the babysitting universe was that? Wasn't I JUST freaking out about how everything was moving too fast?

Wasn't I JUST doubting that Aman could very well be a murderer or, worse, a pyramid-scheme salesman?

The minute my brain registered what my body had done, I stiffened and stared straight ahead like I'd been electrocuted. I should have quickly got to my feet and blamed the whole thing on 'weak knees' (it wouldn't be a complete lie), but I stayed put.

I could feel my back pressing against his chest. His hands hovered in the air on both sides of me (like someone was holding a gun to his head), telling me clearly that he was as shocked as I was. His legs stayed frozen under me and I wished that the earth would just split and swallow me up whole. I gulped, pursed my lips and shut my eyes in a silent prayer to whoever was listening. Gods, Satan, spirits, energies, Mark Zuckerberg. My breath stuck in my rib cage and the veins on my forehead were about to burst. I regretted waking up that morning.

And then Aman wrapped both his arms around me and pulled me closer.

AMAN

Lemons, mint, aftershave and regret.

Her hair smelt of lemons and mint. Her back was pressed against me. Her body had frozen, giving away the fact that she'd acted on impulse and was instantly regretting it.

Her spine had stiffened, and before she could convince herself to tear away from me, I wrapped my arms around her and pulled her closer. I liked how perfectly she fit in my arms. I rocked forward and placed my chin on her left shoulder.

'Have *you* been reading my mind?' I whispered.

'Why?' she responded breathily.

'Because I've been wanting to hold you in my arms ever since I walked through that door this morning.'

She stilled for a bit. A moment passed. And then another. She remained silent.

I instantly regretted saying anything. Maybe she wasn't looking at this the same way I was.

'Tell me a secret,' she said softly.

'A secret?' I wasn't expecting that.

'Yes, anything. That tells me you aren't God's favourite child.' She half-turned to look into my eyes, and then looked down.

'I hate tomatoes,' I said.

'That doesn't count. Tell me another one.'

'I'm deathly scared of dolls.'

'Not good enough. Another one.'

'I sing Britney Spears songs in the shower.'

'Now we're warming up,' she smirked. 'Another one.'

Why was I not backing down when she asked me for ONE secret, you ask? The girl I had thought about every waking minute now for the past few weeks was sitting in my lap, snuggled in my arms. She smelt like fresh summer mornings and her skin was soft against my fingers as I traced tiny circles on her arms. She could ask me to run naked on the streets of Mumbai and I would do it without batting an eyelid. Sharing embarrassing secrets was a fairly easy deal.

'I haven't stopped thinking about you since the first day I saw you,' I said quietly.

'That's not a secret. You've made that clear with all the blatant flirting and smouldering eyes.' She again turned slightly to face me. I noticed little freckles on her nose that I'd missed before. Her cheeks were slightly pinker than a while ago and her big eyes looked into mine.

'Tell me something you've never told anyone,' she said.

Her eyes dropped down to my lips and back to my eyes.

'I've never been in love.'

She stilled in my arms. Her smile dulled ever so slightly, giving away that this wasn't the answer she was looking for. She let her breath out and parted her lips to say something.

'Yet …' I said quickly, before she could let a word out.

Something changed in her gaze. We must have sat like that for a few seconds before she spoke.

'Tell me one more secret.'

'I'm going to kiss you now,' I said. 'But that's not a secret.' My voice sounded raspy.

'Why?' she asked, swallowing.

'Because …' I cupped her face with my hand and she turned her body towards me. I gently held the back of her neck and pulled her face closer to mine. 'You knew that already.'

And then my lips were on hers.

AVANI

This guy is mad.

I gave in to the scent of Aman's aftershave as I ran my fingers through his hair. I had rehearsed this moment in my mind a thousand times before. For a brief second, he pulled away to look into my eyes, and then his lips were on mine again. Gentler this time, but more deliberate.

I felt my lips spreading into a smile when his hand dipped to my waist.

'You're ticklish,' he murmured, like he was making a note rather than asking me a question.

Slowly, he slid his other hand along my waist, and I squealed.

'Stop!' I said, holding his face in my hands, wriggling to stop the tickles.

He paused, but just for a second, and went right back in.

'Amannnnnnn! Pleaseeeee!' I laughed uncontrollably. 'Stoppppp!' I twisted and turned in his lap. 'I'll do anything. Pleaseeee!' I screamed.

He paused. 'Anything?' he asked, with one brow raised.

'Yes!'

When he stopped, I took a few breaths, still giggling in between.

'Be my girlfriend,' he said. The words rolled off his tongue like they'd been sitting there for a while. He sat up straight and tucked a lock of hair behind my ears. He brushed his knuckles softly against my cheek as his eyes bore intensely into mine.

And there it was. The other shoe. It had dropped.

This guy was mad. Delusional. Not in his right mind. Couldn't he see it was too soon? We'd known each other for just about two weeks and he wanted me to be his girlfriend? My mind was in a daze. I felt a strange tightness in my chest. This was stupid. This wasn't right. Relationships don't just start like that. On a whim. With no thought of the past or the future. Had he even figured out what he *didn't* like about me yet? There was a lot to not like ... How could he want me to be his girlfriend? What about love?

All I could do was stare. Which I did for an obscenely long time before following it up with the one thing that I should have avoided when I couldn't find any words to express what I was feeling.

I got up and walked away.

AMAN

Half-boners and goodbyes.

All right. What just happened?

One minute I was kissing her and the next I was sitting on the floor cushion with a ridiculous half-boner because she had simply got up and left. What was I not getting here?

When I finally had a grip on my thoughts, I slowly got to my feet and followed her.

'I'll take that as a no, then?' I said. The words came out snappier than I had intended them to. I couldn't put a finger on what I was feeling, but it was not pleasant. The slight sting I felt in my chest was unmistakeable.

'What?' she said, now pacing up and down in her kitchen.

'It's okay, Avani,' I said, steadying myself. 'I overstepped. I'm sorry.'

She stopped and looked at me. Maybe it was too soon, but I didn't regret telling her how I felt. God knows I fell for her the day I walked into the bookstore, and I would say I've not really hidden the way I feel. So why the sudden withdrawal? Was there something I didn't know? Or *someone* I didn't know about?

'I have to get back to my notes. I'll call you?' she said, her mind clearly elsewhere.

I felt a physical ache stemming from the centre of my chest and radiating to my shoulders. I wasn't expecting her to come running into my arms, but surely we could have had a conversation? Could she not see we'd developed a relationship that was a little different from the usual? Why was she looking at me like she didn't know me?

With no words to express my thoughts, I walked over to the table where I'd kept my car keys, picked them up, walked back to her, placed a kiss on her head and said, 'Okay.'

Then I walked out the door.

AVANI

It's for the best, I think.

I must have stood frozen where I was for a good while after Aman left. My brain was annoyingly silent now that I'd ruined a perfect moment.

Genius. Where exactly did you want to walk away to, Avani?

I was in MY house! A modest one-bedroom flat with a sad excuse for a balcony. It was so tiny that if I drilled for a little too long into my living room wall, I would have to gift Mhatre Kaka a painting to hang in his living room too.

Maybe I should go after Aman? Ask him to come back? But I'd done the right thing, hadn't I? It was right of me to not lead him on any more than I probably already had.

The voice in my head sighed, almost in relief, now that it could put the turbulent thoughts about Aman to rest. Now that it was over.

But there was another voice inside of me that had started whimpering. Like it was already heartbroken. Like it had let go of something that could've been magical.

But was the uncertainty worth it? What was I thinking going into this with my guard so low? I had never done that before. I'd been looking out for myself like I always had. Everybody got infatuated with someone every now and then. Especially if that someone was Aman.

I felt tears pricking the corners of my eyes, and forced them shut. There was no reason to overreact. I took in a deep breath and let it out, repeating the sequence a few more times. I'd decided to stay home that day, but I knew that would mean more moments of doubt and regret over the events of the morning. I took a quick cold shower to calm my nerves, threw on a T-shirt and leggings, and walked to the bookstore.

On the way, I messaged on the group chat to let the girls know I would be chilling at the bookstore for a couple of hours, and asked them if they wanted to join me for coffee. Maya responded saying she'd see me there in thirty minutes and Rhea texted saying she'd stepped out for an errand and would be back in twenty.

When I walked in, Martin was at his usual spot behind the coffee counter, his nose dipping alternately into a book and a big mug of coffee. I sat down heavily on the bar stool opposite him.

He looked up, then back at his book.

'Why are you here? Didn't you take the day off?'

'I did.' I shrugged. 'But I didn't feel like staying home by myself. Also, I was craving your eclairs.'

'Babe, my eclair is off-limits. It's reserved for hot strangers who promise to never call me after we bang once.' He winked.

'Yuck.' I hopped off the stool to pour myself a cup of coffee.

'Is everything okay? You look off.'

'Wow, thanks, Martin. Apologies for not looking perfectly presentable to you on my day off,' I snapped. It kind of slipped out before I could really think it through.

'The fuck is up with the sass?'

I shook my head and glared at the coffee that was filling up my mug.

Martin took two steps forward so he was now standing between the coffee machine and me.

'Talk, bitch,' he said. But his tone was softer than before.

'It's nothing,' I replied, trying to keep my voice from shaking. 'You want another coffee?'

'Avani?' Martin said, his hand on my shoulder. 'Talk.'

'Nothing. Like I said.'

'Is everything okay with your boo?'

'He is NOT my boo, Martin. Honestly, calm down. Everything is not a joke.' My voice was louder this time, though I didn't particularly know what I was mad about.

I picked up my coffee mug and made my way to the seat by the window. I knew I wasn't being fair. Martin was only checking on me. I looked down at my coffee and muttered a curse. What the fuck was going on with me? I took a few more deep breaths, then got up and walked back to Martin, who was now behind the coffee counter.

'Sorry ... I had a weird morning,' I said. 'I didn't mean to snap at you.'

'Like hell you did. What the fuck? What happened?'

'I kissed Aman.'

'Can't wait to see you burn this store down when you guys fuck, then.' He rolled his eyes. 'And why was that strange?'

'It wasn't.' I sighed.

Martin's brows drew together and he cocked his head in confusion, like I was talking to him in Mandarin.

'Are you high?' he asked, sounding almost worried. 'You kissed that fine piece of man real estate and came back with a frown and a fuck-all attitude?'

I looked at Martin.

'Was it bad?' he asked.

'Nope. It was perfect. Better than anything I'd ever imagined. It's what happened after that that was strange.'

The bell at the entrance dinged as Maya walked in.

'What's wrong? You both look like you've eaten worms,' she said as she settled into the chair opposite me.

'Avani kissed Aman and then came here in a bad mood and a killjoy vibe. I'm just trying to understand what's wrong,' Martin said.

'You KISSED him?' Rhea squealed from the entrance of the store as she put a big brown box of something on the floor and rushed towards us.

'Seriously, Rhea, read the room.' Maya took Rhea's arm and forced her to sit on a chair next to hers. She turned to me. 'We're here to help, Ani. We can figure this out. Talk to us.'

'It's not a big deal, guys. I don't know what's wrong with me.' I sighed again.

'Just walk us through your morning,' Maya said calmly.

I told them. About the texts, about the breakfast, about the conversation that followed, about the lap-sitting, about the kissing ... about the G-word. If ever there was a group of people who knew me better than I did myself, it was this one. I didn't even have to finish the story after that. All of them collectively sucked in their breath and hissed.

'Please tell me you stayed there and had a conversation, and DID NOT run away as soon as you heard "girlfriend"?' Maya said with her eyes closed, like she already knew the answer but was willing it to be otherwise.

'I ... umm ... walked away ... and then ... umm ... told him I would call him,' I said, now regretting every word I'd uttered all over again.

'YOU SHOOED OFF THE GUY YOU'VE BEEN OBSESSING OVER FOR THE PAST FEW WEEKS AFTER SHARING THE MOST AMAZING, TOE-CURLING KISS WITH HIM?' Rhea screamed. 'DID YOU FORGET WHAT HE LOOKS LIKE??'

'Rhea ...' I started.

'ARE YOU INSANE?'

'That's exactly my point, okay?' I retorted. 'Is that all that matters? How good he looks, how he's saying and doing all the right things? Yeah, he looks great. Yes, he's thoughtful and charming and respectful and funny. Yes, he's focused and successful and close to his family. He has dogs and loves them enough to leave everything and fly a thousand kilometres when one gets stung by a bee. He knows exactly what to say and where to be, and he brings me a lot of joy ...'

'Bitch, you're really not making a case for yourself here,' Martin said, his voice quiet.

'Yeah ... I don't understand ...' Rhea added.

'My point is that ... how do you guys not see it? It's all too good. How can someone be everything? He's too perfect. He's too good.'

There. That was it.

'And ... that's a problem, why?' Martin asked.

'Because it doesn't seem real. I don't believe he—'

'But you don't even know the guy,' Maya said. 'How do you know he's perfect? Maybe if you spend some time with him, you'll learn about his flaws.'

'We've been speaking to each other every waking minute for the past two weeks. And nothing about him seems off yet. How do I know if there's something wrong with him?' I asked.

'You *want* something to be wrong with him?' Martin asked.

'Seriously, Ani, all the guys who show interest in me end up stealing my credit card or keying my car. And you have this perfectly yummy, charming guy asking you to be his girlfriend and your problem is that he has no flaws? Unbelievable ...' Rhea said, shaking her head.

'I know this sounds ridiculous when you say it like that, but you guys don't get it.' I picked up my phone from the counter. 'I'll see you later.'

I walked out of the store without looking back. A strange feeling clawed at my chest. I had hoped for the conversation with my friends to go differently. Yes, they were right about Aman. But they knew Aman slightly less than I did.

Things weren't always simple. A guy like Aman didn't just waltz into your life and ask you to be his girlfriend. He was successful, older, sorted. He lived in a luxury penthouse and had a mansion in the hills, and I was just a student who worked at a bookstore to be able to afford rent—that, too, because one of Aaji's friends had a place that was just sitting there gathering dust and she wanted to rent it out for peanuts so it would not just come crumbling down one day. Aman and I weren't in the same league. He had his ducks in a row and my ducks were basically floaty plastic bath toys. If he was ready to be my boyfriend in the few days that we'd spent together, maybe he'd meet me with a cushioned velvet ring box the next time we went to dinner. Who knows?

So this was for the best. Before more damage was done.

I think.

2 MAY 2023

AMAN

Had I jumped the gun?

I hadn't texted Avani or attempted to call her since I'd walked out of her apartment almost two weeks back. I needed to work things out for myself first, clear my head of the thoughts crowding it.

I hadn't felt this way in a very long time—not since I was twenty-four, when my girlfriend of six years had moved to Australia and ended things with me the minute she'd settled in there. There hadn't been much of a conversation then either. With Avani, I wished the conversation had gone differently. Or at all. Her sudden withdrawal and reaction indicated I'd hit a nerve, but I couldn't figure out what it was. Maybe I should've been a little more careful, taken things slower.

Not in a million years had I thought I would be this involved with anything—or anyone—that wasn't to do either with my family or my work. I had trained myself to be a fairly realistic and clear-headed person, until Avani had come along and disrupted what I thought I knew about myself.

Avani wasn't just another girl who'd caught my attention with her expressive eyes, thick brown hair and infectious laugh—she was the calm that had settled comfortably into my otherwise hectic, work-driven life. She wasn't a distraction—she was the counterpoint to the hyper-focused, disciplined routine that my days were. She made it all lighter, and filled it with pleasure and excitement and wonder.

And being with her had made me realize the 'why' of it all.

Suddenly I knew WHY I worked maniacally every day. Because before her, there'd been no one who'd made me want to take the focus away from work, or find joy in anything else. I hadn't met anyone before Avani whom I wanted to spoil, pamper or provide abundantly for. As the youngest of the family, I grew up being the pampered one. And now I'd met someone *I* wanted to protect and keep in the warmth of my arms on every windy day.

I knew WHY I now walked with a spring in my step, especially when I knew it was leading me to her. Because I was ready to go a long way with her.

I knew WHY none of my other relationships had felt like anything more than effort. Because they weren't with her.

So why couldn't I ...

I sat up and held my phone tightly with both hands ... but dithered.

This was stupid. I was a grown man and the CEO of my company. Making decisions was what I did best. I could do better. I knew better. This was getting very desperate very fast. I contemplated calling Jogi to hear his two cents on the matter, but decided against it when I played out the lines in my head.

Jogi, so you remember Avani, right? Yeah, I asked her to be my girl and she kind of asked me to leave her apartment. And ... well ... I've no idea what to do about it now. What should I do?

No, that wouldn't do. So I called up the one person in my life I knew could help me look at things from Avani's perspective.

'Hi, Babu.'

'Hi, Ma.'

'You've called me on a Tuesday afternoon.'

'I'm so glad old age hasn't hampered your time-telling skills.' I smiled into the phone.

'And you are in office and joking with me ...' She let her voice trail off.

'But old age has definitely made you a fan of stating the obvious,' I replied, trying to keep the dullness out of my voice.

'What did you do?'

'How are you so sure it's my fault?' I asked, slightly offended but also curious.

'Because if you'd called her before you called me, you would've known what you've done wrong. And you clearly haven't spoken to her, so here we are.'

I had to give it to Ma. I hadn't even mentioned Avani.

I sighed and narrated the story so far. After which, for a full twenty minutes, Ma proved to me that whatever had transpired was my fault, after all.

Maybe I'd got a little too excited and jumped the gun with the whole thing. It wasn't completely fair of me to dive into the relationship when baby steps were what had got me to hold her in my arms in the first place. I could've taken it slow and met her midway instead of pushing her that day because I was so sure of how I felt. And though I had kind of known she was it for me the first time I had met her, two weeks was indeed a very short time to expect a commitment from anyone.

'So what should I do now? Did I scare her off? Should I then just let her go?' I asked Ma.

'That's up to you to decide, son.' Papa had joined our chat midway. The two of them were inseparable, especially when it had something to do with Gagan or me.

'We can't tell you whether or not you should give up or work harder to be with her,' Ma said. 'But if you carefully consider all angles, I'm sure you will get your answers. Whether you like them or not.'

More points to Ma for being crystal-clear in the first part of the conversation and then painfully cryptic in the end.

I had to admit I felt calmer, though. I took a deep breath till the strange tightness in my throat and shoulders eased. I told them I loved them, ended the call, leaned back in my chair and let out another long breath.

I knew what I had to do. I picked up my phone and began to type.

Hey, gorgeous. I'm going to get right to the point. I'm sorry for springing the relationship stuff on you the other day. I might've gotten ahead of myself. However, we still deserve a conversation, don't you think? I won't rush you. I'm here whenever you want to talk. Can't wait to hear your voice. It's been too long.

I hit send. My knee tapped against the bottom of my desk as I stared at my phone, waiting for a response. Was I going to get one? I told myself that even if I didn't, it would be okay. As romantic as it sounded to follow a girl to the ends of the earth because real love didn't take no for an answer—or whatever else the movies taught us—I'd been raised to respect it when a woman said no.

My phone pinged.

Avani: *Dinner at mine? 9 p.m.?*
Me: *I'll get dessert. :)*

My mother was a magician. Or maybe it was simply that she was a woman.

AVANI

Wise and stupid.

I'd lost count of the number of days that had passed since I'd handled yet another simple situation with my brilliantly complex emotional reflexes. I wasn't proud of myself. I played and replayed the entire sequence with Aman in my mind, and redirected minute details from each scene to remake the memory of when I'd seen him last. I could've explained how I felt, told him it was perhaps too soon, that I needed time. Instead, I'd walked away and asked him to leave.

This was so not how it went in the romance novels I read. I mean, what happened to the classic third-act break-up? Wasn't I supposed to mindlessly fall for him for the first two-hundred-and-fifty pages before I found out that he'd fucked up big time? Instead, I'd ended the story before it had even begun. A part of me was curious to find out how it would've gone, but the bigger part of me felt a certain comfort in staying curious. It was true. He was ... too good to be true. Anyway, it was easier to get over a small disappointment at the start of things than to get over a heartbreak later.

It had taken me about two weeks to feel as close to Aman as I did, so I imagined that's how long it would take for me to undo those feelings for him.

I had forced myself back into my regular routine.

Wake up. Chai and gossip with Shanta Tai. Bookstore. Classes. Coffee or dinner with the gang. Study. Late-night comfort shower. Scroll through my last text thread with Aman. Fall asleep.

Every morning I woke up telling myself that I would call him and deal with the situation like an adult, but mornings rolled into afternoons and then evenings, and by the time it was night I would push it to the next day. Every time. What could I say to him that would make me sound like a sane person anyway? I'd frozen when I had the chance to say what I felt, and now anything I said, no matter what it was, would be insignificant.

Through all of it, one irritating question repeatedly played on my mind: Was I being wise or was I being stupid? Wise, because I was proud of the fact that I had my own back and could save myself from being further disappointed. I had kept my past in mind and let it be my guiding light for the future. I hadn't been beguiled into believing that life was offering so much so easily. Stupid, because, well, I could deny it, of course, but the truth was that Aman had brought me joy. He'd brought light and laughter into my life and successfully revived my flirting skills from a garbage heap of bad dates and mundane dating-app conversations. He had made me want to spend that extra minute every morning doing my hair so he could brush it off my shoulder or tuck it behind my ear mid-conversation. He had made me want to read the newspaper aloud every day so I could surprise him with the elevated stock price of his company's shares. He had made me want to slow down my pace every time we were walking anywhere together, only so he could stop, turn around and hold my hand to make sure we were walking side by side. It was almost like God had made this perfect guy walk into my life and then thrown in all my trust issues for funsies.

On the weekend after that Thursday, I had taken a bus to visit Aaji in Pune. She hadn't asked me any questions, but she knew that my unannounced visits always came with a need for comfort. She bustled about, fussing over me, cooking and feeding me more food than I could eat in a whole week, and rushed off and bought me two new books. Romance novels, of course, because nobody supported my addiction to them as much as she did. But I didn't feel like reading them. Instead, I found stuff to fix around the house, including the drain of her kitchen sink, and went with her to yoga class. When I got back home on Monday morning, I felt calmer, but as the day progressed, the uneasiness crept in again.

I sat in class the next day, staring into space, thinking of nothing in particular, while Mr Desai droned on about how modern constitutional law was the offspring of nationalism, when my phone vibrated in my bag and I sneaked a peek at it.

Aman: *Hey, gorgeous. So I'm going to get right to the point. I'm sorry for springing the relationship stuff on you the other day. I might've gotten ahead of myself. However, we still deserve a conversation, don't you think? I won't rush you. I'm here whenever you want to talk. Can't wait to hear your voice. It's been too long.*

I mean, COME ON, Avani! How can you not want to be around this guy?

I read and re-read the message, and every time I did I felt a tiny sliver of joy warming up my chest. I had done a pretty great job of convincing myself that not being near him wasn't a big deal. That was until now, until the possibility of actually seeing him again became real. He was right. We did deserve a conversation.

Me: *Dinner at mine? 9 p.m.?*
Aman: *I'll get dessert. :)*

I needed to get home. I waited for Mr Desai to finish whatever he was talking about, packed my stuff quickly and bolted out of class. I had just enough time to rush home, shampoo my hair and order Chinese takeout. But first ... I fished my phone out of my bag and pulled up Martin's contact card. I hit the call button and he answered almost instantly.

'Ssup, babe?'

'I asked Aman to come over for dinner.'

'You did?'

'Yeah.'

'Was someone holding a gun to your head?'

'Martin, please.'

'What do you need to hear?'

'That this is just dinner and I don't need to freak out about it.'

'This is just dinner. You don't need to freak out.'

'And?'

'And it's okay even if you do freak out. Just put your thoughts into words so it's a healthy conversation.'

'Okay.'

'He's a good guy.'

'I know.'

'And you are a great girl.'

'Yeah?'

'Babe, you're one of the nicest, most caring people I've met. You'd guard your people with your life and you have impeccable taste in friends ...'

'I knew I should've called Maya.'

'Love you too. Call me after,' he said before hanging up.

I got into a taxi to head home, and had just tapped open my phone again to call Maya when I saw her name flashing on my screen.

'I was just going to call you,' I said as soon as I answered.

'Martin just called saying you're meeting Aman for dinner.'

'Yeah, I should talk to him.'

'Do you want me to come over later?'

'Not really, no. I'll be fine.'

'Ani?'

'Hmm?'

'It's okay to do something and regret it than to regret not knowing what it would've felt like.'

'I'll call you after, okay?'

'I'll be here, cutie. I love you.'

'I love you.'

Maya. I wish I could put her in a locket and wear her around my neck all the time. That woman worked better than crystals. She'd made me feel instantly calm, and I let that feeling seep into my being—before following it up with a flutter of excitement that I hadn't felt in a while.

I was about to rush into my building when I stopped in my tracks and turned around to see a car parked outside.

And there it was.

Aftershave.

Aman walked towards me, that familiar, dimpled smile lighting up his face.

'Hi, gorgeous.'

White shirt, blue jeans, holding bags of what looked like too much food for two people. Hadn't he said just dessert? For a second I wasn't sure if he was walking towards me in slow motion or if I was dizzy from all the extra oxygen reaching my brain because I was finally breathing after the twelve days that I hadn't see him.

God, I'd missed him. And now that he was here, whatever little restraint I had imposed on myself vanished. He'd set the bags of food down on the floor, and I let him scoop me up in his arms as I wrapped mine around his neck and buried my face in his shirt's collar. He smelt of shower gel, laundry detergent and aftershave, and suddenly my eyes burnt and tears began to roll down my cheeks as I held on to him tighter.

There was absolutely no need for this to get so dramatic so quickly. We hadn't even got to whatever conversation we were supposed to have, and I was already a mess. Maybe it was the guilt of having behaved the way I had. Maybe it was the utter confusion about why I had issues with trusting this man who had given me nothing but happiness in whatever time I'd spent with him. Maybe it was just the relief of having him close to me again, smiling at me and holding me like he never wanted to let me go.

'I missed you too,' he whispered as he placed a kiss in my hair before lowering me back to the ground.

I smiled against the fabric of his shirt as my hands moved from the nape of his neck to his chest. My head rested against it so I could hear his heart beating.

At a very normal rate.

'Your heart's not racing,' I mumbled.

He laughed. 'What?'

'My heart's beating so fast. Yours isn't. I thought you were excited to see me.' More mumbling.

Aman held my face in his hands and tilted it up. 'It was racing until I saw you,' he said.

'So, you're saying?'

'I'm saying you bring me calm.'

I gently ran my thumb over the stubble along his jawline. He turned his face so he could place a kiss in the palm of my hand.

We picked up the bags of food and walked in silence into the elevator and then into my apartment. The energy between us was familiar, but still a little tense. Maybe he was wondering how to begin the conversation we'd decided to have, just like I was wondering how much to reveal to him and how much to keep safe. I didn't know yet what he'd want to know, but more than that I didn't know exactly how much I wanted to share. It had been more than a year since I'd sat down and actually spoken to someone about all the things that haunted me. I didn't know if I was ready to bare myself just yet. What I did know was that I had to apologize to him for being a complete ass. So I spoke before he could.

AMAN

There she is.

We'd barely walked into her apartment when Avani turned to me and said breathlessly, 'I'm so sorry. I've acted like a complete and utter brat, and I want you to know that that's not who I am. At least not all the time. I mean … I'm better than that. I'm sorry I froze. I'm sorry I was rude. I'm sorry I didn't call or text you. I thought of it, I went over all our chats, over and over again, but for some reason I couldn't get over whatever I was feeling. I don't know how to explain it and I know it wasn't nice. I'm sorry I acted selfishly and didn't give a thought to how you must've felt. But I want you to know that whatever I did or did not say wasn't because of you. It was because of me. It was because I have … these issues … that make it tough for me to simply believe that a perfectly great guy like you would want anything to do with me. My life in the past few years has been weird and I didn't know it would creep up on me like it did the other day. I like you. And I like spending time with you. So please believe me when I say I really am sorry.'

She took a breath, shut her eyes tight, then opened them and looked at me earnestly. I wanted to gather her in my arms and hug her so tight that all her broken pieces would be glued back together. I wanted to tell her that she shouldn't feel guilty for feeling the way she did. I wanted to kiss the tears off her cheeks and pull her to my chest so the world wouldn't be able to get to her in whatever way it had in the past.

Instead, I smiled. 'Okay.'

'Okay?' she asked, surprised.

'Yeah. Okay.'

'That's all you want to say? You don't need to know why I acted the way I did?'

'The only thing I NEEDED to know was that you like me.' I tucked a stray strand of hair behind her ear.

She looked at me with those big, beautiful eyes of hers and an expression that looked like a mixture of amusement and relief. Like she wanted me to say more but was relieved that I had accepted her apology without any more dialogue. A ghost of a smile tugged at the corners of her lips and her eyes lit up in the way they always did when she was about to say something playful. She got on her toes and placed a soft kiss on my chin before she turned to walk towards her bedroom.

'I'm going to take a shower,' she announced from her bedroom door.

My eyebrows shot up of their own accord. 'Are you going to leave the door open?' I asked.

'Umm, no.' She narrowed her eyes.

I sighed. 'Then don't tempt me with details I have nothing to do with, sweetheart.'

'Why will I leave the door open if you're in there with me?' She winked.

'Really?' I blurted out.

'No!' She laughed an exaggerated laugh as she went into the bathroom and locked the door.

And there she was, my little flirt.

MAY, JUNE, JULY 2023

AVANI

Playing with fire.

If I said what followed over the next few months was fun, it would be an understatement. What followed over the next few months was a fucking fairy tale! It was like someone had installed new batteries in my clock and given every wall in my mind a fresh coat of paint. Let me walk you through it.

I had almost the whole of May off from classes, and then some more. I spent more time at the bookstore. Maya, Rhea and I went on several museum and art gallery dates. I spent a whole week with Aaji, helping her pack for her trip to Kashmir with her gal pals (her words, not mine). Martin and I hosted baking lessons for kids at the store on alternate weekends. Martin baked and I was just the guinea pig used for tasting all the shit the kids made. I might or might not have got a terribly upset stomach for all of the following week, but it was nothing Shanta Tai's rasam and regular cuddles from Aman couldn't fix.

Speaking of Aman, we spent most of our evenings together. After the conversation at my house and the heartbeat-calming shower, which I sadly took by myself, we came to the conclusion that we should take it slow and see where it goes. We agreed we both loved spending time with each other, so we decided to start there.

'So you'll be my time-spender?' he asked goofily, his mouth full of the world's best spring rolls from Prashant Chinese Corner.

'I can be your money-spender too, Daddy,' I shot back, winking.

He laughed so hard that I was sure the rest of the spring roll would come out of his nose, while I cringed visibly at the words that had left my mouth. I spent the rest of the dinner convincing him that I had no interest in his money and he spent it laughing at me for the shit I sometimes blurted out.

That was the evening I knew exactly what I wanted to spend all my time with him doing. Making him laugh. He had the brightest laugh I'd ever heard, and it came from deep within. His brows bunched up, little lines appeared in the corners of his eyes, which turned into slits, and his dimples put on a full show. He also had rich-people teeth, that were unbelievably clean and white and perfectly aligned. And sometimes—just sometimes when I absolutely killed it with my one-liners (especially the flirty ones)—he pressed his face into the palms of his hands and his shoulders slumped, as did his neck, in the sense of a subtle surrender. Which told me I'd won that round. And I didn't have to try too hard either. He laughed easily and at all my jokes, so he was great for my already inflated ego.

The other day we were rearranging the books in his gorgeous library at home (my idea!) when, without any explanation, he cleared a tiny corner shelf at the top.

'We can leave that empty,' he said.

'Why would we leave a whole shelf empty? We have so many books that can go there.'

'That shelf isn't for those books.'

'You're doing that thing where you use a lot of words to get to the point, sir.' I rolled my eyes as I wiped another leatherbound Jane Austen clean and placed it on the opposite shelf.

'I want you to give me a list of your favourite romance novels. All the dirty ones with the dirty covers. This shelf's for those.' He carried on with the task at hand like he hadn't just laid me on a table, made careful incisions in my chest cavity and sliced a piece of my heart out for himself.

I slowly turned and stared at the back of his head, till he laughed and, without turning around, said, 'Don't look at me like that.'

The god of guts and overconfidence must have shone her brightest spotlight on me, because I strode over to him, turned him around, lowered that gorgeous head of curly hair with both my hands and locked my lips with his. I knew I'd caught him off guard, as his face showed equal parts surprise and delight.

'Wow,' he breathed. 'What was that for?'

'No reason. Just felt like it.'

He broke into a wide grin, grabbed my waist and picked me up like I was a bag of feathers and floof. He carried me to the coffee table, raised his left leg up on it so I now had the world's most comfortable seat as I wrapped my legs around his waist. We must have made out for a minute—or twenty—when I finally pulled back and looked into those deep brown eyes.

'Going forward, please always do whatever you feel like. Whatever,' he said, smirking.

'I always do!' I blushed as I dismounted from his leg. (It wasn't as dirty as it sounds.)

I know, I know. We'd decided to take it slow, but ... let's be serious, I was taking it slow by not ripping his clothes off and stripping down to do something I haven't stopped thinking about.

On days when we weren't eating Chinese takeout on my couch or making out in his library, Aman and I took long walks in the city. I hated, hated, hated the summer heat that Mumbai spat up all through May, so Aman would pick me up late at night, when the roads were emptier and the breeze cooler. We would walk along Girgaon Chowpatty, Marine Drive and the bylanes of Colaba, or sometimes just sit by the sea at the Gateway of India. His company made the flags that were hoisted on all official buildings and historical sites in the country, so he got special access to sit right under the Gateway at any time of the night after the place had been closed to visitors. I wasn't surprised. He could tell me his family owned the Gateway of India because Queen Victoria lost it to his great-great-grandfather in a taash party during Diwali, and I would have believed him in a heartbeat.

We would talk about video games, comic books, pet peeves, twerking and just about anything that came into our heads. Or we'd stare at the sea while I rested my head on his shoulder and he drew little circles in my palms with his fingers. I would try to match my breaths with his just so our bodies moved together.

We were a fucking postcard, y'all!

Later at night, I would lie in bed smiling to myself like an idiot. I tried to warn myself about getting ahead of things, but mostly just immersed myself in the calm I felt every minute I spent with Aman. I hadn't felt that in a very long time.

Baby steps, Avani.

Baby leaps.

June started with me visiting the private airport in Mumbai for the first time. Did you know Mumbai had a private airport? I always thought chartered flights flew out of rich people's backyards. Turns out I was wrong. Aman had to fly to Italy for a couple of weeks for a work conference, followed by a family vacation, so I graciously offered to drop him to the airport. In his car, to his private jet.

'I would say I'll miss you, but Professor Umbridge says one must not tell lies,' I said, pretending to be coy.

'In that case, I'll miss you too. And I will definitely not be checking out the half-naked Italian women on the beaches of Sicily.' He smirked as he hooked one arm around my waist and pulled me closer.

'And I ...' I started. 'I ...'

'Yes?' he drawled.

'Fine, I'll miss you for real. Ugh. Don't look at Italian boobs, please.' I rolled my eyes and tucked my head in his chest. 'Not that I care,' I added.

'Absolutely love this carefree side of yours. No Italian boobs, I promise,' he whispered, holding me closer still.

'Good. And get me a fridge magnet, okay?' I said as I hugged him tight.

'Avani?'

'Hmm?' I murmured against his chest.

'Who's Professor Umbridge?'

I looked at him squarely in the eyes and said, 'Aman, don't dare walk into my bookstore again.'

I still had a week before classes would start after summer break, so I took an impromptu trip with the girls, Martin and Dhruv. Our destination wasn't Italy, but a close second. Mahabaleshwar.

The six-hour-long drive to the hill station felt immeasurably long till we got to our hotel just in time to witness the sunset. The world made sense again. The view from our room's balcony was to die for and the breeze was cool with the anticipation of the monsoon. Maya, Martin and I bunked together in one room, and Rhea and Dhruv took the second one. By this point we had all kind of started pretending that we were blind and didn't bother asking them about their relationship status—even though we had a million questions. Are you two dating? Is it serious? Is it casual? Does Rhea know what casual means? Do you guys think we are stupid?

But Rhea looked happy, so we let them be. Which meant that Maya, Martin and I spent most of that weekend together, chatting, (over)sharing, laughing, doing extensive skincare routines, taking long untimely naps and longer rambling walks.

'Babe, when Aman asked you for pictures from the trip, I'm pretty sure he meant ones of you, preferably naked. Haven't you sent him enough pictures of the sky already?' Martin joked on the second evening, after the sun had sunk below the horizon and I had reviewed the photos I'd taken of a perfect painted sky.

'Yeah, there is a sky where he is.' Maya laughed. 'And maybe a much prettier one.'

'Speaking of pretty ...' I picked up my second glass of Long Island Iced Tea from the side table and lay down on my stomach on the bed, where Martin and Maya were lounging. I increased the brightness of my phone screen and turned it around towards them.

'Mother ... fucker,' Martin whispered, bending forward to take a closer look.

'I call Photoshop,' Maya said, one eyebrow raised. 'That can't be real.'

I proudly shrugged and turned the screen back towards me to gawk at the image Aman had sent of himself earlier that morning.

Sit back, relax, let me paint a picture for you.

Aman. In white swimming trunks that hung low, low, LOW on his toned, tight waist. He was kneeling on the beach, flashing those high-grade man thighs, with sand peppered across his legs and chest. His right hand gripped the neck of a beer bottle tightly enough for those veins in his forearms to pop, and his left hand rested carelessly on his thigh. His toned, muscled torso was tanned and glistening like he'd just stepped out of the ocean after a swim. There were specks of crystallized salt on his collarbone and his neck muscles were flexed in the way I knew they did when I said something goofy. And there it was, that gorgeous, gorgeous smile on that gorgeous, gorgeous face. His wet hair was brushed back like he had just run his fingers through it and his eyes were hidden behind what must have been a stupidly expensive pair of sunglasses.

I'd always wanted a tattoo. But I could never decide what would make me feel hot enough to get an image of it branded on my skin for the rest of my life. Now I knew. This exact picture of Aman, tattooed in colour on my left fucking butt cheek—because the right one was reserved for Daniel Radcliffe's autograph whenever I saw him.

'How the fuck have you kept your hands to yourself?' Martin asked.

I took a huge sip of my drink and replied, 'I mean, I've barely managed to keep my pants on when he walks towards me in those dress pants and shirts with the sleeves folded up to his elbows. If he ever wore his swimming trunks when I was around, I would lose it.'

Too Good to Be True

I made a mental note to never go swimming with Aman. Or to the beach. Or to the sauna. Or anywhere that would require us to not be fully clothed.

'Bitch, lose it. PLEASE!' Martin exclaimed.

I smiled to myself, rolled on to my back and opened Aman's chat.

Me: I think you should wear your swimming trunks every day. To work, to the gym, on our walks. Every day.
Aman: You're still staring at that photo from this morning, aren't you? You little creep.
Me: Listen, I've had a couple of LIITs and the true beauty of that photo is just beginning to shine through. Let me admire it.
Aman: You haven't sent me any pictures of your pretty face, you know that?
Me: Your face was in that picture too?
Aman: Funny.
Me: Yummy.
Aman: I gotta go. Everyone's waiting for lunch. Call you tomorrow?
Me: Have fun. Can't wait.

One more LIIT and I would have typed, 'I love you.'

I could barely sit still through the first week of the new semester because Aman was going to be flying back to Mumbai that weekend. I finished all my laundry, cleaning, bill payments and other adult bullshit before that, so I could spend every minute possible with him. He, obviously, hadn't made any such plans with me, but in my head it was all decided.

I was sitting in the last class of the day when my phone pinged.

***Aman:** What's my girl doing?*
***Me:** Who's this?*
***Aman:** I'm sorry I didn't text earlier.*
***Me:** Do I know you?*
***Aman:** Do you think you can be mad at me while I feed you dinner?*
***Me:** Did that line work on the Italian women?*
***Aman:** I know you're hungry! I can practically hear your stomach growling. Also, Italy has women?! I didn't know.*

Idiot.

I was staring at my phone with a wide, goofy smile on my face when the professor announced the end of class.

I texted 'Where are you?' as I packed up, said goodbye to my classmates and walked out of the university campus. I was about to refresh the chat window to see if he had replied when I looked up, and there he was. Leaning against his car, parked right opposite my university gate, looking all tanned and gorgeous and completely clothed. (Dammit.)

I crossed the road and walked towards him.

'Hi, gorgeous.' He smiled as he took my face in his hands.

I tried to keep it together, but my lips continued to stretch into a smile till I was sure my gums showed. Aman was finally back home. Where I could watch, smell and touch him …

'Hi,' I said breathily and leaned in closer to his chest. I wrapped my arms around him and tucked myself in. He placed a soft kiss on my head and hugged me back.

We drove back to my place and ordered in our favourite dinner—Chinese takeout. I was in the kitchen putting away the dishes when Aman dashed in, took my hand and pulled me out to the balcony. The monsoons had arrived.

I may have mentioned this before—I've never really been a fan of the rains in Mumbai. Growing up, I loved it when it rained in Pune, because that just meant better weather and a day off from school. But the rains in Mumbai? They were a whole different monster. The roads got messed up, water clogged every other lane in the city and traffic became a worse nightmare than it already was. Although the city still functioned as though the shower had just gently moistened its spirits, I hated going to uni on rainy days, hated how gloomy and wet it got for days on end and hated how my books began to smell all musty. But this year, the monsoon felt new. Less annoying. Maybe slightly beautiful too.

The blue-and-white overhead canvas had been pulled back, and Aman stood in the centre of the balcony, getting drenched in the rain, with his hand stretched out towards me.

'Come on! Don't leave me hanging. It's the first rain of the season!' he said, eyes glowing with excitement.

'This is all incredibly movie-like.' I laughed.

'Are you just going to stand there?' he asked as I hovered on the threshold of the living room.

'Your shirt is very see-through right now. Don't mind if I do,' I teased.

He took two big strides towards me and caught me by the waist. And before I could protest, I was scooped up like a toy and out to the balcony, getting drenched with Aman.

'I'm wearing contact lenses!' I gasped as soon as I felt the sting of the water in my eyes.

'Close your eyes,' he said, setting me down.

I closed my eyes and lifted my head up as I let the rainwater wash away the heat from my body. The past few weeks had been horribly hot in the city and this was much needed. I could still feel my cheeks glowing red from being so close to Aman after almost two weeks and I moved closer to him as I gripped his shirt like I never wanted to let him go. I could feel his hands move from my waist to my shoulders, to my neck and then on to my cheeks. I could feel his breath as he closed the distance between our faces and leaned in so our lips were just an inch apart.

'Next time, if I'm leaving the city for more than a day, I'm taking you with me,' he murmured against my lips.

'Clingy,' I murmured back. I felt him smile before he held my neck and kissed me.

Now I get why the poets go on about romance and the rains.

The monsoons were really going at it this year. Most of my classes through July had turned into online lectures as none of our professors were badass enough to swim through the city's gutters, jump waterlogged railway tracks or simply teleport themselves to university. Losers.

So that meant that my days included spending a few hours at the bookstore, coming home before rush hour—to avoid pedestrian traffic (yeah, that's a thing in Mumbai)—attending online classes till 8 p.m. and then spending time by myself, with my friends or with Aman. Or reading. Or catching up with Aaji. Or chilling with Aman.

Yes, there was a lot of Aman. My days would start with butterflies in my tummy from playing and replaying in my mind every touch and every kiss we shared, and end with the anticipation of more. Whenever I felt like an obsessed teenager, with the hormones doing all the thinking for me, I took a couple of minutes to have a serious one-on-one chat with myself in the mirror. But the stupid smile that invariably appeared on my face even as I reasoned through things was bribe enough to make me to feel everything I was feeling without assuming the worst. So I did just that.

Occasionally, to keep myself in line, I dissected every meeting and scrutinized every conversation I had with Aman, but every time the familiar feelings of doubt crept up on me, he did something to push them away.

One Saturday we were chilling at my place with a 3,000-piece Disney puzzle, with no plan of action for the rest of the day. It was a rainy afternoon, so we'd ordered takeout khichdi and chicken tandoori, and Aman made me a drink of rum and hot water.

'Aaji drinks rum and hot water on rainy days too,' I said. 'With a stick of cinnamon in it.'

'You should be having a drink with her then,' he said simply.

'Maybe someday soon.'

'Today?'

'Today?' I exclaimed. 'We can't just go to Pune today.'

'Why not?'

I had no answer.

So, in the next few minutes, I found myself packing an overnight bag to visit Aaji. With Aman.

He casually offered to fly us in his private jet so we could be there in fifteen minutes—of course I should have guessed that would be his solution—but I pointed out how we would then not be able to take a detour for corn fritters and chai in Lonavala on our way. Also, hello, what about climate change? Ashok was immediately asked to arrive, and off we went. I had high expectations from the drive, but both of us passed out in the car the minute it hit the highway.

I woke up when we were about forty minutes away from Aaji's home and turned my head sleepily to look at Aman, whose head was resting on my shoulder and his fingers intertwined with mine. His shoulders moved in a relaxed rhythm as he breathed in and out. His perfectly shaped lips were parted just slightly. I gently reached for my phone and indulged in a selfie with the most adorable man in the world.

A strange feeling started pooling at the bottom of my stomach as I stared at that picture of us. Was I leading him on? Why hadn't he asked me anything after that conversation we'd had two months ago? Did he look at this as just a casual relationship? Was he seeing other women on the side? Was he seeing me on the side? What was I doing in his life?

'You're a creep, Avani Joshi.' His voice brought me out of my trance. He was sitting up now, though his head still rested at a lazy angle on the seat. I glanced at his sleepy face and bit my lip to hide a smile.

I reached over and ran my fingers through his tousled hair and then over his cheek.

'Why am I a creep?'

'Because you take pictures of innocent men while they sleep.' He stretched and put his left arm around my shoulder, pulling me close. 'Are we there yet?'

'Almost.' There it was, that feeling of calm again. All the doubts vanished and a fine cocoon of joy enveloped my heart.

Feelings were so deceptive. Which ones was I to believe?

What started off as a weekend in Pune at Aaji's house ended up becoming two nights and two whole days of overeating, yoga classes and endless discussions, most of which were strangely titled, 'Oh, do you know what Avani did when she was six (and seven and ten and fifteen) …?'

Aman decided to work from home on Monday and I took a sick day. I texted Martin to tell him I'd see him on Tuesday morning.

Martin: Have fun, Virgin.
Me: I'm in my grandmother's house, you pig.
Martin: If you can dry-hump your man in the bookstore's supply closet, your childhood bedroom is far from inappropriate. Unleash those whore-mones.

I rolled my eyes, locked my phone screen and made a mental note to make out with Aman in my bed at least once before we left for Mumbai. Martin knew me too well.

'Where did you find him?' Aaji whispered as we sat chatting in the living room on Sunday night after Aman had gone to sleep in the guest bedroom.

I laughed at the thought of what a simple, yet ridiculous question that was. He wasn't a sweater I'd picked up at a thrift store. He was a man. A beautiful man.

'We met at the bookstore, Aaji,' I said, laughing, reaching out to give her hand a squeeze.

'And now he is your boyfriend?' she again whispered.

'No! I mean, we're hanging out … I don't know.'

'Hanging out? What are you, laundry?' she snapped.

'Aaji!' I let out a snort. 'I've just met him. We're taking it slow.'

'How old is he?'

'He's thirty-one.'

'Then *you* are taking it slow. He isn't,' she replied calmly.

'What do you mean?'

'Have you seen how that man looks at you? If you weren't my granddaughter, I would marry him.'

I raised my eyebrows and looked at her in surprise. All those yoga classes and sangria nights she had been attending with her 'gal pals' had made her feistier than I remembered.

'I could if I wanted to,' Aaji added nonchalantly.

I shook my head and stifled a laugh. I leaned over and hugged her.

'I like him,' I said softly.

'I can tell.' She smiled.

We stayed like that, hugging each other on the couch, as my mind started going to places I feared and my eyes began to sting from tears I hadn't anticipated. I missed feeling like this. Protected, tucked into Aaji's arms when life seemed a little too much. She always knew what to do and say. And although I knew she was always a phone call away, I missed how she stroked my hair when she understood I was silently fighting the demons nobody could see.

Like I was in that instant.

'Not everyone is the same,' she said quietly after a while.

That opened the barrage I was holding back. I cried softly as I held on to Aaji. She gently patted my head and rocked me in her arms.

I could pretend all I wanted, but I was taking this anything but slow.

I knew I was playing with fire, and I liked it.

---

2 AUGUST 2023

AVANI

First fight.

The thing about getting overly attached—emphasis on 'overly'—to someone is exactly that. You don't realize how deeply you feel about them until something comes along to shake you into reality. Or in this case, someone.

Now, I've known me for, what, twenty-three years? Yeah. And I've known Aman for … four months, approximately. So I wish someone would help me understand why I did what I did and how I did it.

'How come we don't hang out with your friends much?' I asked. 'I haven't really seen them after that night at your house.'

Aman and I were chilling on my living room couch on a Wednesday evening after my classes and all his long business calls were done for the day. He was reading some smart leatherbound book while I was filing my toenails.

'My friends?' he asked absent-mindedly.

'Yeah. We never see them. Don't you like meeting them?'

'I do.'

'Then why don't you?'

'No reason.' He shrugged.

'Is it because of me?' I asked sharply.

'What do you mean?' He put his book down.

'I mean, do you not meet them because of me?'

'I've been spending all my time with you lately. I haven't got around to making plans with them. It doesn't really matter—they can make plans if they want to meet.'

'Oh, so you're saying it *is* because of me then?' I snapped.

He sat up, a confused look on his face.

'What's on your mind?'

'Nothing.'

'You've met most of my friends. Do you want to meet them again?'

'No,' I replied, biting the inside of my cheek, wondering why I'd even started this conversation.

'Okay,' he said simply and turned back to his book.

We sat there in silence, which was perfectly okay. So I don't know what came over me that I opened my mouth and said a little belligerently, I have to admit, 'You've met all my friends, you know. *And* you've met Aaji. You've seen where I work. You've come to my university. You've even seen embarrassing pictures of me as a child.' I raised my eyebrows. 'And I guess all I get in return is watching you read a book in my living room.'

'You want more?' He bit his lips to hide a smile.

'No,' I replied curtly. 'It's okay. Go back to your book.'

'Okay.'

'Okay.'

Silence again.

'Are you ashamed of me?' I said before I could really think through what it was that I wanted from him.

'What?'

'Are. You. Ashamed. Of. Me.' I repeated in my most annoying tone.

'Why the hell would I be ashamed of you?'

'I don't know, you tell me.'

'What's going on, Avani?' Aman asked gently, scooting closer to me. 'Did I do something?'

'Nothing,' I replied and went back to filing my nails. In my head I decided that I was done with whatever this tantrum was and that I needed to have a little internal dialogue before I said things out loud. Aman, however, wasn't on board with this plan because of course it had all happened inside my thick head. I'd riled him up. So I deserved what came next.

'I really can't tell with you sometimes,' he said. 'Can't you just say what you're thinking and make it easier for both of us?'

'What I'm thinking is, maybe you don't want me to meet all your friends because ...'

Don't say it, don't say it.

' ... I work at a bookstore and all those other girls you know are like Victoria's Secret models or some shit.'

There, done now?

Aman looked at me, incredulous. Honestly, the fuck was wrong with me? I never got this insecure. I loved myself too much to compare myself to anyone else. However, I'd been scrolling through Aman's socials, and there was a particular handle that kept commenting on every picture he posted, someone I hadn't met at Aman's party all those months ago. I'd told myself it was probably an ex-girlfriend or just a friend, but something about the comments nagged at me.

Anyway, coming back to the stupid situation I'd put myself in, Aman's response was sharp when he said, 'I don't understand what that means. What *is* going on, Avani?'

'I want to meet your friends more often—all of them—but I don't want to tell you that I want to meet all your friends more often. I want you to know that maybe it's time I met all your friends, all of them, again,' I blurted out.

His eyebrows were now raised to his hairline. I looked down at my nails, hoping he wouldn't read too much into this—or just fling his book at me. I would have if I were him. I was being a brat for no reason. When I looked up, I saw he'd crossed his arms across his chest and a smile had appeared on his face.

Was he amused?

He shook his head, chuckled and pulled me towards him, tucking his face into the crook of my neck. I tried to fight it, but he looped his hands around my waist and hugged me tightly.

'You're cute when you're needy, you know that?' he said.

My jaw dropped. 'I'M NOT NEEDY!' I said as I slapped his arm. I felt half annoyed that he'd called me out on my moody nonsense, and half relieved.

'How about dinner on Saturday? My place? My brother is in town and a couple of friends will be coming over. These are the ONLY friends that matter. Okay?' he whispered into my neck.

'Oh, we're going straight to "brother"?'

'Why not? And then maybe you and I can have a little after-party of our own once everyone leaves.' He placed a gentle kiss on my shoulder.

'You're going to make me clean the dishes, aren't you?' I said.

'You know I love it when you get dirty.' He winked.

5 AUGUST 2023

AVANI

Woke up to deal with needy Avani.

It was Saturday. I looked at my reflection in the mirror before I met Aman downstairs. The needy girl who had thrown a tantrum for this party to happen was not there any more. This morning I'd woken up as the introvert who blamed her briefly extroverted alter ego for making a plan that involved skinny jeans and concealer and stepping out of home. I took a deep breath and locked the door behind me.

Downstairs, by the car, Aman pulled me into a hug and placed a soft kiss on my cheek. 'You look beautiful,' he said.

'I promise I didn't spend the past hour trying out a bunch of clothes so I could get this reaction from you,' I said with a serious expression.

That brought on another hug. 'Let's go!' he said.

It was a much more intimate affair than I'd imagined. We entered Aman's apartment to see a bunch of servers placing expensive-looking silverware next to expensive-looking plates on expensive-looking place mats on a very expensive-looking dining table. A proper sit-down affair with catered food and service, not what I was expecting.

'Wow,' I started.

'Yeah, I didn't want a hectic scene, so I kept it simple.'

Sure. This was all pretty simple. Nothing over the top or unusual at all.

I walked around the table, taking in the finery, and then peeped into the kitchen, which was buzzing with chefs. The anticipation of a boring evening lulled as I poured myself a glass of wine and went to get comfy at my regular spot on Aman's living room couch.

Aman was busy talking to the head chef when the doorbell rang. Before anyone could respond, he practically jumped out of the kitchen and sprinted to answer the door. I heard faint chatter from the hallway for a few seconds before he walked over to me with what I can only describe as an older, more intense version of Aman.

'Avani, meet Gagan, my elder brother.'

I put the wine glass down and went over expecting to hug Aman's brother, when he stiffly stuck out his hand.

'Pleasure,' he said curtly.

A little thrown, I retracted my outstretched arms and shook his hand. Firm handshake. A little firmer and it would have cut off blood supply to my arm.

'I'll get you a drink, just give me a second,' Aman said, and went off to the kitchen, completely oblivious to my eyes pleading him to not leave me alone with this new person.

'So, are you in town for business or pleasure?' It was the first question that sprung to my mind in the absence of my ability to make small talk.

'Business,' he said, not really making a move towards the couch or any other seating area.

'Nice, nice.'

I rocked back and forth, mentally screaming out to Aman to come back.

'Aman tells me you're based in London?'

'That's correct.' He stood there stiffly, his arms crossed before him.

It didn't look like this invitee would be the life of the party, did it, I thought, and felt immediately guilty. As someone who was socially awkward, I had no business judging someone else for not being personable with a person he'd just met. It was unlike me to want to make more conversation. In any other situation I would've been relieved that Gagan was okay with his monosyllabic responses, but this was Aman's brother, and something about Aman's excitement at seeing him made me want to try a bit harder.

'So do you come to Mumbai oft—'

'I have to go. Excuse me.' He walked off towards the kitchen. In the middle of my question, no fucks given.

I stood there, sweat gathering on my forehead, ready to curl into a ball and become one with the couch cushions, when I heard the brothers emerge from the kitchen, chatting, and move towards the main door.

'Oh, Avani,' Aman called out to me, looking over his shoulder. 'Gagan can't stay for dinner.'

'Oh,' I managed to reply before walking towards them.

'Nice meeting you ... Avani,' Gagan said, before hugging his brother and stepping out of the door.

'I thought the dinner was for him.' I looked at Aman as he shut the door and returned to the living room.

'Yeah, well, that's Gagan for you. You can never really make plans with him. His schedule is too erratic.'

'That must suck. I can tell you miss him.'

'We've grown used to it,' he said. 'Should we head to the dining room and get comfortable there? Jogi's almost here, and Nikhil and Khushi texted to say they'll reach in fifteen.'

'Yes, let's.'

The evening went fine after that, but I couldn't get the weird encounter with Gagan out of my mind. In all his reluctance to engage, I'd felt he was watching me closely, almost scrutinizing me. I wondered what Aman had told him about me, if anything at all. I looked at Aman and saw him guffawing at something Jogi had said, and figured I should stop overthinking it. That was just how his brother was, maybe, a man of few words and fewer facial expressions.

Later that night I lay in bed, wondering how strange the past week had been with my moods and emotions running untamed, and then woke up the next morning to the answer. My period was here.

11 SEPTEMBER 2023

AVANI

Taking a chance on the universe.

Does anyone else suck at multitasking as an adult too? And I don't mean the pay-bills-while-getting-three-meals-a-day-and-not-die-of-dehydration kind of multitasking.

That's basic survival shit. I've lived by myself long enough to have cracked that. I'm talking about the kind of compartmentalization of priorities that needs to come with being an adult. I visualized it as many lateral charts of to-dos placed parallelly in your mind, with all of them needing to be accomplished together.

Like wanting to have a steady source of income while studying, while also making time for skincare before bed and clocking in eight hours of sleep. What do you prioritize?

Like spending money on avocados but also fighting with the dry-cleaner guy for bumping up the prices. What do you prioritize?

Or, in my case, like wanting to be a successful lawyer but also not wanting to stop thinking about a certain billionaire CEO who was the embodiment of every romance-novel hero ever.

How. To. Prioritize.

My life had been so much simpler six months ago, when I would wake up thinking of no one in particular, get through my morning routine, then get to work and listen to Martin tell me about his latest fuck. Study for a few hours, come home, cook dinner and then eat it while watching reruns of *The Office*. Even for someone who is all about enjoying her own company, the last few lines are sad. Maybe it was, until Aman walked into the bookstore all polished and perfect. But at least those six months ago I wasn't sitting at my study table at 8 a.m. on a Monday morning, staring at an unfamiliar word that flashed across my semester results displayed on my computer screen: 'REAPPEAR'.

Yes, that—next to three of my five courses.

Practitioner's Approach to Competition Law: 53%

Commercial Contract Drafting: 81%

Advanced Company Law: REAPPEAR

Banking and Financial Law: REAPPEAR

Corporate Insolvency Law: REAPPEAR

Shit.

I stared at my report sheet. This was worse than the time I'd fallen off my friend's moving motorbike because I wanted to lie back and enjoy the rains in Pune. That was plain stupidity. But this? What was this?

I stared with my eyes wide, waiting for some kind of pep talk to come through. From somewhere. None came. I had never slacked at school. And that, too, because of a boy? Never ever. If Aaji saw this, she would probably come hug me for taking a break from being a nerd for once. 'Thank god something pleased you more than company law. It's okay, I'm sure you will do better next time,' she would've said and patted me proudly on my back while the world collapsed around me.

But no, this was not my life. I needed to get my shit together. I picked up the phone and called Maya. I needed to get an earful from someone.

No answer. Ugh.

I called Martin next.

'It's 8 a.m., bitch. Who died?' he answered in a groggy voice.

'My career.'

'I don't have any coffee in me for your quarter-life crisis. Do I need to make a mug first?'

'Martin, I failed three out of my five courses. And I'm freaking out. This has never happened before and I don't know what to do.'

'You failed three classes?!' he yelled.

'Yeah,' I whimpered.

'Well, can you attempt them again?'

'Of course I can. But that's not the problem.'

'What's the problem, then?'

'The fact that I failed them! I don't fail! I've spent the last few months being focused on everything but my career, and the results clearly show that if I keep going like this, I may not even *have* a career.'

Martin laughed. 'Calm down. It's okay.'

'What? It's not okay. I can't keep doing this with Aman.'

'How is this Aman's fault?'

'It's not his fault. It's mine. I need to take a step back and focus on my career. He's well settled anyway. I don't want to be the loser who got too caught up in her feelings.'

'Ani, breathe. So you flunked a couple of classes. It's okay. Everybody does. That doesn't mean you've failed as a lawyer.'

'Are you dumb?' I snapped. 'That is exactly what it means, Martin. Oh my god.'

Feelings of instant regret and panic were starting to settle inside my chest and my hands were going numb from holding my phone to my ear with white-knuckled force.

'Calm down. Seriously. You have another chance to clear these courses, right?' he asked calmly.

'Yes.'

'All right, so let's focus on that. And, Avani?'

'Yes?'

'Aman might just be the best thing that's happened to you in a long time.' He paused. 'You know I'm right. He's good for you. Don't mess this up because you don't see it yet.'

I relaxed as I felt my nerves calm a bit. Why did Martin have to wake up and make sense? I wouldn't have minded freaking out about the situation a bit more before logic took over. I told him I'd call him back when I saw Maya's call waiting on the other line.

'Morning, cutie,' she said cheerily. 'Sorry, was in the gym when you called.'

Of course, she was running to perfect her already fit body and glowing skin, while my life was falling apart.

'I failed three courses this semester,' I said in a low voice.

'Okay. What are you doing now?' she asked.

'You mean other than freaking out about my future? Nothing.'

'Brush your teeth and get dressed. I'm picking you up for breakfast in twenty.' She hung up.

I had a couple of hours before I had to be at the bookstore and I needed to hear what Maya had to say. I needed to be in sane human company so I wouldn't spiral to dangerous places in my mind. So I did as I was told. Half an hour later, we were sitting across the table from each other at our favourite breakfast joint not very far from home, sipping our coffee and waiting for our toast and omelette to arrive.

'What are you doing in this part of the city so early in the morning?' I asked.

'I had to make a delivery to this snooty client who's becoming a bigger pain in my ass with every passing minute.' She rolled her eyes.

I chuckled and looked into my coffee mug.

'But you tell me,' she said. 'What's on your mind?'

'I've never been distracted, Maya. I don't know how to deal with failing courses.'

'Like the rest of us, Ani. You study harder and get through them the second time. But you knew that already. Now tell me what's really on your mind.'

She tilted her head as she waited for me to answer.

'I don't know what I'm doing with Aman,' I said as I let out a long breath. 'It started out as an innocent, flirty friendship and now we're in uncharted territory, where strange feelings and thoughts are taking over.'

She sipped her coffee and nodded at me to continue.

'I love spending time with him and I miss him when he isn't around. But the more time I spend thinking about him, the more I feel like I'm getting blindsided by something that should be in plain sight. Like I'm walking on a tightrope without knowing how far I'll fall if I don't make it to the end, you know?'

'Are you, maybe, feeling like that because you're stuck in the middle?' she asked, articulating each word slowly.

'What do you mean?'

'Maybe you know you like Aman but are too worried to label those feelings. So it's stuck between being a friendship and something more. And maybe that uncertainty is what's playing on your mind. You're one of the smartest, most intelligent people I know, Ani. You've always lived by your own rules. I've watched you deal with whatever life has thrown at you and never felt you needed a reality check. You're careful and conscious every day. Maybe, somehow, Aman has challenged that part of your being. And I'm not saying that's a bad thing, but you can't fool yourself any longer than you already have. For the first time I feel like you're not being honest with yourself. And that's concerning.'

As I listened to her, the reality of her words slowly dawned on me.

'I don't know what it is, Maya, but with him, I'm constantly waiting for the other shoe to drop. When I'm with him, life is perfect. But the minute he drops me home, I silently wait for a message or a call or a news article that will tell me that he isn't as great as he seems. And I know how stupid that sounds when I say it out loud like that. But it's tough to not be able to trust someone even when they've given you more than enough reasons to trust them. My life is the opposite of what I read in my books. Ugh.'

Maya smiled as she held my hand in hers.

'I guess you'll never know if you don't take a chance, Ani.' She paused. 'And that's a choice too. You could choose not to take a chance and walk away from Aman because you believe he isn't right for you. But it's a choice you'll have to make. Things aren't going to sort themselves out on their own. You can't be on the fence about it any more. For your mental peace and clarity, make that choice.'

I bit my lower lip as I contemplated her words. She was right. It had been six months since I'd met Aman and he'd given me no reason to be so broody about us. He'd been nothing but supportive, respectful and charming, and maybe it was time I got over my insecurities and took a chance.

Chances were that I would have to live with a gaping hole in my heart if my fears were to come true, but there was also a chance that the universe would come through and give me what I deserved.

Maya dropped me home a while later and I went straight into the shower to let the new thoughts settle. I got ready soon after and left for the bookstore. I put my bag down on the billing counter and stared into nothingness for a minute before I fished out my phone and dialled Aman's number.

If there was anything I was sure about when it came to him, it was that he was definitely worth the risk.

'Hi, gorgeous,' Aman said as soon as he answered my call.

I don't care how cheesy I sound when I say no words hotter have ever been spoken by any man who walked the face of this planet. Ever.

It was 10.30 a.m., so I guessed he was on his way to office. His tone was relaxed, not like he'd been in the middle of prepping for a work call. Bottom line, I couldn't have timed it better.

'Hi,' I said. What was it about this man's voice that turned my insides to gravy? How had it taken him two words to make me forget what an introspective morning I'd just had? Two hours ago I'd been contemplating moving to a new country and selling momos for a living, and now here I was, sitting at my day job, smiling into my phone and talking to a guy who I might or might not be falling for.

'Did my girl sleep okay?'

'Kind of, until she woke up to utter doom and panic.'

'Your period's back so soon?'

'Worse.'

'Your semester results? I completely forgot. What happened? They couldn't have been …'

'I failed in three out of five,' I replied, feeling sad just hearing myself say it again.

'Can you reappear?' he asked, not missing a beat.

'Yeah.'

'Baby, it's going to be fine. I can help you with classes in any way you want. I can get Sheryl to look for a tutor. A close friend of my father's is a judge at the Supreme Court. I can quickly call him to check if he can find someone who can tutor you for this semester. I'm sure we can get through this. I know it might not look like it, but it's going to be fine, I promise.'

I bent my head down and smiled to myself. 'We can get through this,' he'd said, and what was better was that I knew he meant it. I could stall what I had to say till dinner. Maybe I could ask him to pick me up after work, and then cook for him while I told him what was on my mind. Or I could spare both of us the nerves and come clean with it now.

'Avani, you there?'

'I'm here.'

'You want me to pick you up after work tonight? Let's get some dumplings for dinner.'

See what I mean? It's like this guy was made by God when She was two glasses of wine down. Because that's when you make the best decisions. You have just the right amount of liquid courage to push your limits and you're sober enough to tell right from wrong. I say, a woman with two glasses of wine can win the world like it's just another Monday.

Without further thought I said, 'Aman?'

'Yes?'

'Remember the time you asked me to be your girlfriend and I freaked out and ruined everything?'

'Vaguely.'

'Does that offer still stand?'

There was silence on the line. I bit my lip nervously. Why wasn't he saying something? Was it too late? Did I take too much time reaching this decision? Should I have just shut up and eaten the dumplings later tonight?

'Aman …?' I said, tentatively.

I heard him draw a breath to say something on the other end of the line and started preparing casual answers to his response.

Option 1: No? Okay, good. Thank god we're on the same page about this.

Option 2: You met someone else? I'm so happy for you.

Option 3: Sorry, what? I think there was a cross connection just now.

The last was by far the safest.

'Hello?' I said again, and heard the phone line go dead.

He'd hung up.

I stared into the space around me like I'd just seen a ghost. He'd chosen to hang up on me rather than answer me. I quickly pinched myself to make sure this wasn't some fucked-up nightmare. How did I mess up my career and the possibility of a future daddy to my twelve puppies all in one morning? I hopped off my stool and walked towards the café, where Martin was busy talking to some guy who had come in. There must've been something about my expression, because I saw him stiffen.

'OMG. What did you do?' he asked in panic. 'Sit, sit.'

He indicated the stool next to the guy he was talking to. 'Okay, boo. Take five. I have a crisis at hand,' he told the guy and walked around to me.

'Speak!' he barked.

'Don't yell at me!' I barked back.

'Sorry, your face is really freaky right now. Just tell me what you did.' He put one hand on his chest and the other on my shoulder.

'I asked Aman to be my boyfriend and he hung up on me,' I said.

Martin looked at me like I'd told him Michael Jackson was still alive. What was it about these words from my mouth that just stunned men into silence?

'Say something!' I yelled.

'Did you try calling him back?' he blurted. 'Maybe he was in a bad network area.'

'Nope.'

'Uhhhhh ...' I felt bad for him because I knew I'd put him in a spot too, and to think I had been mad at him for making too much sense when I'd called this morning.

'Ugh, this is the worst day ever! Why did I have to open my fat mouth and say stupid things? I could've just shut up and mulled over my feelings for a day or two and then made an informed decision. Why, why, whyyyy did I have to be impulsive and embarrass myself like this? When am I going to learn, Martin?'

But Martin said nothing. He just looked at me, his lips pursed. For a second I thought he was going to have a laughing fit. I fisted my hands on my sides because if he was going to laugh at me, he was going to have to do it with no teeth. I straightened up, rolled my shoulders back, tilted my chin up and took two long breaths before I decided that I was not going to stand there waiting for Martin to say something. I was going to go back to my workstation and call Aman back and get this straightened out. I'm a lot of things, but a coward isn't one of them. I gave Martin five more seconds before I turned to leave ... and walked bang into a strong, broad chest which had been just inches away from me. Before I could look up or process what had happened, I felt two strong hands around the back of my neck and my face being tilted up. It must've been all the overflowing emotions, but my vision was so blurry I couldn't comprehend anything. It happened so fast that my raging heart went absolutely quiet the moment I felt Aman's lips on mine. I took a long breath to inhale the familiar scent of aftershave and my shoulders slumped in submission. His hands moved from my neck to my waist as he picked me up and gently put me down on top of the coffee bar. He moved in closer as he deepened the kiss and ran his hands up and down my back. When I finally gained control over my limbs, I cupped his face with my hands and pulled back from the kiss with wild confusion and anticipation in my eyes.

'Yes.' He kissed my cheek and buried his face in the crook of my neck as I felt him smile against my skin.

He was here. He came. He did not run away and block my number. I heard myself let out a short laugh as relief washed over me. Having him in my arms had calmed down every little annoying voice in my head. I buried my hands in his thick brown hair and hugged him. Even if I died right then, I wouldn't mind. Not even a little bit.

'You could've just said that on the phone and saved me a whole-ass panic attack, you know?' I murmured against his suit jacket.

'I know. But what's the fun in that?' he replied.

Idiot. *My* idiot.

How had I woken up so badass today? How had I dealt with a massacre of a report card and cemented a relationship all in a few hours on a Monday morning? And to think I'd done that with no wine in my system. Well done, Avani.

20 SEPTEMBER 2023

AMAN

I must have done something right.

'I'll pick you up after class then?' I said as my car halted outside the bookstore.

'Spending that extra hour studying with Dhruv after my last class today, don't forget,' she replied as she stuffed her phone back into her bag and turned to look at me.

'Oh, yes. How's the tutoring going?'

She shrugged. 'As well as it can, I guess. His notes are really helping me, I have to say.'

'Be good. See you later.' I leaned in to kiss her cheek. '9 p.m. it is.'

She kissed me back and stepped out of the car, saying, 'Best of luck with your meeting today …'

'Avani?' I called.

'Hmm?' She peeked in through the window.

'I love you,' I said, smiling.

'Whatevs.' She rolled her eyes and smirked playfully, and swayed her hips a little extra as she turned and walked into the store. Oh, she knew I was looking.

I sat back as Ashok turned the car in the direction of the office. I was about to open my e-mail app to check how my day was planned when the phone rang. It was Ma.

'Babu!' came her voice.

'Ahh, you know how much I love that name, Ma!' I said, faking annoyance.

'That's why I call you that every time I miss you a little too much,' she responded cheekily. 'Are you at work?'

'Just dropped off Avani at the bookstore. Heading to the office now.'

'Oh, which reminds me, I hope you're getting her to the party next weekend. It's been too long now … We have to meet her.'

'I haven't asked her yet.'

'Why? We won't judge you for dating a girl with eight eyes and three noses. Aliens are in this season.'

'Ha ha. Rich of you to assume it's her that I'm embarrassed of,' I teased.

She laughed heartily in response.

'I've just not had the chance, Ma. Maybe I'll ask her later today.'

'Nothing doing. You *are* getting her with you, and that's that.'

'All right, Ma'am. I'll talk to her today. I've got to go now. Love you.'

'Love you, sweetheart. See you soon. We miss you.'

I hung up with a smile on my face. I missed them too. Their thirty-fifth anniversary was around the corner and Ma had been planning the celebration for weeks. It was to involve only close family and a few friends, and it was to be a surprise for Papa. Except that she'd not been able to keep it a secret from him. She'd confessed to me that one evening last week, when Papa had casually asked her what she was doing up late in the study, she'd replied, a little irritated, 'I'm planning a surprise wedding anniversary party for you, Anil. Stop interrupting me.' So the party had gone from being directed by one crazy party planner to two crazy party planners—which is why I've had nothing to do with the planning. The happy couple had gone all out, I was sure, and I was looking forward to it because my folks had always been excellent hosts and knew how to ensure their guests had a great time. And I was looking forward to spending some time with Gagan too. As for Avani, Ma had been asking me to invite her over to meet everyone, but I'd been hesitating about bringing up the 'meet the parents' thing. I'd met her Aaji, of course, but she hadn't spoken much about her parents. There was something there, I guessed. I noticed the way she went quiet and pensive at any mention of my folks.

'Morning, baba.' Sheryl smiled as I walked by her desk and entered my cabin.

'Morning, beautiful. What's happening? What's on the cards today?'

'I've set up your meeting with the ConsciChic guys in meeting room 2, for 11.30 a.m.'

'Yes, I read the e-mail.'

'Oh, so you dressed like your meeting was on the beach on purpose then?' She raised an eyebrow at the shirt I was wearing.

I pursed my lips. 'Avani's idea—and to answer your question, yes,' I smirked.

The meeting went well. I loved it when the room was filled with minds that were receptive to new ideas. The only downside of becoming the CEO of a company with a wide range of operations at the age of thirty was that you'd probably be the only one who was thirty in most boardrooms. On most days everyone around me was close to twice my age, so this meeting had been quite exciting for me. The conversation was productive, and I saw a lot of potential in ConsciChic joining hands with Raina Textiles.

'Make sure we set up a follow-up call in a week, once the contract is sent,' I told Sheryl. Then I nodded at the two young entrepreneurs as I stood up to leave the meeting room. 'Thank you for your time. Please get in touch with Sheryl if you have any questions at all. I'm an e-mail away too.'

I entered my cabin and sat down as my phone rang. It was Avani.

'How was it? Shit. Are you still in the meeting? Okay, call me when you're free.' She hung up.

I smiled at my phone and called her back.

'Hello to you too!' I said.

'Hi! It's over, na? How was it?'

'Went very well. They might come on board by the end of next week.'

'Oh great. I knew it would work out. I think it was the shirt I picked that did it.'

'Oh, definitely the shirt.' I smiled. 'Where are you?'

'On my way to the next class.'

'Okay, have a good one. I'll see you later tonight.'

'Aman?'

'Yes?'

'I love you.'

'Whatevs,' I said, and we both laughed.

The rest of the day in office was busy, as always. We'd been working on some interesting projects with the government and the internal teams had been driving themselves hard to deliver. Papa's credibility was at stake here, so I'd taken it upon myself to look into every detail.

Before I knew it, it was 8.30 p.m. and most of the office had cleared out. I finished sending the last few e-mails and shut down my laptop for the day. I stepped out to see Sheryl still at her desk.

'It's late,' I said.

'Almost done. I was just getting a present for your parents' anniversary.' She smiled.

'You don't have to, you know. They'll be glad to just see you.'

'I know. But they are very special to me. I've knitted a tablecloth for them—you know how much your mother likes handmade stuff—and just ordered a painting from a Pichwai artist she loves.'

I gave her a quick sideways hug. 'Shall I drop you home?'

'Oh no. I'm meeting a friend for a drink at the bar down the street,' she said as she got up to leave. 'I'll walk over.'

'Goodnight. See you tomorrow,' I said and walked to the elevator.

I was sitting in the car outside Avani's university campus thinking of ways to bring up the Mussoorie trip when I heard the door open.

'Hey, gorgeous. What do you feel like having for dinner?' I placed a kiss on Avani's cheek as she settled beside me in the car.

'Can we just go home—yours—and eat ramen?' she asked, kissing me softly. She settled her head back on the seat and turned to me.

'Of course we can.' I tucked her under my arm and asked Ashok to drive us home. I loved how Avani felt when she was close to me. Her hair smelt of coconuts and jasmine and her body was always warm. Her jhumkas made a faint chiming sound every time she moved and her fingers absent-mindedly drew invisible circles on my forearm as she told me about her day.

In the elevator, she tugged me into a hug and rested her head on my chest. 'I'm so tired today,' she said, sighing.

'A shower will help,' I said, wrapping my arms around her waist and resting my chin on her head.

A half-hour later, I was standing at my kitchen island pouring her a glass of wine and fixing myself a green tea, when Avani walked down the stairs from my bedroom in my bathrobe, her hair dripping wet and smelling like a million bucks. I watched her walk towards me, like that was all she had been created to do. Be mine.

I swallowed. My throat was dry.

'Your robe was just hanging there. I couldn't help myself. It's so soft. What is it made of? Clouds?'

'I think you should wear only this every day.' I turned away reluctantly. 'Wine?'

'Yes, please.' She settled into my couch and folded her legs under her. 'What are we eating?'

'You said ramen,' I replied, 'so I ordered ramen. And sushi.'

She took the glass from me and raised it high, saying, 'Cheers to Japan!'

'Cheers!' I laughed.

'So,' I began as I sat down next to her, 'what are you doing next weekend?'

'Not sure. Why? Do you want to fly me to Paris in your private jet and feed me escargot on top of the Eiffel Tower?' She tilted her head and smirked.

Okay. Time to take the leap.

'Close,' I said. 'I want to fly you to Mussoorie for my parents' wedding anniversary party.'

Silence. Then, after what seemed like ages, she asked, 'For real?'

'Yeah. It's a special day and I want you to be there with me.'

'Do your parents know I'm coming?'

'They want you to be there. But it's your choice. I don't want to make you uncomfortable if you think it's too soon.'

'Is it too soon?'

'Not for me. I've wanted you to meet my family for a while now.'

'And what about Gagan?'

'What about him? He'll be happy to see you too.'

'Are you sure?'

'Are you going to only answer in questions?' I laughed. 'Baby, I'm sure I want you to be there. But it's up to you.'

She took a large sip of the wine and looked into the glass. I could see the wheels turning in her head, since she did little to hide it. I told myself that I would settle for whatever answer she gave me. I couldn't choose how fast or slow she wanted to go in this relationship. That was not my place.

'Take your time ... if—'

'I want to go!'

'You do?'

'Yes! I do. I've heard so much about your parents. Also, you have dogs there. Ha ha.'

'I do!' I exclaimed, relieved. 'Wow, cool. They'll be really happy.'

'What am I going to wear?'

'Baby, you could wear this bathrobe and you'd still be the most beautiful girl in the room.'

I kissed her on the neck, with just one thought in my head: I'm one lucky asshole. I must have done something right.

29 SEPTEMBER 2023

AVANI

Nothing to wear.

'What kind of party is this?' Rhea asked as she lay on my bed, popping butter-smothered popcorn into her mouth.

'The fancy kind, I gather,' I said. 'From the sound of it, everyone Aman knows is going to be there. Ugh! I have zero fancy clothes! Where the fuck is Maya? Was she not supposed to be here like an hour ago?'

'Calm down, Ani,' said Rhea. 'She said she's right by the corner. Should be here any minute.'

It was Friday afternoon and I had exactly three hours before Aman picked me up for the airport. Rhea and Maya had promised to help me pack for this Rich People's Royal Ball, and, characteristically, Rhea had arrived with tequila and popcorn while Maya was on her way with designer clothes from her wardrobe. The bell rang as I was about to plunge into my minuscule closet one more time for an appropriate 'private airport OOTD'.

'I'll get it,' Rhea announced as she sprung off the bed and bolted to the door.

'Good. That way you're of some use here,' I muttered under my breath. All she had done for the past thirty minutes was chug tequila shots and freak me out about how difficult rich people were to be around.

'I heard that,' she yelled from the living room.

I rolled my eyes and held my head in my hands as I stared at the pile of clothes lying at my feet. Crumpled T-shirts, faded pjs, shorts I would never fit into again, a frilly peplum top ... Was this for real?

'Who robbed you?' Maya said, walking in with two suitcases.

'This is all I own, Maya. Please tell me you've got your expensive shit.' I exhaled loudly.

'Calm down, Ani. Here,' she said, carefully setting down her suitcases and unzipping both. She proceeded to swiftly pull out coats, sweaters, belts, bags and dresses one after another, and carefully lay them down on my bed, organized by colour and size, quite unlike my jigsaw-puzzle wardrobe situation.

The next hour was a classic rom-com montage. The one in which lively music plays in the background as the dorky girl's besties give her a makeover while chugging alcohol directly from the bottle and she walks around modelling outfits and making goofy faces. I have to admit that in reality it was a lot more of me saying 'OMG I can't wear this' or 'You paid how much for this again?' and 'I'm sure it'll fit fine—I don't need to try this on'.

One hour later, we were finally there, all outfits selected and planned, and packed neatly into my suitcase.

'Umm ... *that's* what you're going to wear to bed?' Rhea asked as I held up my raggedy Superman tee in one hand and an oversized white kurta in the other when she announced 'nightwear'.

'Yeah. Why?' I asked, looking from one to the other.

Rhea ignored my question and turned to face Maya. 'Maya, could you *please* ...'

'Ani, I think you should pack something cute,' Maya said, her lips pursed, holding back a smile.

'Why?' I retorted. 'Who's going to care what I wear to bed?'

'Umm ... Hopefully Aman?' Rhea said with exaggerated sarcasm. She always got so squeaky on tequila.

'Why will Aman ca—' I started protesting and froze mid-sentence.

One second. Hold on. Did they mean sex was on the cards? Was I going to have sex with Aman? Aman, who was sculpted by the Greek gods and possibly slept only in his hot boxer shorts? Me, who slept in old, oversized clothes with holes in them, hair tied into braids, and possibly snored like a generator? I had NOT thought of that!

Okay ... that's not true. I *had* thought of that. A million times. The time it had rained so hard I'd had to stay over at his place, the time we'd napped on my living room couch after watching *La La Land*, the time he'd spilt ketchup on his white shirt and changed out of it into my old, ratty tee ... But it had never got so close to becoming real.

My chest suddenly felt tighter.

'Guys,' I said, 'I'm not ready for this.'

'Of course you are. Stop acting like you didn't anticipate it or haven't had sex with anyone before,' Rhea squealed.

'But ... you don't have to do something you aren't ready for. It's up to you. It's your choice.' Maya, giving me the birds-and-bees talk like I was a teenager. Right. 'I mean, yeah. It has to be consensual. And—'

'Oh my god, guys!' I erupted. 'When I say I'm not ready, I don't mean mentally. Of course I want to ... I mean, it's Aman. What I mean is ... physically.'

They stared at me like I was speaking French. My eyes bounced between my two confused friends. 'I'm not ready! I haven't prepared for this. Physically,' I repeated, gesturing wildly at my body.

'You wanna stretch?' Rhea asked blankly.

I gave them a few seconds to get what I was saying. Then I sighed. 'Dear friends, this is to inform you that I have not manicured the garden in a while. It's all quite ... bushy.'

'Ah,' both said in unison.

Maya giggled. 'We've still got about two hours before Aman picks you up. I can book you at my regular place. Or just mow the lawn when you get there.'

'I think I'll do just that.' I nodded and went on to pack my trusty razor.

'Or leave it be,' Maya added. 'Who cares? It's Victorian.'

'Right?' I laughed.

We giggled as I added my make-up pouch and my hair-styling tools to the suitcase and zipped it close.

We moved my luggage to the living room, and the girls settled on my couch and turned on the TV, while I walked back into my room and shut the door. I had some time till Aman got here, but my nerves were getting the better of me. I decided to take a quick shower and then sat on my bed blankly with dripping wet hair and a towel draped around my body.

I hadn't been to a family event in quite some time. I'd left my parents' home when I was still a teenager and Aaji had hardly ever hosted family at her house. It had always been her and me. I had attended a few birthday dinners with Rhea's family over the past few years but nothing of the scale that I assumed Aman's parents' anniversary party was going to be. I wasn't a textbook introvert, but families weren't my strongest suit. I took in a few deep breaths and told myself that Aman would never make me feel uneasy. I could count on him to read my mind if I got into a sticky situation with his family.

Overthinking as usual, Avani. These are just your demon thoughts clouding what could be a fun and easy weekend away.

True. No place with six dogs could be anything less than pure heaven, right? This could actually be great. I would have Aman to myself, and then maybe I wouldn't have to worry about how cute or sexy my clothes were in bed if I didn't see a reason to wear them.

I smiled to myself.

I might or might not have rehearsed my seductive door-to-bed walk before getting rudely interrupted by rapid knocks on my bedroom door.

'He'll be here any minute, Ani! Are you ready yet or not?' Rhea's voice came from behind the door.

'Coming!' I yelled and picked up the outfit Maya had left hanging for me on my wardrobe handle.

I quickly slipped on the classic blue jeans and white shirt, carefully folded the sweater I was instructed to wear before landing in Mussoorie and put it inside my oversized handbag. I checked on my air-dried hair and touched up my minimal make-up. I picked up the tan trench coat that Maya had brought for me—the one that made you look instantly rich—and threw it over my forearm as I opened the door and stepped out into the living room.

'So chic!' Rhea exclaimed. 'Maya, I think you should style Avani every day!'

Maya whistled. 'You look great, cutie!'

'Thank you.' I let out a heavy breath and looked at the girls with grateful eyes.

'Please, please, PLEASE don't forget to water my plants over the weekend, Rhea. Shanta Tai is on leave till Monday,' I said as I took my phone off the charging port and stuffed my charger into the handbag. I wore my white sneakers and was just about to call Aman to check on his ETA when my phone lit up and his name flashed on the screen.

'You ready, baby? I'm here,' he said as soon as I answered.

'Be right there.'

I slung my handbag on my shoulder, turned to give my besties a hug and rolled my suitcase to the door.

Maybe it was that I trusted Aman and was looking forward to learning more about his life or maybe it was that I knew what I was going to wear while I did that. Either way, I was ready for Mussoorie.

AMAN

We were doing this.

'Yes or no? HELLO?'

'Ma!' I couldn't help laughing. 'Yes. YES, Ma. Listen, I've got to go now. I'll see you in a bit,' I replied as Avani walked up to me. I wrapped my free hand around her and kissed the top of her head. 'You okay?' I whispered into her hair.

'Can't wait to see you, Babu!' Ma's voice sang cheerily into my ear. I had forgotten to hang up.

'Bye, Ma,' I said and quickly stuffed the phone into my pocket as Avani giggled.

'Babu?' she said, an eyebrow raised.

I grinned. 'You'll meet her soon ...'

I held the door open for her as Ashok carefully placed her suitcase in the trunk of the car. I got in and instructed Ashok to head to the airport.

AVANI

The Mile High Club.

I stood at the foot of the six-step ladder that famous people pose next to when they enter or leave their chartered airplanes, wishing I'd worn a polka-dotted dress, dark shades and a large straw hat to hold on to against the wind. In large lettering on the side of the plane was stencilled the name 'RAINA'.

Right.

But why would you spend so much money on an airplane and then write your last name on it when you could literally write anything you wanted to? Plane and Simple. Wingin' It! Nimbus 2000?

'Why the face? You don't like it?' Aman interrupted my thoughts.

'Do I not like your private jet?' I raised my eyebrows at him.

'Yeah.' He smiled cheekily.

'It's okay, I guess. I've seen better.' I shrugged as he grinned and shook his head, and we made our way up the steps.

Just as I reached the entrance, I was swept off my feet as Aman literally carried me over the threshold and into the cabin.

'Amannn!' I whispered, conscious of the waiting crew politely trying not to look shocked. 'Put me down!'

He just chuckled and continued walking until he slowly lowered me into a seat and leaned over, his hands on the armrests. His face was mere inches from mine, the scent of his aftershave like fucking morphine. I stared at him as he gently lowered his head and placed a kiss on my lips.

'The airplane needs to take off for us to enter the Mile High Club, Mr Raina,' I said, kissing him back.

'I'm so glad you said yes to this,' he said as he settled opposite me and got busy adjusting his seat belt.

'Speaking too soon, aren't you?' I said as the captain locked the doors and announced that we were clear to take off.

He laughed and brought my hand to his mouth to place a kiss on my wrist.

I turned to look out the window. The retreating monsoon was blessing us with a light shower and the city lights twinkled in the droplets sliding along the glass as the plane smoothly took off.

There was no going back now.

AMAN

All the heaven and stars.

'How long is the flight?'

'A little over an hour.'

'Mussoorie has an airport?'

'Nope. We land in Dehradun and then go up to Mussoorie.'

'How far is that drive?'

'It's not a drive.'

'OMG, is it a cable car? They really freak me out.'

'Nope. Papa has a chopper waiting for us at the Dehradun airport.'

'Of course he does ... What happens to this plane then? Does it fly back to Mumbai?'

'No, it stays in the hangar at the Dehradun airport for when we fly back.'

'And the staff stays there too? Do they sleep in the plane? Like a camper?'

'No, we put them up in a hotel close to the airport.'

'You pay for their hotel? Or do you own that hotel too?'

'Something like that.'

Avani had a lot of questions. About everything. And I couldn't help smiling as I answered all of them.

We were thirty minutes into the flight to Dehradun. Avani had her legs folded under her, snacking on popcorn and leaning forward eagerly like I was revealing the hidden secrets of the universe.

'Do you want to know something about my family too? Or are you only interested in the Raina Assets?' I smiled as I moved a stray strand of hair off her face.

'I mean I'm clearly interested in the Raina ASS-ets. Why else would I snag the most perfectly round one?' She winked.

'Oii! Behave!' I said. 'But seriously, aren't you at all curious?'

She settled back into her seat and said after a pause, 'I'm terrified, Aman. Have you not seen how quickly I downed those three glasses of champagne?' She sighed. 'Tell me about your mom.'

'She's really excited about meeting you. She's been asking about you very often, so I'm looking forward to the two of you spending time together.'

'She knows we're together?'

'Of course she does. She was the first person I spoke to about you.'

'What did you say?'

'That I've met a girl.'

'Wow.' She rolled her eyes. 'Iconic.'

I laughed. 'I told her what I had to, and now she'll see for herself and know that I was right about everything.'

'What's everything?'

Avani rarely fished for compliments, but when she did I made it a point to indulge her shamelessly.

'Hmm …' I began, 'just that you love your books, particularly the dirty romances, the covers of which you try to hide from me very often. You pretend to garden when in reality Shanta Tai does the watering and plucking and pruning, and you just click pictures of the hundred plants you have in your apartment. You're witty, intelligent and you make me laugh even when you aren't trying. You're pretty, and very hot, but you're so clueless about it that it makes you even hotter. You own some three thousand pairs of silver jhumkas in all sizes and they are clear indicators of what kind of day you're anticipating ahead.'

'What does that even mean?' she asked, crinkling her eyes.

'As in ... when you've got your tiny jhumkas on, it's go time—you have errands to run, bills to pay, kitchen counters to clean, tests to appear for, assignments to submit. When you've got your big, dangly jhumkas on, it means that you woke up earlier than you intended to. You had time to make your breakfast, do your hair, choose what you wanted to wear and possibly had a light day ahead. You spent an hour talking to your Aaji on the phone before leaving for work, and you will have an extra croissant from Martin's tray that day for fun. And then there are the jingling jhumkas ...'

'What about them?' she asked, clearly amused.

'When you have those on with your chikankari kurta and kohl in your eyes, I know you've been thinking of me. So those are the days I know I'll have you all to myself.'

Avani parted her lips like she wanted to say something but chose to just draw a quick breath in. She put the tub of popcorn down on the island between us and got up to come stand next to me. She took my face between her palms, touched her forehead to mine and shut her eyes. I pulled her closer to me as I felt one lone drop of tear fall on my shirt.

'Baby,' I whispered as I wrapped her in a hug. 'Too much?'

'Not enough.' She snaked her arms around me and hugged me tightly.

The rest of the flight went by with me telling Avani about every person who was expected to attend the party. I told her about Gagan and his pragmatic thinking. About Papa and his bad jokes. And about how I could not wait to show her every corner of the house that was so close to my heart.

'You think they'll like me?' she asked as the pilot announced our descent to Dehradun and the seat-belt signs dinged on the display above our heads. She slipped on her sneakers, settled into her seat and fastened her seat belt as she turned to me with nervous eyes.

'They'll love you.'

'Be by my side, please. I'm not the best in family settings,' she said quietly.

'Always.'

The cabin lights dimmed as the twinkling lights of Dehradun homes came into sight from the plane window. I rested my head back on the seat and took a deep breath. Anybody looking from the outside would question what the big deal was about this one weekend. But something told me that the time we were about to spend over the next sixty hours or so was going to decide where we were headed.

I wanted to be everything Avani needed.

Because if I hadn't been sure enough thus far, I knew it clearly now—I could not live a life that didn't include her. Not now. Not ever.

AVANI

What in the Karan Johar cinematic universe is going on here?

A cool breeze and the fresh smell of damp earth hit me as I stepped off the aircraft about an hour and a good few glasses of champagne later. A black SUV was waiting on the tarmac to transport us to an adjacent helipad, and before I knew it Aman was strapping me into my seat on the chopper and fixing his own seat belt as the ground staff quickly loaded our luggage.

I shut my eyes tightly as my stomach rolled when the chopper took off, leaving Dehradun looking like a canopy of fairy lights under our feet. I looked at Aman with a wide smile as we flew further from the city towards the less populated, remote mountainside. The noise-cancelling earplugs and the headphones reminded me of how fast my heart was beating as every breath I took sounded like a huge ocean wave in my ears.

It was almost 7.30 p.m. and the sky looked spectacular, the twilight hour painting the mountainside in fading gold. I looked at Aman and realized he was watching me, a faint smile on his face.

'We're almost there,' he said over the headset, his voice in my ear startling me.

'OKAY!' I yelled after fumbling and failing to find whatever magic button we had to press while speaking into the microphone protruding from the headset.

The chopper took a slight turn to reveal the silhouette of a gorgeous mansion sitting atop the highest hill in the area. A siren light on a tall tower turned green, presumably signalling to the pilot that it was clear to land.

'We're here,' Aman said, looking out and then back at me.

That's when the mansion came into full, glorious view. You've watched *Kabhi Khushi Kabhie Gham...*, right? Now take the Raichand mansion and make it slightly more believable. It wasn't as huge as in the movie, but it could easily pass off as an entire private school. Or a secondary royal residence, the kind a queen would go to if she fought with the king. It had a sloping brown-tiled roof and countless little windows on all sides, rays of golden light streaming out from them to the surrounding lawns.

I could see a group of people standing at the main entrance of the house, with five big, fluffy dogs, ranging from the size of a wolf to a baby bear, and a small, furry puppy, held back by leashes.

I bit the inside of my cheeks and took a deep breath as the pilot announced our descent. I adjusted my sweater and fixed my hair.

Aman's smile grew wider as we got closer to the helipad on the sprawling estate. As soon as we landed, he jumped out to greet the six dogs charging towards him. The helicopter blades gradually stopped whirring and the sound of happy yelps filled the air. I unbuckled my seat belt and took my headphones off. The wind was much more chilly up here and the tip of my nose instantly went numb. I thanked the pilot, jumped out of the chopper and quickly wore the trench coat that I had lugged around for this very moment. I wrapped the coat tighter around me and looked up to see where Aman was when I was quickly pulled into a tight embrace.

'Welcome home, beta. I'm Aman's Ma.'

She had a strong, kind face with Aman's brown eyes and a wide smile.

I felt something foreign and gooey in my chest. 'Hi, Aunty,' I managed to say. 'Thank you so much for having me here.'

'Come,' she said and, placing her hand on the small of my back, directed me towards the house.

All of a sudden people were milling around us, wanting to be of service in every way possible. Some went to pick up the luggage, others stepped forward to tame the excited dogs who were jumping all over Aman, someone came forward to offer me a woollen scarf and a line of people stood at the main entrance with trays of what looked like steaming cups of tea. I was still taking it all in when I felt a strong arm around my shoulders and was tucked into Aman's side.

'I see you've met Ma.' He smiled at me and lowered his head so his mom could place a kiss on his cheek.

'Let's get you both inside. It's colder today than the past few days.'

'You ready, baby?' Aman whispered, rubbing my arm affectionately.

'As ready as I could be,' I murmured, looking at the grand doors that swung open for us to enter.

I took a deep breath. Who was this man who had convinced me to leave every insecurity behind and follow him to a mansion on a faraway hill, with this warm, fuzzy feeling in my heart? I looked at Aman and our eyes met.

He could ask me to accompany him to the ends of the earth, and all I would ask is, 'Am I driving, or are you?'

I vigorously rubbed the soles of my shoes on the rug outside the main entrance as I stared into the lobby with my jaw touching my knees. If the lobby was bigger than my entire Mumbai apartment, the rest of the house could easily host Badshah's next concert.

The floor was black-and-white stone tiles arranged in a chequered pattern and there were large leafy plants in white stone planters along the walls on both sides. Aesthetic artwork adorned the walls and gorgeous wicker lamps hung from the ceiling. There were two ornate benches at the entrance, presumably where one could sit to wear or take off shoes (or perhaps sit and stare into nothingness, thinking about how to spend all the money one had).

Aman slipped his hand into mine as he led me through the lobby to an expansive living room beyond. The room was … honestly, let your imagination run wild. Everything that anyone could ever want in their home to make it look like it came out of someone's dream was there. Yeah, they had all of that and some more. Each item was carefully curated and set in its designated spot, adding to the tasteful aesthetics.

There were floor-to-ceiling glass windows with linen curtains in soothing pastel shades carefully tied to the ends of the window trims. The wall on the right had pictures of the family, the dogs and of holidays, illuminated by stylish light fixtures. A massive painting in a distinctive style, clearly an original, covered a large part of the wall on the left. A gigantic, cloud-like couch was placed a little away from the wall, with smaller couches placed at different angles to it and a bunch of floor cushions strewn around. A grand armchair stood in one corner. It looked like a family catch-up area. Warm rugs on the parquetted floor and blankets thrown into huge bamboo baskets added to the warmth of the space. The heating had been turned on and the temperature was set just right. I took off my coat and carefully placed it on the armrest of the couch that I settled into, next to Aman.

I did a quick sweep of the remaining space. Massive bookshelves, a large wooden swing hanging from brass chains, two stately armchairs next to a marble table with a vintage chessboard placed on it and more comfy couches at intervals.

Aman's mother sat across from us on one of the smaller couches. She picked up the intercom from the side table and dialled a number.

'They're here, Anil!' she said, excitement brimming in her voice.

A house so big they had a private telephone line to be connected to each other. What was next? Horse carriages to take us from the living room to the bedroom? A zipline from the terrace to the garden? An airlift from the backyard to the pool?

A server politely offered me the tea I'd had my eye on from the minute I'd got off the chopper. I picked up a delicate cup and handed it to Aman. Then I took one for myself and nodded at the server. She smiled and moved on to Aman's mom.

'*Rakh do, beta.* Thank you.' She smiled at me. 'This is Pooja,' she introduced. '*Yeh Avani didi hain. Bhaiyya ko bolo bhabi banane ke liye.* Ha ha ha ha!'

I choked on my fancy tea and Aman's head snapped up.

'Ma!' he half-whispered, half-yelled.

'Kidding. Don't mind me, Avani. I will never let a chance to annoy my baby boy pass.'

I smiled awkwardly and hurried to change the topic. 'You have a lovely home, Aunty.'

'Thank you, beta. It's part of our hearts. I'll give you a tour tomorrow. You must see the tulip garden.'

'THERE THEY ARE!' The booming voice was Aman's dad announcing himself from atop the majestic staircase on our right that led to the upper floor. I looked up to see a man with a pleasant face. He quickly descended the steps and walked towards us with a wide smile and open arms. He was dressed in a grey-and-white striped polo tee and grey pyjama bottoms, with furry slip-ons on his feet. His hair was silver with strategic strands of black placed like they had been painted on. His smile, which reached his eyes, was kind and generous. Something about his presence made me feel welcome and wanted in that huge house. Like Aman's mother, too, had made me feel out by the helipad.

Aman got up to hug his father while I put the cup of tea on the table and got to my feet.

'Sit, sit, beta. Please. Be comfortable,' he said, after hugging Aman and patting him proudly on the back. I waved a weak hi at him and immediately felt self-conscious.

'How was the journey?'

Aman made a thumbs-up sign. 'It was perfect, Papa. Thanks for sending the chopper.'

'That wasn't for you. I wouldn't want Avani's first time here to be a tiring mountain drive.' He turned to me. 'Are you cold, beta? Should I turn the heat up?'

'No, I'm fine, Uncle. Thanks.' I smiled.

I sat there in silence, sipping the tea, while Aman and his parents caught up. His father and he started discussing business when his mother interrupted them and said, 'We are being so rude. Please don't mind them, Avani. You must be hungry, yes?'

Now I don't know if this is just me, but every time I'm awkward or uncomfortable, I deny myself the pleasure of any comfort or any remedy for discomfort.

Cold? No, I'm fine.

Bored? No, I'm having *so* much fun.

Thirsty? Nope.

Hungry? No, no.

'No, no, Aunty. I'm fine.'

'Fine? How? It's dinner time or well past it.'

'Actually ... umm ... I don't eat dinner, Aunty. Intermittent fasting ...' I heard myself say, and followed it up with a fake laugh.

I stole a glance at Aman, hoping he wouldn't call my bluff and force me to eat something. Needless to say, I was starving. But he just smiled and said, 'That's fine, Ma. Don't worry about us. We ate on the flight too.'

We had not, but I was relieved when his mother stopped insisting and replied, 'Oh, okay. If you get hungry in a while,

I can always send some food up to your room. Aman, beta, go get some rest. Your Papa and I need to rest too. The guests will start coming in early tomorrow and we need to be ready. Lots to do!'

'Isn't Gagan arriving tonight?' Aman asked.

'Oh, he'll be here in a while. He likes heading straight to his room as soon as he gets home. We can catch up at breakfast tomorrow,' his father replied as he got up and walked us to the stairs. 'I'll have your bags sent up. Goodnight, beta.'

'Goodnight, both,' Aman said, turning around to give them both pecks on the cheek.

His father placed a gentle hand on my shoulder. 'We are so happy to have you with us, Avani. Please feel free to ask if you need anything at all.'

'I will.' I smiled. 'Thanks, Uncle. Goodnight, Aunty.' Aman's mother reached out, took my hand in hers and gave it a warm squeeze.

After they had left, Aman wrapped an arm around my shoulders and led me up the gigantic staircase, to the right and then down a passage with two rooms on either side.

'Which one's mine?' I asked.

Aman scoffed and grinned as he opened the door on the right. 'This one's *ours*,' he said.

In a daze, I stepped through the door into a cozy lounge area with low cabinets and a tall shuttered cupboard on one side, and a living area, complete with a massive TV and recliners on the other. Straight ahead there were sliding glass doors, through which I caught a glimpse of a plush four-poster bed with a fur rug on the floor and floor-to-ceiling French windows that seemed to open out to a huge balcony.

'You have an apartment inside your house?' I exclaimed as I set down my handbag and trench coat on the console table next to the door, and walked towards the balcony.

The sky was dark outside and the crisp chill in the air was a welcome change from the humid heat of Mumbai. I pulled down the sleeves of my sweater and leaned against the railing, looking out at the sprawling gardens, the majestic property gates and stretches of forested land beyond that for as far as the eye could see. I felt Aman's strong arms envelop me as he hugged me from behind, pulling me towards him and against his warm chest. I turned my head slightly to take in my favourite scent and he lowered his head to nuzzle against the crook of my neck.

'Welcome home,' he whispered.

I leaned back into him and sighed. 'This is gorgeous, Aman.'

'I knew you'd like it. You'll love it during the day. It's magnificent, this view.'

We stayed like that for a while, staring at the moon-washed landscape before us as a cool breeze brushed lightly against our faces. I could feel Aman's breath on my neck and his warmth against my back. I stood there in his arms, feeling ... safe.

'I'll call for dinner in the room, then,' Aman said as he kissed my cheek and headed back into the room.

I turned to rest my back against the railing as I watched him call someone on the intercom. He placed the handset back in its cradle and walked up to lean against the door of the balcony. 'I've requested for some basic dal-chawal and aloo ki sabzi. That's cool?'

'Yes,' I said. 'It's perfect.'

AMAN

Elephant.

'Are you sure? What if they mind?' Avani had asked me, again and again, her eyebrows creased. I was clearly doing a bad job of convincing her that my parents were okay with us sleeping in the same room while we were here.

'Baby, like I said, I'm thirty-one years old, an adult. It's *okay*,' I'd said, perhaps for the thousandth time. After some more nervous pacing around the room, she'd finally unpacked her suitcase and begun to settle in.

I poured a glass of wine for Avani and made a cup of green tea for myself, and settled into the cane couch on the balcony, staring at the night sky while my mind wandered to new places. This was the first time we would be spending the night in one room ... There had been many nights when I'd secretly wished it could be so, and I suspect she had wanted to too, but we'd never expressed it out loud to each other, so it had never happened. Except that one night when I'd found Avani snoring on my couch after four glasses of wine as I returned with one more, and unwilling to wake her up or leave her sleeping there alone, I had slept on the floor on a mattress.

My chain of thought was broken by a sound from the bathroom. I stood up and walked over to the door, which was slightly ajar, and knocked twice. 'You okay, Avani?' I asked.

'Is this it?' she replied in a raspy voice.

'I'm coming in!' I announced as I slowly pushed the door open and saw Avani leaning against the bathroom cabinet with a bottle of my aftershave held to her nose.

I couldn't help laughing.

'This!' She sniffed at the bottle again. 'Oh my god.'

'What about it?' I asked.

'It's my favourite scent in the whole world.' She took a deep breath, her eyes closed.

I walked over to her and placed my hands on the cabinet on either side of her.

'Is it?'

'Yes.' She looked up at me. 'It's how I know you're close. I'm like a sniffer dog.'

'You're *my* sniffer dog.'

'Aww, you say the most romantic things, Aman.' She made a funny face to underline her sarcasm.

'I can do the most romantic things too,' I said, leaning forward to kiss her neck.

'I'm not in the mood for another Ryan Gosling movie, haan. I'm tired.' She laughed, ducked under my arm and stepped out of the bathroom.

'Hey, that was just one time!' I sighed. Long story, that, don't ask.

I changed into my sleep boxers and returned to the bedroom to find Avani pulling the duvet back from the bed and fluffing her pillow. She flung off her slippers and tucked herself under the covers. I slid in under the duvet from my side and lay down.

'Won't you get cold?' she asked, her eyes wide. No matter how freezing the weather was, I always slept in my boxers. She'd turned to her side, facing me, her hands tucked under her face. Her hair fell over one side of her face and in the dim light of the room her eyes looked shinier than I'd ever seen them.

I tucked the duvet around me and mirrored her posture. Reaching out, I pushed a few strands of her hair away from her neck.

'I'll be fine,' I said.

'Okay.'

'So?' I said after a few moments of silence.

'So?'

'It's our first night together.'

'Is that why I suddenly have this mad headache?' she asked, looking serious. 'I thought it was just an excuse women made to get out of sex.'

I burst out laughing and pulled her closer to me. She tucked her face under my chin and took in a long breath. 'I love how you smell,' she whispered, her face buried in my chest.

'I love how you feel,' I replied, running my hands down her back and resting them on her waist.

She raised her head to trace a queue of kisses from my neck to my jaw. My hand on her waist stiffened as our lips met and then our tongues.

The wine and the green tea lay forgotten.

AVANI

Taking matters into my own hands.

There are times when you pray to God. Like when your exam results are due, or when you're hoping the pimple on your face disappears before a party, or when you want your favourite player to score the winning runs in a cricket match. And then there are times when you just want to hug God for giving you exactly what you want. Like when you get that dream job or, in my case, when you're lying next to a half-dressed Aman.

The anticipation of the moment hung so low that I could feel the weight of it pressing against my chest as I fumbled to find the right words. 'So what happens now?' seemed too demure and innocent coming from me, given the dirty day dreams I'd had about this very moment. Also, a really stupid question, because … umm … I knew what happens now. 'Let's fuck?' seemed too aggressive and shallow. So I led with, 'My feet are freezing.'

Without a word, he moved closer to me and gently tucked my cold feet between his, and I took the opportunity to scooch in closer, into the already non-existent space between us.

I watched his eyes flicker down to my lips as I took a slow breath. The corners of his mouth twitched up, just a bit, like he could read every thought going through my mind. My hand drifted up to his chest. I smirked, feeling bold despite the loud pounding of my heart.

'So ... is this the part where I say something clever and mysterious?' I murmured, my fingers tracing his collarbone before resting on his sharp jawline. 'Because I'm fresh out of mysterious.'

Aman chuckled, a low, delicious sound that rumbled under the palm of my hand. 'Oh, I think you've already ruined mysterious,' he replied, his hand skimming down my side and stopping at the curve of my waist. 'But I'm all for bold honesty.'

'Well, then,' I said, pretending to muse as I leaned closer, our noses almost brushing. 'Bold honesty would be saying I'm thinking less about this conversation and more about ... other things.'

'Other things?' His eyes gleamed with mischief blending with an intense, unmistakeable heat.

'Other things ...' I echoed with mock seriousness, which crumbled as he inched closer, his lips hovering over mine, close enough to drive me insane, '... that we can do with our hands and mouths and tongues ...'

Before I could finish, his hand firmly grabbed the back of my neck to pull me closer and his mouth was on mine, his lips warm and tasting faintly of mint and trouble. His kiss was slow and deliberate at first, like he was savouring every second, like he would ensure he took all the time in the world to explore every inch of me. And for a moment it felt like the two of us were locked in this perfect moment. But then something shifted. The gentleness melted away, replaced by an intensity that was raw and unapologetic. His grip tightened and his lips pressed harder against mine, turning the kiss into something fierce and consuming, like he was done holding back. The air between us thickened and, suddenly, every breath, every touch felt charged with an undeniable urgency that left me dizzy and wanting more.

When he finally pulled back, his fingers still tangled in my hair, he looked at me with a knowing grin. 'Still cold?'

I let a moment pass before I replied, 'Freezing,' and pushed his shoulders down, pinning him to the bed as I climbed on top of him. I was done taking measured steps. I was done thinking and rethinking. I was done being the girl who knew what she was doing. I was done being wise and reasonable. I wanted this. I wanted him. And now that he was right here, vulnerable, almost naked and mine for the taking, nothing was going to stop me. So, what's that saying again? I threw caution to the winds and took matters into my own hands.

Make what you want of that last line. Who am I to tell you what to think and what not to?

All I can say is that he hums when he ...
Wink wink nudge nudge.

I smiled to myself as every second of the last hour—was that really an hour, or was it two, or did it last three days?—played out in my mind in vivid detail. My stomach did a swoop every time a certain visual or sound echoed in my mind, causing my breath to catch and my heart to skip a beat, every few seconds.

'You're thinking about it, aren't you?' Aman whispered into my hair and pulled the blanket tighter around us. We were on the couch on the balcony, cuddled up, processing our first time together.

'I'm sorry, can you not talk?' I shushed him. 'I'm very busy replaying what that mouth can do when it's not interrupting my very graphic visions.'

Aman dropped his jaw in fake horror, then suddenly stood up and gathered me up in his arms, blanket and all. He flung me over his shoulder and smacked my ass playfully as I mock-screamed and play-fought his grip. Inside the room, he threw me down on the bed on my back, then crawled over me till his face was directly over mine.

Aaaaaaand fade to black!

30 SEPTEMBER 2023

AVANI

My new wallpaper.

I'm not particularly grumpy or unpleasant in the mornings, but let's say I'm also not like Barbie on crack. So the fact that I woke up this morning with a smile on my face even before my eyes had fully opened is journal-worthy. The sheer curtains drawn across the balcony door danced in the slight draft entering the room, causing the golden rays of the sun to form waves and patterns on the wooden floor. I slid my hand over Aman's on my waist and let the familiarity of his skin fill my heart.

Wow, so one night with the man and I'd woken up as a Rumi knock-off? But as much as I loved every bit of snuggling with him in bed, there's only so much a girl can be dreamy about when she desperately needed to pee. I could feel Aman's steady breaths on my neck, so I knew he was fast asleep. I carefully plucked his hand from my waist and slid off the bed. As an afterthought, I picked up my phone from the nightstand and tiptoed to the bathroom. My business done, I stood before the mirror, looking at the girl with crazy bed hair and flushed pink lips. So this is what writers mean when they describe the 'morning-after look', without ever mentioning its inevitable companion ... I have two words for you: Morning. Breath.

I quickly fished out my toothbrush from my toiletry pouch and tied my hair into a topknot. A wash, moisturizer, lip balm and a mild spray of perfume later, when I somewhat resembled the Avani Aman had seen last night, I sat on the edge of the marble bathtub and pulled up the Triple-decker chat window and quickly typed.

Me: Guys.
Maya: Do we still like him?
Rhea: You're up early. Or ... did you not sleep?
Me: He he.
Rhea: OMG! How was itttt???
Me: I'll tell you everything when I'm back home but ... guys ... my brain is mush right now!
Rhea: Ohmygawwwwwwd! I can't wait!
Maya: Are you happy, Ani?
Me: I am! More than. Okay, just had to tell you this. Gotta go now. Bye.
Rhea: Haffunnn!

I scrolled through my contact list and quickly pulled up Martin's contact card. He was away that weekend with his current girl on a 'bartending retreat' in Goa, so I wasn't sure if he was going to answer my video call so early in the morning. But before I could finish that thought ...

'The only reason you would call me this early in the morning after your first night in Mussoorie has to be that you shagged Hot-Rod-Raina! Just say yes and make my day, babe!

I need at least one of us to have started the weekend with a bang.' He stared into the screen expectantly.

I opened my mouth to tell him, but decided to just go with a light nod of my head and tight shutting of my eyelids.

'FUCK YES!' he exclaimed.

'Shhh!' I replied. 'He's sleeping in the bedroom.'

'And you are on your phone in the bathroom when you could be staring at his god-like naked body right now? Bitch, the fuck is wrong with you?! Hang up and go juggle his moneybags, ugh!'

He hung up.

Right.

Stepping out of the bathroom, I saw Aman still fast asleep. I wrapped the throw blanket from the couch around my shoulders and tiptoed to the fancy espresso machine placed next to a wicker basket full of coffee pods of all kinds—light, medium roast, dark, decaf—beside another basket with a million different teabags and pouches of brown sugar.

Coffee and mugs selected, I faced off with the espresso machine. I stared at it, trying to figure out how it worked, and then gave up, fishing my phone out of my pocket so I could google a solution.

'It's the button at the bottom right of the machine, baby.'

I screamed and turned to find Aman smiling at me from the bed, complete with wild bed hair and sleepy eyes, dimples on full display ... and those perfect lips.

'Aman! You scared me!' I pressed my palm to my chest.

'Good morning,' he said in a sexy, sleepy voice. 'Why are you out of bed already? Come back.' He patted the duvet.

'I was going to wake you up with coffee and then we were going to snuggle. Now you've ruined that plan by waking up before I could figure out how this stupid coffee machine works.'

He laughed, pushed off the covers and stepped out of bed. Walking over to me, he pulled me to his chest and rested his chin on the top of my head.

'I like waking up to you fiddling with my coffee machine in the morning.'

'And "coffee machine" being code for …?' I started.

He tucked me into the hug a little tighter, laughing. Then he reached over and pressed the button at the bottom right and the espresso machine kicked into action with a sharp whistle that turned into a rumble and then a long, loud hiss.

'Wow. So if you hadn't woken up by yourself, this little shit would've put a spanner in my plans anyway,' I said.

'Mm-hmm.' He turned me around so I was now facing the coffee machine, and still standing behind me, proceeded to make us coffee. 'Why don't you go pretend to be asleep, and I'll wake you up with surprise coffee?' he whispered into my hair.

'And then can we snuggle?' I whispered back.

'One hundred per cent!'

'Yesss,' I said and ducked out from under his arms and got into bed.

I sat there, under the covers that smelt deliciously of Aman, watching him walk to me in his boxers with a tray of coffee mugs and biscuits, the sexiest man alive. I reached for my phone and opened the camera app.

My phone screen would now have a new wallpaper.

'Gagan's here. He's meeting us for breakfast in thirty,' Aman said without looking up from his phone. We'd finished our coffee, spent another hour playing tonsil tennis and other spicy games that grown-ups play and were now lying back in bed, scrolling through our phones. Like a real couple.

'Will everyone be there?' I asked, swinging my legs off the bed.

'Oh yes, the Rainas love their breakfast-table catch-up sessions,' he said, looking at me. Then, reaching out to stroke my cheek, he added, 'They're looking forward to having you there.'

I raised my eyebrows and stretched my mouth wide to indicate what I was feeling: Shit!

'Baby, it'll just be the family. But ... you can stay in if you feel like joining us later. I can always—'

'No,' I cut him off. 'I want to be there, with you.'

'Okay.' He propped himself up on his elbow and kissed the tip of my nose. 'Now, we need to take a shower.'

'We?' I asked.

'No?'

'Yes.' I chuckled.

Without missing a beat, Aman sprang out of bed, scooped me up and carried me to the bathroom, his eyes not leaving mine for even a second. He set me down on the bathroom vanity and kicked the door shut behind us.

And we went on to lather each other's bodies till they were nice and foamy, and then engaged in deep passionate lovemaking ... Just kidding.

I was still sore from last night—all the nicknames that Martin had given Aman were actually quite accurate—and quite tense about the breakfast coming up, and we had to keep an eye on the time. So, yes, we kissed, and there was a lot of touching, but just a shower it was. Not that it didn't have its moments—particularly the one of complete vulnerability when I sang in my shower voice and Aman laughed in my face. But I blamed it on the expensive marble. Not the right acoustics for my middle-class bathroom voice.

A little while later, I was rummaging through my suitcase looking for the breakfast-appropriate outfit Maya had so carefully curated for me, when Aman stepped out of the bathroom looking like a dream in a pair of light blue baggy jeans and a grey knit sweater, and sat on the couch to wear his white sneakers. Watching me scramble around, he walked over.

'Nobody cares what you wear, baby,' he said, kissing the side of my head.

'As if!' I huffed and puffed into my black leggings and powder-blue oversized sweater and rushed to the bathroom, where I quickly filled in my brows, put on some blush and lip gloss, and tied my hair into a low ponytail. I rushed out again and pulled on the tan boots Maya had packed in and sat down on the bed to take a breath while a serene-looking Aman leaned against the coffee table with his arms folded across his chest and a smile on his face.

'I'm not late, okay? You just get dressed in minus-three seconds. That's not on me.' I pointed a finger at him.

'I didn't say a word.' He raised his hands in the air. 'Shall we?'

'Where's your bottle of aftershave? Can I have it for a moment?'

'Why?' he asked, walking to the bathroom to fetch it.

'Because ...' I said, as he handed me the bottle and I undid the cap of my love potion and dabbed two dots behind my ears and on both my wrists, 'I need to smell exquisite!'

'Creep!' He laughed. 'Let's go!

So here we were, on the back porch of Aman's lavish home. The air was chilly and the sky bluer than I had ever seen in Mumbai or Pune. The lush lawns were interrupted only by a near-Olympic-sized swimming pool a little ahead. A long table made from the most exquisite piece of natural wood had been set for breakfast. Aman's parents were there already and broke into wide smiles as they spotted us walking towards them hand in hand.

'Good morning, my loves!' Aman's mom sounded as gleeful as ever. 'Slept well?'

'Good morning, Ma,' Aman replied, pecking her on the cheek. 'Morning, Papa!'

'Good morning. I slept very well, thank you,' I said.

'Good morning, beta. Come. Sit.' Aman's dad rose and came around to pull back the chair opposite his.

'Thank you, Uncle.' I took my seat and Aman sat on my left.

'This looks great,' I said, glancing around the table to see at least a hundred items laid out. All of it looked delicious.

I hadn't realized I was so hungry until the smell of steaming hot waffles reached my nose. Aman must've noticed my eyes light up, because he picked up the plate of waffles and served us both and went on to offer the fruit platter to his parents. Meanwhile, his mother had poured me a glass of what looked like apple juice and placed it on the table in front of me.

'It's from our apple garden. Fresh as it could be. Taste?' she said, smiling wide.

I took a sip, relishing the scent and taste of fresh apples long forgotten, thanks to my habit of OD-ing on store-bought juices out of tetra packs.

'It's amazing!' I said, gesturing 'perfect' with my fingers.

I turned my attention to the tall plate of waffles before me as the others engaged in regular family chatter. Servers walked around us every few minutes, offering omelettes and parathas, breads and more waffles, jams and cheeses and cold cuts. I think I ate like a starved cavewoman.

I was almost done with my second glass of apple juice and my waffles and jam when a deep voice interrupted the chatter at the table.

'I see everyone is here already.'

'Gagan!' Aman's mother threw both her hands in the air, her face radiating joy. Aman and I turned to see his elder brother walking towards us.

He wore a navy blue sweater and dark jeans, and had the same slightly cold look in his eyes and the defiant upward tilt of his chin that I remembered from Aman's party a few months back.

He gave his parents polite hugs and walked around the table to greet Aman. 'You look good, man,' he said, as Aman stood up and the two exchanged some sort of a complicated handshake that ended in them entwining their right arms and half-hugging each other.

'I wish I could say the same. London really has worn you down,' Aman replied, mischief in his voice. That earned him a playful punch in his gut and then Gagan turned to face me.

'And ... the famous Avani who has our man wrapped around her little finger ... Good to see you again.' He gave me a tight smile.

I smiled back politely and extended my hand. 'Hi. Good to meet you again,' I said evenly.

'Too soon to be sure of that, Avani. We don't really know each other yet.' He winked as he shook my hand quickly and went on to take the empty seat next to his mother.

Suddenly I felt the air shift in a way I couldn't quite understand. I told myself that Gagan was much older and maybe his sense of humour just wasn't as easy and free-flowing as Aman's. I had reasoned, after we'd first met at Aman's place, that he was perhaps awkward during first encounters—many people were—and that this time in Mussoorie would be different. But here I was, my guard back up just as I had begun to get comfortable.

'So ... Avani ... where do you work?' he asked as he cut into an omelette with surgeon-like precision.

'I'm just—' I began.

'Let's not scrutinize the guest already, Gagan,' Aman's dad cut me off. 'It's her first time in our home.' He smiled, though his voice was graver than I remembered it from just minutes ago.

I returned his smile and went back to my plate of waffles, but not before noticing Aman's parents signalling to each other with their eyes. Clearly, subtlety was not the family's strongest suit.

'Avani ... Come, you have to see my tulip garden,' Aman's mom piped up.

'I'd love to, Aunty.' I understood what she was doing and was thankful for it.

'Come on, then. Let the boys talk shop.' She came around and extended her hand towards me. I felt Aman's hand lightly squeeze my thigh under the table, encouraging me to go with his mother. I stood up and took his mother's hand.

'Don't mind Gagan, beta. He takes a bit of time adjusting to people, especially if they are new to the family,' she said in a low voice as she led me away.

'That's fine, Aunty. Everyone says that about me too.' She turned to meet my eyes and flashed me a smile.

As I walked beside her, her arm linked into mine, the tiny knot in my chest slowly loosened. She had something to tell me about every bush and tree we walked past on our way. She knew each one intimately—names, ages, varieties, how they changed with the seasons, odd facts—and I let myself settle into the warmth of her company.

The last time I had walked through a garden was when I was seven, holding my mother's hand. A trip had been arranged from school to the Sanjay Gandhi National Park and my parents had followed the school bus on their Scooty to make sure I would be okay. It had always taken me time to make friends and they were worried that I would be sitting alone somewhere while the other kids ran around and enjoyed themselves. They were right, of course. So when my mum arrived and saw me standing by myself next to a bench, she snuck me off on our own little walk around the play area. She told me all kinds of stories, none of which I remembered now, but what I did recall was walking barefoot on the grass, my hand in hers and her voice reassuring me softly with stories. I remembered feeling safe. And not alone. The memory felt so real that it scared me, and I shook my head to clear it.

'Here we are,' Aunty said, her eyes shining in anticipation, as we reached a narrow, cobbled path that I assumed led to the tulip garden.

'Give me a second, Aunty,' I replied, as I let go of her hand to undo my boots so I could take them off when I walked on the grass barefoot.

AMAN

What am I not seeing here?

'When did you get in last night?' I asked Gagan as Avani left the table with Ma.

'Late,' he said. 'When did you get here?'

'Late evening … 8ish.'

'I was planning on flying out immediately after the party today, but if you're staying on for a day, I'll stay too.' He looked at me and flashed his usual half-smile. I responded with a thumbs-up. It felt good to be back home with everyone there. It had been a while. Gagan was three years older than me, but he was like a secondary parent figure in my life, and his general demeanour had always been authoritative and reserved. I'd grown up going to him for life advice on everything—parents, career, friends, love. He was the pragmatic one, annoyingly practical, and I'd needed that outlook more times than I could count.

We finished our breakfast chatting about work and life in general, and left the table to walk into the house. The sun was getting hotter, and some of our relatives and family friends had slowly started coming in. We followed Papa into the living room, where we saw Sheryl bustling around, welcoming Arvind Uncle, Papa's oldest friend from school, and his family. Gagan and I followed Papa to greet them and then moved to the tea room annexe. Ramesh, our housekeeper, arrived, asking us if he could get us something, and Gagan and I agreed on tea.

'How's office?' Gagan asked as we settled on the couch.

'Office is great. Learning a lot from doing things myself, though Papa's very much there when I need him, of course. And it's been good to have Sheryl around. She ensures I don't mess up,' I replied, grinning, and he nodded in agreement.

'How have you been, though?' I asked. 'We haven't caught up properly in over a year.'

'Busy with work. Global marketing head now, so …' The glint in his eyes reappeared and he sounded almost sheepish.

'What the hell? And you're telling me this now?' I punched his arm. 'Do Ma and Papa know?'

'Not yet. I don't want them making a big deal out of it.'

'Dude! It is a *huge* deal! We all know how hard you've worked for it.'

'Yeah, but everything doesn't need to be celebrated with catering and a tent in the backyard,' he replied. 'If I tell them, Ma will throw another one of her parties, and I'm maxed out on small talk, honestly.'

'They're proud of you, Gagan.' I grinned widely and thumped him on the shoulder. 'So am I.'

He nodded, his lips stretching to one side in a semblance of a smile. 'But tell me about you. I see a lot has changed from the last time we caught up. You have someone in your life now.'

'Life's good … great, actually. Avani makes it better in every way.' I was about to tell him how we met when I noticed the expression on his face change. I knew this look only too well.

'Something going on?' I asked.

'Nothing. Just that … I worry about you. You're quite stupid when it comes to matters of the heart.' He turned away to pick up one of the two cups of tea Ramesh had left on the coffee table.

I reached across and picked the other up for myself. Settling back, I said, 'Tell me what this is about?'

'You seem to have set all these levels of commitment in your mind. That bringing a girl home makes everything serious. Or telling Ma about your feelings changes things. When are you going to get a little practical in life and see things as they are ... and not as they could be?'

'Okay, I've got a bone to pick with that tattletale we have for a mother, but, hey, it's not like that. I've been with Avani for a few months now and I'm feeling good about this.'

'Isn't that what you said about the last one? What was her name ... Aanchal?' He looked up from his cup.

Aanchal and I had been together for a few months before I spoke to Gagan about her. She wasn't my brightest decision, I have to admit, but Avani was nothing like her. Gagan's words weren't any harsher than they would be if this were a discussion about anything else, but something about his refusal to give Avani, or anyone else, a chance didn't sit well with me.

'You've barely spoken to her, Gagan. I think you should give her more than one tiny conversation before you make up your mind about her,' I said, a little more curtly than I would have liked. I knew Gagan was looking out for me, but this time I decided I wouldn't back down. Avani deserved more.

AVANI

Comfortably numb.

'This one is a red cross tulip. And that one is a lady tulip, Anil's favourite. My favourite, however, is the Yokohama tulip. It's right ahead ... here.' Aman's mother and I were walking through never-ending rows of gorgeous flowers. When she had mentioned a 'tulip garden', I'd imagined a few tulip bushes scattered aesthetically across a lawn. Instead, I was now walking through what looked like the tulip fields of The Hague.

'Our company did a lot of work with the Japanese government in the early days. We still do. The consulate general gifted me a bouquet when I visited Japan in 1997. I knew immediately that I had to have these in my garden. It was also easier to fly back with seeds then. It wasn't as strict as it is now.' She proudly caressed the gorgeous yellow bulbs.

'They're stunning, Aunty, just beautiful.' They really were.

'Here, love.' She bent down, plucked a few stems and handed them to me. 'For your bedside table. They'll bloom some more tomorrow.' She smiled at the flowers and then at me.

'Thank you.' I brought the bunch to my nose to take a sniff.

'Oh, tulips don't really have a scent,' she said. 'Wouldn't expect that, would you, from the way they look?'

I nodded, and we walked on, me in her footsteps, till we reached a glass house in the centre of the garden. She opened the door and let me in. It was beautifully lit by the sun streaming in. A long dinner table, neatly laid, took up most of the space inside it, with at least twenty intricately carved vintage-looking chairs arranged around it. Cozy but still very stately.

'We like to eat our brunches here in the winters. The sun keeps us warm and I love listening to the chatter of a big group of family and friends over food and mimosas.' She took the seat at the head of the gigantic table. I placed the bunch of tulips on it and took the seat next to her, around the immediate corner.

'Aman tells me you work at a bookstore. That must be magical. Tell me about it.' She rested her chin on the palm of her right hand and leaned forward, looking at me intently.

'Oh, it's the best! It's called Bombay Bound.'

'What a lovely name!' she exclaimed.

'Yeah, it's a beautiful space. My best friend Rhea's family owns it. I work there part-time. In the mornings, usually.'

'How I would love to spend my mornings surrounded by the smell of books.' She sighed.

'That's my favourite part too!' I laughed. 'Her family is sweet and I get to earn while getting through classes. I love it.'

'I can imagine. Living in Mumbai as a student is criminal! Everything is so expensive. And I'm sure your big fat law books must cost a limb!'

'You have no clue,' I said, glad that *someone* understood.

'Actually, I studied law too. I wish I had been smart like you and taken up a part-time job alongside my studies. By the end of every month, I was scraping leftovers.' She laughed. 'Until I married Anil. Then we scraped leftovers together.'

I couldn't help laughing. I remembered Aman telling me about his parents starting the company in his uncle's garage and building it up from there.

We spent close to an hour in the glass house, chatting about everything from law to our hobbies to Aman. She told me funny stories from his childhood that I carefully filed away in the must-tease-Aman-about-this cabinet in my head. I told her about my childhood and growing up with Aaji in Pune, and she shared how she'd always thought of Pune as a lovely place to live in.

'I never really got to meet my grandparents, you know,' she said. 'I wish I had. They passed away when my mother was still a teenager, but she had the most beautiful memories of them that she would tell me about as bedtime stories.'

'I'm sorry. That must've been rough.' I reached across and gently placed my hand over hers on the table.

'Not at all. I only have the most amazing stories as memories of them. And their pictures.' She paused. 'Oh, I must show you the family albums. You have to see how gorgeous my grandma's dimples were,' she exclaimed, clapping her hands together.

'So that's where Aman gets his from!' I said.

'Ha ha! Yes, he does! Come!' She got up and extended her hand to me again.

Our minds are such weird little places, I thought as we made our way back through the rows of gorgeous flowers. It stores our insecurities and issues so close to our joys and laughter, like rooms sharing walls. Sometimes a loud noise on one side echoes in the other and sometimes the wall is so thick that you forget there is a room on the other side at all.

As we walked back to the house, I let my mind wander to a place where there were no walls, only postcard photos of Yokohama tulips and people sharing a laugh in the warmth of the sun.

It was 11.30 a.m. by the time we got back to the house. A lot had happened already. Gagan's brusqueness this morning notwithstanding, spending time with Aman's parents, especially his mother, had made me feel a lot more confident about my decision to have taken this trip with him. For a large part of my life, well into my late teenage years, my biggest achievement had been making more than one friend whose family I was comfortable around, so this was new to me, and being able to enjoy it made my heart sing.

As soon as we stepped into the living room, Aman pulled away from an intense discussion that he was having with Gagan and his father, and Aunty left us together to join them, cupping Aman's face in her hands with extra affection as they passed each other.

'Had fun?' he asked, taking my hand in his.

'Yeah. She's so sweet.'

'That's where I get all my sweetness from,' he said with a smirk.

'You really think highly of yourself, don't you?'

'Might I jog your memory to a time not too long ago when you took my name very "highly" yourself?' he said with mischief in his voice. That earned him a slap on his chest as I shushed him and glanced quickly towards his family, who were standing quite close to us, to see if they had overheard.

He laughed, then squeezed my hand and said, 'Okay listen, I've got to go meet some of Ma and Papa's friends. Something tells me you'd prefer reading a book in the room while I am away.'

'You know me so well.'

'I'll see you upstairs in a bit?' He gave me a quick peck on the cheek before walking towards a big group of people greeting each other raucously at the far end of the living room as I made my way upstairs.

Thirty minutes later, I was in our bed, staring up at the ceiling, my book resting upside down on my tummy. I hadn't got beyond two paragraphs since I'd started as my mind kept wandering to imaginary (mostly disastrous) scenarios from the party later that evening. Me standing alone in a corner while Aman folded over laughing at an inside joke with his family. Me spilling wine on the expensive ivory dress Maya had lent me to wear that evening. Me drinking too much too quickly to get over my nervousness and then waking up tomorrow regretting doing some shit like getting everyone to form a human pyramid for a group photo. The last one had the most potential to come true ... I closed my eyes in dread.

I threw my book down on the bed and got up to make some coffee. I'd slept like a baby, but that breakfast binge was making me sleepy again, or maybe it was just my overthinking brain. I'd settled on the balcony couch with my cup when I heard a knock on the door.

'Come in, no!' I yelled, sure that Aman was going to walk in.

Nobody entered. Instead, there were two more knocks. I walked over to the door and pulled it open, expecting him to give me one of those 'Ma'am, your order for a hot man is here' dialogues.

It was Gagan.

'Hey,' I said, trying to hide my shock in an awkward smile. 'Are you looking for Aman? He's …'

'Hi. No, I was just with him. I was actually looking to have a word with you,' he replied. 'Can I come in?'

'You MAY come in,' I said, deliberately correcting him as I stepped away from the door. The sour expression on his face was starting to get to me. All that expensive Ivy League education, and still this.

He strode in and sat down on the couch. I left the door slightly ajar and walked to the bed, but didn't sit down. Leaning against one of the poster frames, I said, 'I've heard so much about you—'

'We can cut the small talk, Ananya.'

WOW.

'Umm … Avani.'

'Avani. Sorry. That was rude. Avani … I knew that.'

'That's okay. So, since you obviously haven't come here for friendly banter, what's up?'

'Yeah ...' he said, and then fell silent. I waited for him to voice whatever it was that was important enough for him to seek me out and call me by a wrong name.

'I don't want you taking this the wrong way ...' he started.

I nodded, indicating I wouldn't, and waited for him to continue.

'But Aman is ...' Long pause again.

I wasn't sure if this was just his style or if he sucked at putting words together in general. You never know, staying away from home with such an unsociable personality—maybe that made one lose basic communication skills.

'Aman is ...' he said again, '... naive.'

He looked at me. His gaze was empty—not warm, not ice-cold like it was this morning at the breakfast table, but indifferent.

'What do you mean?' I asked, confused.

'I mean, between the two of us, he's the emotional one. And sometimes he tends to make decisions that don't quite stand the test of time. You know what I mean?' His right eyebrow flicked up. I could hear my heart beating in my ears.

'I don't ... sorry,' I said awkwardly.

'I mean, don't read too much into this.' He made sweeping gestures at the room.

'Into what?'

'You being here, with my family.'

'Uhh ...'

'We're very protective of each other. We try to ensure that we prevent each other from making bad decisions ... mistakes.'

'I'm not sure I understand ... I ...'

'Didn't think you would.' He slapped his thighs and sprung to his feet. He took two very slow steps towards me. 'Have fun this weekend. Walk through the property, enjoy the party, get your selfies and then let things run their course. As they must.' He smiled tightly and walked to the door.

'Gagan,' I called out. 'Are you asking me to leave Aman?'

'I'm asking you to not get your hopes up. Usually that only brings disappointment,' he said, half turning around. Then he walked out and shut the door behind him.

I froze, my eyes fixed on the door. What the fuck was that?

I could feel chills running up my limbs to the centre of my chest. I took a few deep breaths, trying to bring my brain back from the very unpleasant direction in which it was heading. I told myself that this—whatever it was—had to be a misunderstanding. That maybe Gagan had misjudged something I had said or done, and assumed the worst. Maybe he was tired. What could be the intention of being so square with me? Had he just called me a 'bad decision' and a 'mistake'? Had I not met him warmly enough this morning?

No, Avani. No. This isn't the time to doubt yourself. Aman was right next to you at that breakfast table. If you were in any way rude or disrespectful, he would've told you. You know that.

I took another deep breath.

His mother apologized for Gagan's behaviour too. This isn't on you.

I sat down on the bed and drew the duvet around me. Nobody had ever spoken to me like that before. I had been in my fair share of uncomfortable rooms, but I had never been made to feel so unwanted or undeserving. And that is what Gagan's words had made me feel.

Unwanted …

I pulled my phone out to call Aaji or Maya or anyone I could talk to, but the door opened again and Aman walked in, a spring in his step. He had a basketful of fruits and breads in one hand and what looked like a box of sweets in the other.

'I almost expected you to be napping,' he said breezily as he placed the basket on the console table. He walked over with the box of sweets and sat next to me on the bed.

'These are Mussoorie's best gulab jamuns,' he said excitedly. He took one out and brought it close to my mouth. 'I had Ramesh order them fresh this morning.'

I took a bite and let the sugar rush calm my nerves down to some semblance of normalcy.

'You like?' he asked as he took a bite too.

'I love.' I smiled, wiping the syrup trickling down my chin with the back of my hand.

You should say something. He should know. Maybe he knows?

How? He wouldn't know. He would never let Gagan talk to me like that. I trusted him. I had no idea what Gagan had meant, but for the sake of sanity I was willing to consider that it was all a big, ugly misunderstanding. Would it be right to make a big deal of it by discussing it with Aman on the morning of his parents' anniversary dinner?

Yeah, maybe not.

Aman was saying something, oblivious to the storm raging inside me.

'Sorry? Didn't hear that …' I said.

'I was saying, baby, that I have more things to show you that you'll love. Come on, we've got to go!' Before I could respond, he got up excitedly and strode out of the room.

AMAN

How do I slow down time?

'Dress warm and meet me downstairs,' I called out to Avani as I took the stairs down. I called Ramesh to have the car readied for us, and as I made my way out, I passed my parents conversing animatedly with another lot of friends who had just arrived. I made a mental note to chat with Ma about her 'small gathering of close family and friends' way of going about this party—any party, really—and waved politely at them as I walked by.

My dad's vintage red Hindustan Contessa was waiting for me in the driveway, glistening in the sun. Papa never tired of telling us the story of how he had bought this beauty after their company had closed its first big client deal. We must have heard it at least five times a year since we were old enough to listen to stories, and at every family Diwali card party after his third drink of whisky. The high point of the story for Papa was when he had told Ma he'd won it in a lottery so she wouldn't throw a fit. He guffawed loudly every time he narrated that bit, and then went over to Ma to hug her while she sat shaking her head. Ma always joked that she'd raised two kids, but Papa had raised three: the Contessa was his firstborn child. It was the first thing he had got transported to Mussoorie when they decided to move from Mumbai and not a day passed without Papa polishing it squeaky-clean before his morning runs every day.

It took me many, many years to gain Papa's trust enough to take her for a spin. Gagan still didn't have that privilege because he banged up the first car he got when he joined college. But the Contessa was ethereal, and as much as I loved driving her around the town now, as a child I would simply take my book and sit inside her while she was parked in the garage. She felt like a friend, a place of comfort. So when I decided to show Avani around town, I knew I had to take the Contessa.

Ramesh handed me the keys from across the hood and I walked around to get into the driver's seat.

'Oh my God, who *is* this? Introduce us, please.' I looked through the window on the passenger side to see Avani, her eyes wide in awe, walking around the car, her hand stroking the side. I laughed and stretched my left arm over to open the door as she came around the back. 'Meet my dad's firstborn child,' I said.

'She's beautiful!' Avani got in and pulled the door gently shut, like it was a precious, fragile object that needed to be handled with care.

I beamed, put the car into gear and drove out.

Every trip I'd ever made to Mussoorie included one afternoon of driving through the lanes of the town, getting a coffee and cake at my favourite café, and then driving uphill to catch the most magnificent sunset. My date was usually Ma or our caretaker's twin toddlers. But today I had with me the one person with whom I wanted to share all of my favourite things to do.

We drove through the gorgeous hills as the radio shuffled between songs and presenters.

'Where are we going?' Avani asked as she turned to face me. She'd rolled down her side of the window a few inches to breathe in the fresh mountain air without freezing her button nose off, but before that she'd reached over and zipped my jacket all the way up to my neck and planted a quick kiss on my cheek.

'To get some coffee or hot chocolate to warm you up.'

'Okay.' She signalled a yes with a beaming smile and went back to watching the trees rush by. She'd been quieter after breakfast with the family this morning. I'd decided against asking her what she was feeling. She was probably just overwhelmed. Together, we Rainas could get a little too much sometimes. In any case, Avani liked to take time to process things by herself and would figure if she wanted to talk about anything. It could equally be that I was reading too much into things ...

I slowed down as we made our way to the Hathipaon area and pulled into the parking space next to Ballu Coffee House.

'Who's Ballu?' Avani asked, reading the old wooden signage above the entrance to the quaint café.

'Nobody knows,' I replied. 'The owner was apparently drunk when he got this board made. Every time I come here, his grandson makes up a new story about the cafe's name. I strongly recommend you ask him about it. Maybe you'll hear a version no one's heard before.'

She threw her head back, laughing. 'The coffee and shakes here are the best, though,' I added.

We walked in and took a corner table overlooking the gorgeous valley, and I raised my hand to summon the waiter.

We spent the next hour alternating between laughter, conversation and comfortable silence as we took in the views of the beautiful town and sipped on the excellent coffee (mine) and hot chocolate (Avani's). Avani clicked pictures to send Aaji, Maya, Martin and Rhea. I clicked pictures of her for myself.

'Where to now?' she asked.

'You'll see,' I said, reaching over and wiping the chocolate-milk moustache off her upper lip.

I got up and held her coat for her. She slid her arms through and turned to face me with the cutest smile.

'What?' I smiled back.

'It's just strange when you're putting clothes *on* me,' she said, grinning.

I draped her scarf around her waist, spun her around and pulled her closer. She squealed as she looked up at me and I placed a soft kiss on her lips.

'I can't wait to be back in the room with you,' I whispered. 'You're too far when you're not cuddling with me in bed.'

'Not even now?'

'Nope. Not close enough.' I kissed her again and turned her towards the door.

'Oh, wait!' she said and moved towards the billing desk, where the owner's grandson was sitting at his usual place behind the counter. 'Hi!' she said to him. 'Why is the coffee house named Ballu Coffee House?'

'They say there is a secret tunnel under the coffee house that leads to the grave of a man named Ballu and that he comes here at night to have coffee with the love of his life, who used to work here 200 years ago,' he said, unblinking and impassive.

'Wow,' she said, turning to me with eyes wide.

I laughed and thanked the man as I led Avani towards the exit.

Outside, she stood by the car, tapping her feet to stay warm as she waited for me to unlock it. I stopped a few steps away and pulled my phone out to take a picture of the girl I'd got to call mine, looking stunning in the early afternoon sun against the backdrop of this gorgeous town.

When had life become so fucking perfect? What could I do to slow down time?

AVANI

Blame it on the mountains.

'Where to now?' I asked him, looking out the window as we began driving further uphill.

'You'll see.' He smiled, giving my thigh a slight squeeze.

We drove for another ten minutes up through the mountainside till we reached a tabletop. There were no other cars in sight, no people. Aman parked the car near a makeshift shed that had a bicycle kept inside it. It was colder up here, windier, and the clouds were so low I felt I could touch them if I wanted to. There was a lone bench that faced the valley flowing off the edge of the flat land we stood on.

I wished suddenly that I was the kind of person who viewed a landscape in numbers. You know, how some people say, 'Oh, this cliff must be 3,000 metres above sea level' or 'This land must be around 9 acres' or 'It's so cold, it must be as low as 8 degrees here'. But here I was, happy to simply be high in the hills and enjoying the crisp, cold air.

We settled on the bench and Aman put his arm around me, pulling me closer.

'This feels like something out of a movie,' I said dreamily.

'It must be one if it feels like one.' He lowered his head to kiss my forehead.

'That line can fit into a lot of conversations.' I smiled tightly.

He hugged me tighter.

'So ... what's the story?' I asked.

'Huh?'

'About this place?'

'Didn't get you …'

'I mean, why have we come here? What memories do you have of this place?'

'None.' He paused, and then said, 'Yet.'

He turned to hold my face delicately between the warmth of his palms and placed his lips on mine. My hands moved from my lap to the collar of his sweater. He winced a bit when my ice-cold hands touched his warm skin, and pulled me closer into the kiss. His hands moved from my face to my hair, to my neck. I found my right leg moving of its own volition to fling itself over him, and in one swift movement I was straddling Aman.

Was it like me to lose all sense of place and just get into a full-on make-out session with a hot man on a park bench in public? Absolutely not. But this was Aman, so … fuck, yeah. Our lips didn't lose contact for a single second as our bodies started moving in urgent chaos.

I felt a brush of cold air, his hands sliding up my sweater and resting firmly, almost possessively on my back. Instinctively, my hands moved from his neck to his broad chest and then slowly towards the button of his jeans.

'You're never going to forget this place,' I whispered as I undid the button and leaned in closer to kiss him.

'Promise?' he rasped back.

'Promise.'

AMAN

Took me thirty-one years.

Sucky inventions, these cellphones.

I was in the middle of what could be the hottest make-out session of my life when my phone rang and rudely interrupted us.

'Take it,' she whispered when I let it ring.

'No,' I said, gasping a little.

'Aman!' She got off me and settled back on the bench, adjusting her sweater and scarf.

I groaned and pulled out my phone. Gagan. I straightened and buttoned up before I answered the call, like my brother could see us getting down and dirty on the hilltop.

'Hey!' I said.

'Where are you?'

'Avani and I are out for a drive.'

He took a split second before saying, 'Don't you want to be home with your family, now that we're all together?'

I frowned involuntarily at his tone. Gagan could get prickly, yes, but he was being particularly thorny this time.

'Be right there,' I said and hung up before he could reply. For a second I wondered if he was annoyed because I wasn't home or because I was away with Avani. I pushed the thought from my mind as I looked at her. 'Gotta get home. The party starts soon, baby.'

'Okay ...' She made a sad face but stood up immediately and pulled her scarf tighter around herself.

'I promise we'll pick up where we left off.' I pulled her to my side as we walked to the car.

We drove back in silence, mostly. 'You're not nervous about the party any more, are you?' I asked as we neared the house.

'Umm …' She shifted in her seat. 'Not really. No. I'm fine.'

'Are you sure?'

'Yes.'

'I'll be right next to you the whole time.'

'I know.'

'I love you, baby.'

She looked at me and smiled, squeezing my hand over the gear.

We entered the house twenty minutes later to see the staff making the final arrangements for the party. Ramesh was giving the dogs their meals so they were well fed and rested by the time the guests started arriving. Ma, Papa and Gagan were nowhere to be seen, so I assumed they were in their rooms, getting ready, and Avani and I headed to ours.

A few minutes passed. Avani was taking a shower behind the curtains and I was shaving by the vanity mirror. And just like that, she stepped out with a towel wrapped around her chest, and kissed my back as she walked past me into the bedroom, as though we did this every day. I looked at myself in the mirror and shook my head. It really didn't get any better than this.

I finished shaving and stepped out to see Avani struggling to zip up her dress. She was facing the wall, so I paused a moment to take in her naked back and the curve of her hips.

'No,' I said.

She turned towards me, confusion on her face. 'Huh?'

'Absolutely not.' I walked slowly towards her. 'You're not wearing that tonight.'

'Why?' she asked, irritation lacing her voice.

I rested my hands on the wall behind her. 'Because I can't walk into a family party with a full-on boner, baby,' I whispered into her ear.

She burst out laughing and slapped my arm. 'Shut up, Aman! It's Maya's, by the way.'

'Then ask her to name a price because you're *not* giving this dress back.' She gasped as I kissed the side of her neck and brought my arms around her waist to pull up the zipper.

'Thank you,' she said when I was done.

'You're welcome ... and you're gorgeous.'

I watched her as she walked away towards the bathroom. The thought that she'd been quieter crossed my mind again, but I forced it away to stay in the present. If there was anything brewing in her head, she would share it with me when she wanted to and we'd get through it together.

I decided to get ready.

I was pouring myself a glass of water when Avani returned to the bedroom, looking like the dream she was. Her cheeks and her eyelids glittered with whatever she'd applied on them, her hair fell loosely around her shoulders in waves and her legs looked like artwork in the deep-red heels that she'd slipped on.

'You're telling me I lucked out so much that I get to have you by my side when I walk into the party tonight?' I said.

'You really should thank your stars.' She smiled gently as she draped a delicate bag on her shoulder and dabbed some of my aftershave on her neck. 'Shall we?' she asked, her hand outstretched for me to take.

How could one person make me want to give everything up so I could run my fingers through her hair while she fell asleep beside me? How could one look from her make me want to build walls so high that nothing and no one could get close enough to hurt her? And how could one touch from her make me want to tell her to be mine forever?

I was losing my mind, I know. But if I had to, I would fall in love with Avani exactly like this all over again.

AVANI

Empty pockets and stomachs.

One evening, I told myself. Just one evening. That's all I had to get through without letting my overthinking mind ruin the absolute dream that our trip had been so far.

We'd had the most gorgeous (and eventful) afternoon, yet Gagan's words still echoed in my ears: 'Enjoy the party, get your selfies and then let things run their course. As they must.'

I rolled back my shoulders, flexed my fingers and gently wrapped them around Aman's arm as we made our way downstairs. Aman remained every bit the Aman he always was. If he'd sensed a change in my energy, he didn't let it show, and I couldn't be more grateful.

The party looked like it had just begun. Guests were rolling in in small groups and the main living area was quickly filling up. If this was what his parents thought of as an 'intimate' gathering of people, their more inclusive guestlist must be the entire state of Uttarakhand, I thought.

Servers looked exactly like they did in books and movies. Textbook appearance. Almost stereotypical, walking around with trays of drinks and small rich-size food items that left the hosts' pockets and the guests' stomachs empty. A live band had been set up at the far end of the living room and was now belting out soft tunes. I spotted Aman's parents by the door, welcoming a family that looked like they owned something or the other. My bet was an airline, but I had no way of checking. My eyes swept across the room, looking for Gagan, but the guests looked like they were having fun and the glass panes hadn't frosted over, so I guessed he must not have arrived yet.

'Let's get a drink? We'll both need the patience to get through all the small talk.' Aman lightly held my waist and navigated me towards the bar.

We ordered a glass of wine for me and ginger ale for Aman. He gave me a quick kiss as he handed me my drink and was about to say something when a gentleman walked up to him and started talking shop. I zoned out after a brief introduction and swept my eyes across the room to take in the lavish anniversary party.

Whenever Aman's parents looked at us, I cheerily raised my glass to them, signalling that I was having fun. Aman was still deeply engaged in a conversation about light bulbs and stocks. I had no clue how the two were related, but the wine was beginning to taste amazing and I could feel myself calming down.

'That was quick. One more?' Aman asked after a few minutes, having seen me down the last gulp.

'Maybe in a while. Shouldn't we go meet your parents?'

'Let's do that.'

We wove our way through the groups of guests, now beginning to get louder, chatting over the increasingly lively music.

'Are you having fun, beta?' Aman's mum asked, giving me a warm hug as I wished them both.

'Of course, Aunty,' I reassured her. 'You look beautiful!' She really did, in a stunning vintage Benarasi sari and dainty gold jewellery that sparkled on her ears and wrists.

'The two of you look good together,' his father said sagely, placing his hand on Aman's shoulder.

'Now go out the back, there's another bar set up for more exciting conversations,' his mother whispered to me, amusement in her voice. 'If you stay here, you will get bored with all the shop talk everyone will want to have with this son of ours.'

I giggled at that and hugged them once more before turning to Aman and said, 'Can I talk to you for a minute?'

He excused himself and led me to a quiet corner of the room, and when I continued to walk towards the door to the backyard he followed me with a confused face.

'Baby, we might get caught,' he whispered.

'What?' I laughed.

'There are cameras everywhere. Let's just go back upstairs.'

I walked on without saying anything, till we stepped out of the back door. He stopped short when he saw the bar, with people closer to our age gathered there. A group of three girls stood at the end of the bar, another group hung out by the pool.

'Oh.' He sighed.

'Oh.' I winked.

It was a lot quieter here and the weather was perfect for the al fresco setting. If I kept drinking wine, with Aman looking the way he did in his suit, we might just have to retire early, I thought.

'Do you want me to introduce you to everyone now or after another drink?' he said.

'You know me too well. What do you think?'

'One glass of wine, coming up!'

He gave me a quick hug before walking over to the bar to greet the girls and speak to the bartender. The girls turned around to check out Aman's ass as he walked back to me with my drink, but I chose not to give that much thought for the moment.

I was about to take the first sip when a familiar voice interrupted my thoughts. 'Hello, Avani.'

And my heart dropped to the pit of my stomach.

I froze mid-sip and took a couple of moments to compose myself.

Confrontations have always been the death of me. If you threw me into a room with someone who could potentially draw me into drama of the negative kind, my cognitive functions would shut down, my self-confidence would dip lower than my standard of humour and forming responses in whole sentences would feel like I was being made to drag a hundred-kilo boulder uphill. In short, I would be depleted in every way. Just another gift my life has given me via childhood trauma. The gift that keeps on giving.

On my way to becoming a fully functioning twenty-three-year-old adult, I've avoided confrontations the best I could.

In sixth grade, I saw Saheli Mistry, my bench mate, stealing my new gel pens from my pouch during lunch hour. Never said a word. Just moved to another seat the next day and never spoke to her again. In college, I caught my first boyfriend cheating on me with the winner of that year's internal beauty pageant, Miss Puneri Pulse 2019, and never spoke of it to anyone because if he knew that I knew, it would become a whole thing that I would have to deal with. I told myself my heart wasn't broken, just slightly scratched, and ended the relationship myself.

And how can I not mention finding out about my parents' decision to separate through a regular phone call from my father when I was staying with Aaji? I didn't ask them what was going on; I didn't scream or cry or protest, even to Aaji. I just convinced myself that it wasn't real until it happened, and bore the aftermath and consequences once it did. It took me years to come to terms with what my childhood had looked like and what it actually was, because I didn't have it in me to sit my parents down and ask them. I didn't even try, and then it was suddenly too late to even do that.

I could feel a slight burn behind my eyelids when I shut them tightly before turning to face the dementor that was unfortunately Aman's mom's firstborn. Just for tonight, I reminded myself and forced a smile as I opened my eyes to lock them with Gagan's. They held the same indifference, same judgement as they had that morning.

'Hey, Gagan,' I said, trying to sound cheerful.

'Hello to you. What are we drinking?' I could feel his words crawl up my spine, one vertebra at a time.

'Wine for my girl and ginger ale for me. What can I get you?' Aman asked as he walked back to us.

'How's the wine, Avani?' Gagan turned to face me, almost ignoring Aman, as he tucked his hands into the pockets of his jacket.

'Good. You should try it,' I replied chirpily.

'Thanks. I'll get myself a whisky.' He pursed his lips into what only he could pass off as a smile. 'Excuse me.'

'I got all the charm genes,' Aman joked as his brother walked towards the bar.

'Clearly,' I said, downing my second drink. I was going to need a lot more than just resolve and positive affirmations to get through this evening. If alcohol was what the lord was offering me, alcohol was what I would take.

The group hanging out by the pool had now moved to the bar, and two of them joined Aman and me, followed by the others, one by one. I realized these were the rich offspring of the various billionaires attending the party. Every few minutes, Aman introduced me to a new pair of eyes that I felt scanned every piece of jewellery on my body and the thread count of the fabric my dress was made of. I really didn't want to stereotype rich people after being with Aman for so many months now, but they were making it very difficult not to. Gagan walked in and out of our conversations as and when he saw people he needed to talk to—that is, those who looked as bored and annoyed as him—but, for the better part of the next hour, I stood sandwiched between the two most opposite types of people in this world. One was sunshine in human form, and the other was ... well ... Gagan.

At some point, we again found ourselves in our little group of three. The wine was beginning to talk back to me, so I stuck to water after that third glass and told myself that I needed to be in full control of my hands, just in case I ended up punching Gagan in the face. A sudden question from him interrupted my very detailed mental rehearsal of how I wanted that fight to go.

'Do you go out often, Avani?'

'Sorry?'

'Do you go out often?'

'Not very. Uni and the bookstore keep me busy.'

'We prefer spending most evenings at home,' Aman added as he slid his arm around my waist.

'And where is home?' Gagan asked as he took a swig from his glass without taking his eyes off me.

'Shastri Road, near Flora Fountain.'

'Wow. Lovely neighbourhood. The rents must be exorbitant. You manage that on a bookstore receptionist's part-time salary?' he asked flatly.

'I see subtlety isn't your suit tonight, Gagan,' Aman replied curtly before I could respond.

'I apologize if that was too personal. I was just trying to get to know her, since—'

'Yeah, let's start with her hobbies then,' Aman cut him off.

'Wow. So wound up tonight, Ace. Chill. We're all friends here.' He patted Aman's shoulder and took another sip of his drink like he wasn't increasingly being an asshole to me as the night progressed.

'I like reading,' I said before either of them could say anything more. The night air had started to prick my skin and Gagan's proximity was making me nervous. 'I like books,' I reiterated.

'And how did you start reading books?'

'My mother used to read a lot. My grandma too. So I grew up with many books lying around the house.'

'And your dad?'

'He worked. A lot.'

'I see. And where did he work?'

I could feel Aman shifting on his feet. I could feel his arm around my waist tense as he stood patiently by my side while his brother interrogated me like I'd fed him the candy that had made his face turn permanently sour.

'He worked as an engineer.'
'And your mother?'
'She was a maths tutor.'
'Was?'
'Yeah. She isn't a tutor any more.'
'What about your siblings?'
'I'm an only child.'
'Your parents must miss you, since you're away for the weekend?'

I knew what he was doing. He was digging for information. He wanted to know more. My guess was that he'd asked Aman about me and Aman had given him no answers, since these were not conversations we had had yet. Aman may have been curious about my family—it was but natural—but he'd never pushed me to share any more than I was comfortable sharing. He was my safe space. I trusted him to be there when I wandered too far, and when I turned around to see if he was keeping up with my whims and insecurities, he always was.

'Avani's grandma raised her in Pune,' Aman answered for me, and then added, 'I think we should head inside and see what Ma and Papa are up to. Maybe they're looking for us ...'

'I see we aren't very open to giving out details. Is there a reason Aman doesn't know much about you, Avani?'

I had expected Gagan to be sharp, maybe even hostile, but I hadn't expected this. What was he playing at? What was it about me that irritated him so much that he didn't even consider engaging in small talk before going at me with what was clearly unconcealed malice?

'Okay,' Aman said finally, his voice cold and emphatic in a way I hadn't heard before. He tightened his grip around my waist as he put his drink down on a tall table next to us and faced his brother. You could cut through the tension in the air with a butter knife.

'Gagan, a word?' Aman nodded towards the door that led back into the house.

'Sure,' Gagan replied calmly. 'See you around, Avani. Nice chatting with you,' he said as he walked away.

'You ... too,' I replied, the words sticking in my throat.

'Baby, I'm so sorry.' Aman turned to me quickly. 'I don't know what's with him tonight. I'm going to talk to him now. Don't move from here.'

He hugged me and I let myself sink into his familiar touch before I pulled back. 'There's something you should know.' I looked up at him.

'What is it? Did something happen?'

I took a deep breath and told Aman everything. I told him what Gagan had said to me, verbatim, and what I'd said in return.

My brain kept screaming at me to shut up. *It's an important weekend for him, Avani. He loves his family and misses them, and he's a good guy ... Don't!*

But I'd said too much already. Saying all of it out loud to Aman instantly eased the tension I'd been feeling in my chest for hours now. He'd know how to fix this. I could lean on him.

I saw Aman's jaw ticking in annoyance when I finished. He may have been a little pale too, I couldn't be sure. I reached out to take his hand in mine and gently asked him to calm down before he talked to his brother about it. I'm not sure he heard me, because before I could say anything more, he pulled his hand out of mine, turned away and strode towards the door through which Gagan had gone in. I'd never seen him look the way he did then. I stood there, stunned, regretting the fact that I'd done the one thing I'd told myself I wouldn't do. I'd ruined the night for Aman.

And something told me that the shit show had just begun.

AMAN

Did I even know what I was doing?

I followed Gagan into the house, fuming at the new piece of information I'd received from Avani. I would've liked to take a moment to process what was going on, but something about the audacious way in which he spoke to Avani compelled me to confront him immediately.

'What the hell is your problem?' I asked as soon as we entered the tea room annexe next to the loud living room. We'd sat there earlier, as brothers. Catching up on life.

I banged the door shut and charged up to Gagan, who was casually sipping his drink. Was he really this calm?

'What is it? Let's hear it. What is it that's wrong with her? What is it?'

'Wow. Look at you. Defending her honour. Tell me, what about the conversation between her and me did you not like?'

'What did I not like?'

'Mm-hmm.'

'I didn't like that you were being a complete asshole to my girlfriend. I didn't like that you made her feel uncomfortable.'

'And how exactly did I do that?'

'Cut the bullshit, Gagan. I'm not in the mood for your patronizing psychotherapy. We both know what you were trying to do there.'

'What I was trying to do was look out for my baby brother.'

'I'm not a baby. Let's get that straight, for starters. I know whom to allow entry into my life and whom not to. And in any case, how would you achieve that—by treating my girlfriend like shit?'

By now I was shaking with rage. How was he being so casual about this?

But Gagan remained unmoved. 'Aman ... open your eyes.' His voice was calm. Cold? 'And for one second just stop being so fucking sensitive about this.' He narrowed his eyes. 'What about my interaction with your girlfriend pissed you off? That I asked her about her job? Or that I asked her about her family? What do her parents do? Where did she grow up? These are all normal fucking questions.' His voice got slightly louder as he said, 'These are the first few questions people ask other people. And if that other person is a girl my brother has brought home for the first time, what's the big fucking deal if I ask her just that?'

'Why couldn't you ask me?' I snapped back. 'Why put her on the spot?'

'Okay.' Gagan took a contemplative step to the side and leaned against the coffee table, crossing his arms. 'I'll ask you. What are her parents' names?'

I stood in my spot, heart beating so loud that I suddenly thought even Gagan could hear it.

'Which school did she go to? Who was her best friend growing up? Where do her parents live?'

Gagan's eyebrows, I now noticed, were raised. The fact that I didn't know the answers to those questions pissed me off. Was he testing me, testing if I had the basic ability to suss out people and build relationships? Did he think I was so stupid that I wouldn't have thought of asking Avani these things? There was a reason we hadn't had that conversation yet, and the reason was between her and me. The way I looked at it, it was her business and nobody else's, so it was up to her when and how she shared any detail of her life with anyone, including me.

'You think I'm stupid, don't you?'

'No, Aman. I think you are naive. You trust people too easily. You let people in too quickly. You let your guard down too soon and I'm just here looking out for you.'

I couldn't believe my ears. Was he being serious?

'Gagan, I'm thirty-one years old. I'm not a fucking child. I know what I'm doing. I can take care of myself.'

'Like you did the last time? Do you want me to remind you how you quit college and flew to London for four months when Aanchal left you? How I was there to make sure you went back to university?'

'I was fucking nineteen!' I yelled. 'That was years ago! You don't think I can handle relationships better now?'

'And are you? Handling it better? Are you telling me you don't feel even a little disturbed about the fact that someone you're in a "serious relationship" with doesn't want to let you in? That she doesn't trust you enough to tell you about her parents? That she doesn't want you to get close enough to have access to information that clearly matters to her? You, on the other hand, have flown her all the way to your parents' anniversary party in Mussoorie and are introducing her to your closest friends and family like you want them to know that this is the person you're going to marry.'

I had to admit that there had been moments when I could tell that Martin, Rhea and Maya knew more about Avani's life and what had scarred her with insecurities and trust issues than I did. That they had been there for her when she'd needed them. They knew how to help her. Even when things between us got strained, I knew she went to them for advice. In those moments I'd told myself that these were things that needed time. But we had known each other for quite a few months now ... How had I not earned that spot in her life yet?

The way Gagan put my doubts into words stirred something inside me. I wanted to tell him how wrong he was, that he was out of his mind to question Avani's intentions. But the words didn't come to me. The sentences didn't form. I could feel my anger growing by the minute. How could he? Didn't he think I could make the right decisions in life? And ... this was Avani we were talking about. I'd never met anyone like her—no one as real and unapologetically herself, for sure.

So I asked the question I'd wanted to ask when I walked into the room.

'Why did you threaten her behind my back? Who gave you the right to do that?'

I saw Gagan's face change when he heard me address him in a tone I'd never used with him before.

'Excuse me?' he asked, his voice low.

'She told me about the conversation you had with her in our room earlier today. What the *fuck* was that about?'

Gagan took a step towards me and then another, slowly and deliberately covering the distance between us till he was standing right in front of me, inches away. He'd always been a little taller than me and, now, the way he was towering over me gave me a sense of how offended he was by the question.

'You know what, Aman?' he said through gritted teeth. 'I had gone up to your room to set things straight with Avani because I was trying to look out for you. You won't believe me if I tell you that I really have nothing against her, but I'll tell you anyway. I don't. It's always been about you. It's always been about us. You and me. Brothers. The world looks at our family and sees the mansions and the cars and the billion-dollar empire. What they don't see is the decades that our parents put into building this shiny life we have today. The sacrifices they made to get where we are, including giving up on the time they would have wanted to spend with us.

I don't know if you care to remember, but growing up, it was just us—always—just you and me. I took you to school. I made sure you did your homework. I learnt how to cook so I could cook you breakfast every morning before we could afford staff in our kitchen. I beat up the guys who bullied you and I picked you up from parties that you lied to our parents about. I was there when you got your heart broken and I was there when you sat on that chair as CEO. I always looked out for you. Not because I had to, but because I wanted to. I have always felt the need to protect you and make sure that everyone around you recognizes you for who you are and gives you what you deserve. And after being in your corner and rooting for you for all these years, if one conversation with a girl can so easily rip us apart and make you question my intentions, I guess I don't have anything to protect in the first place.'

Gagan slowly walked back to the coffee table and raised his glass to me. 'I wish you both a lifetime of happiness. Cheers.'

Then he opened the door of the annexe and walked out, leaving me and my chaotic thoughts to fight it out.

I felt a huge metal ball settling into the pit of my stomach. Had I just made a mistake? Why didn't I have answers to Gagan's questions? Why couldn't I think of a single thing to say to my brother? Why was I getting increasingly pissed off at myself for speaking to him the way I had? Why the hell did I suddenly feel so incredibly insufficient?

AVANI

Almost there.

Ten minutes had passed since Aman had walked away to talk to his brother. Restless, I made my way into the large living room, where the party was now on in full swing. People were laughing and chatting at the top of their voices. Aman's parents were the sweetest sight, jiving to the music being played by the live band, much louder now and squarely in party mode, while others clapped and looked for their partners to join them on the floor. I scanned the room and my eyes fell on Gagan leaning by the bar, chatting with someone.

Where was Aman?

I contemplated looking for him, but my thoughts had begun to spiral and I could feel panic building up inside me. Something had to have gone terribly wrong, because, if it hadn't, Aman would have come looking for me. But he was nowhere to be seen. My gut coiled in anticipation of the nightmare about to unfold.

I was about to fish out my phone and call Aman when I caught a glimpse of his blue suit across the room. I stuffed my phone into my purse, quickly straightened my shoulders and plastered a fake smile on my face as I placed one foot after the other to reach Aman, who looked like he was heading towards the bar.

'Hey.' I tapped his arm. 'I was looking for you.'

He turned to me with an expression that I couldn't quite read, and half smiled. 'Hey ... Sorry. Got caught up with family,' he replied absent-mindedly. His smile remained firmly in place but didn't reach his eyes.

'You okay?' I asked softly, my hand on his arm.

'Never been better.' He slid his hand into mine. 'Drink?'

'Sure,' I said tentatively.

Why did I feel like I was on the brink of a fall? Like the perfect canvas that my life had been with Aman in it up until this evening was creasing and folding at the sides.

I tugged at Aman's hand as we walked together to the bar. 'What happened in there? Are you okay?'

He looked straight ahead without replying.

'Aman?' I asked again.

No reply. His strides got longer as he almost dragged me forward.

'Hey!' I stopped, forcing him to stop as well, a few feet short of the bar.

Aman looked at me. 'Can we talk about this later? It's my parents' anniversary dinner and I would really appreciate it if you didn't mess it up any more than you already have.'

Wait a second.

I opened my mouth to ask what the fuck he was talking about, but he turned his back to me, let go of my hand and walked away.

He was mad? Why the fuck was he mad? And why at me? What was I not seeing here?

I quickly caught up with him and placed my hand on his arm. Gently at first, and then with light taps to get his attention. By now he was leaning over the bar and placing the order for our drinks with the bartender.

'Aman,' I said, a tad sternly. 'We need to talk.'

'Yes, we do,' he said, turning. Suddenly I could see the resemblance between the siblings. Uncanny. He kept his eyes on my face for a split second longer than it felt like he wanted to and then looked away, towards where the guests were.

'Should we step away for a bit?' I said.

'No.'

'Why?'

'Because I'm here to be with my parents. For one evening, we can think past what you want, can we not?'

I felt my ears getting warm as the chill in his voice and the weight of his words settled in my chest. I gulped twice to keep the tears from spilling out and stared at Aman with a frozen face.

Breathe, Avani. Breathe.

I nodded at him, realizing that any words that left my mouth then would only make things worse. I took the drink he offered and turned to face the party. He picked up his ginger ale and stood stiffly next to me.

Over the next twenty minutes, Aman made polite conversation with guests who stopped by to talk to him. I didn't register any of it. My ears were ringing from what I had just heard Aman say. It wasn't like Aman to behave this way. Between conversations with others, there was radio silence between us. I felt as though the music that had filled the space thus far was receding into the distance till the only sound I could hear was the loud thumping of my heart.

I could feel a scream creeping up my throat, and gulped again. I hadn't had a panic attack in months, and now wasn't the best time for it.

'Excuse me,' I said between heavy breaths, and bolted towards the stairway that led to our room, taking long strides at first and then practically sprinting as I felt the tears begin to roll down my cheeks.

'Almost there. Almost there. Almost there,' I chanted to myself until I reached the room, slammed the door shut behind me and turned the latch twice to make sure Aman couldn't walk in to see me melting into a complete mess. And then I let the scream inside my head take over.

AMAN

What did they do to her?

My heart sank when I saw Avani slip out of the crowded room and rush up the stairs. The guilt of having snapped at her now gripped me tight. She didn't know what I was upset about and I should've explained. At the least, I should've given her a chance to speak before I blamed her for whatever this evening was turning out to be. It wasn't like me to speak to her like that. She was Avani. My Avani. I finished what remained of my drink and headed after her.

I reached the door of our room and turned the knob to find it locked from the inside. I took the spare key out of my pocket and knocked twice before using it to open the latch. Inside, there was no Avani in sight.

'Avani?' I called out.

I entered the bedroom and saw movement near the balcony. I took a couple of steps towards it. 'Avani?'

'I'll call you right back,' I heard her say before she disconnected the call and turned to face me. Her cheeks were streaked with tears and I felt my heart break into a million pieces.

'Who was that?' I asked gently.

'Martin.'

Something about that answer flipped a switch in my head. Alien feelings of insecurity and jealousy crept up my spine as I watched her lock her phone and walk past me into the living area.

'Martin?' I asked as I followed her out.

'Yes.'

'You couldn't wait ten minutes before you ran to him with all your life's problems again?'

Mean. I know. My brain was buzzing with that feeling of inadequacy I had felt a little while back. Clearly she felt no shame or nerves sharing anything about her life with her friends, unlike I guessed how she felt with me. She accepted and trusted them more than me. No matter how hard I tried, I just did not seem to qualify. Rage filled my heart.

'Aman …'

'What advice did he give you?' I asked stiffly.

'He was just listening to me ...'

'And what is it about him that makes you comfortable enough to discuss our private issues? Does my consent on this not matter? Since I'm involved?'

'What?'

'Answer the question!' I yelled, louder than I had wanted to. The lack of validation from her had hurt me in ways I hadn't realized earlier.

Her shoulders jerked as more tears spilt out of her eyes. I took a step back and breathed deeply, looking up at the ceiling. This wasn't me. I took two more long breaths before I locked my eyes with her teary ones.

'What is it, Avani?' I started. I needed to have a conversation and get past the angry exchanges. 'What am I not doing right? Where have I gone wrong that you don't think me worthy enough to let me get any closer than I was when we first met? What do I have to do to earn your trust? Every time I feel like I want to know more about you, I tell myself that I'm on your time. And I'll take it. I'll take whatever you give me. But it's been months now. And I'm getting tired of sitting on the sidelines. Waking up every day and hoping that that will be the day you finally let me into your inner circle. I don't know if you've heard me the million times I've told you I love you, but I honestly do. And I hate feeling alone in this relationship. You say you have trouble believing if I'm for real. You say I'm too good to be true. You say you're waiting for the other shoe to drop. So now, I'm not good enough because you think I'm too good? There is no winning with you, is there?'

'Aman ...' She was sobbing now, holding up her hand as if to say 'enough', but unable to say the word. But I couldn't stop either.

'Who did this to you?' I asked. 'What is it that happened to you that you only put up walls? What did your parents do to you that you refuse to forgive them? Why can't you believe a good thing when it's staring you in the face? Why won't you talk about it? Tell me. I want to know.'

'Aman ... stop ...'

I had pushed way past her comfort level. But I needed answers. Where this relationship with Avani was concerned, I was all in. I deserved to know. I deserved to hear her either tell me that she was all in as well, or walk away and never look back.

She sat down on the bed and continued to sob.

'Avani ...'

'Aman ... please.'

'No,' I insisted and took a step towards her. 'I want to know. What did they do? How did they scar you so badly that you only doubt love and trust? What did they do?'

She stared at her clenched hands in her lap.

'Aman, they ...'

'They what, Avani? What did they do?'

'They died.'

I froze.

In the deafening silence that followed her revelation, Avani's eyes stared back into mine with nothing but disappointment and hurt. I took a step towards her, but she gestured to me to stop. I saw her gather the broken pieces of her heart as she looked back down at her hands, now bleeding from her nails puncturing her skin. She drew in a long breath, rolled back her shoulders and wiped her tears with her palms. When she looked up, her eyes were blank, staring right through me at the wall behind.

When she started speaking, her voice was flat, impassive and at first barely audible.

'I was eleven when I found out that my parents were getting divorced. Aaji stepped in immediately and took me to live with her. I was too young to process how a marriage that had seemed perfectly happy could end so suddenly, and I didn't ever ask. Aaji never let me feel alone. My parents started living separately in two different homes in Mumbai and I started a new life in Pune. They'd told me I could take my time to decide who I wanted to live with, but I chose to stay with Aaji. I met them occasionally on birthdays and holidays, but I never understood how they were as happy apart as I remembered them to be together. What started out as confusion slowly grew into annoyance and, I guess, eventually, anger. They never did tell me why their marriage hadn't worked, and their amicable separation just made it that much tougher for me to believe that something was wrong. I kept thinking they had just overreacted, but I don't think they really thought about what their separation would do to me. I slowly distanced myself from them as life began afresh in Pune. I felt peaceful and safe with Aaji—and I decided that was what I wanted. My meeting my parents on and off turned into just phone calls and then into unread texts. As I got older, I let the resentment of their divorce affect my individual relationships with them. They hadn't tried harder for me, I thought. They hadn't thought of holding it together till I was old enough to deal with it.

'What I understood later was that there was no great reason for their fallout. They just happened to realize that they were better apart than together. My mother was a teacher and my father an engineer with a telecom company. They met through common friends and got married in a hurry. The marriage went into a strange, uncomfortable place a few years after I came along. Aaji told me later that they'd tried for a while before deciding that they were better off being friends than life partners. It was as simple as that. They tried harder with me as I got older, but I kept myself away. I didn't want to be hurt by them, or anyone else, again. Everything I'd seen and believed about relationships and love slowly diminished as I got busy building walls around me, higher every time someone came too close.

'By the time I was twenty-two I had completely lost touch with them. Aaji was my world, my everything. Then I moved to Mumbai. There I finally had friends who allowed me to be the person I wanted to be without judgement. I was happy. I began to understand "family" differently. I saw that this lot knew me, and that they were not going anywhere. They'd always be by my side. I started getting better at studies, I dated occasionally ... life was better. I was finding some footing after spending a decade closing myself off to the possibility of making any sense of why my family was so fucked up and yet so sorted. And then, in October last year, I got a call from Aaji telling me that Mamma had had a heart attack. And before I could ask how she was, I heard that Baba had been in an accident while he was driving to the hospital to see her. She survived only to learn of Baba's death and passed away in her sleep the next morning. Another heart attack. My world came crashing down with regret and the thought of everything I'd left unsaid. Every message I'd missed or ignored and every call I hadn't returned. Every gift I'd left unopened and every invitation I'd declined. I'd spent all my teenage years wishing my parents would leave me alone, and then it really happened. I got what I asked for.'

An eerie silence fell around us. Avani had said all that in one breath. She looked spent. Her head hung low, endless tears seeping out of her eyes.

A hundred thoughts crowded my mind at once. Just hours ago we were where she was sitting now, holding hands and planning the weekend. In the hours before that, I had been watching her in deep sleep, thinking how incredibly fortunate I was to have a girl like her in my arms. Only minutes ago, I'd had the chance to salvage the situation we were in, and then seconds ago I'd crushed that chance.

I couldn't imagine the pain she was in.

'Avani,' I said softly as I reached out to take her hand, but she jerked her body away and rose from the bed. She walked to the coffee table and turned to face me. Fat tears continued to roll down her cheeks with no sign of restraint. The face of courage she had put up had cracked at the edges and her shoulders had completely dropped in surrender.

'I'm broken, Aman. I'm not the perfect person that you are. Or the person that you want me to be. I don't have my shit together. I'm winging it every single day, trying to make sense of everything that's happened to me. I don't see things the way you do. I have trouble believing a good thing when it's staring me in the face because good things always turn out to be an illusion. And you just proved me right. Again.'

'No ... No. No. What can I do, Avani? Please tell me. I love you.'

'Do you, really?'

'More with every breath I take.'

'Then let me go home. Where people are exactly who I think they are.'

JANUARY 2024

AVANI

And that's that.

I finished my make-up with a little lip gloss and looked at myself in the mirror of the guest bedroom at Maya's apartment. Though I'd argued with Maya endlessly about booking a salon appointment that morning for my hair to be done, I was glad she hadn't listened. I'd never thought it could look this shiny and set. Hmm ... and she was right—the new powder-blue salwar-kameez really brought out my eyes. I slipped on my Kolhapuris and sprayed on a bit of perfume before looking into the mirror again.

Big day today, I told myself. Almost thought I wouldn't make it, didn't I? Almost gave up midway. But now I could take a bow. The journey, they say, is more important than the destination, but I quite liked the destination and could do without the excruciating journey, thank you.

'Ani, we're late!' I heard Rhea shout through the door for the sixth time in the last two minutes, like I didn't know how to tell time. I let out the breath I was holding.

'Well done, Avani,' I told my reflection in the mirror, picked up my tote and walked out to the living room.

Aaji sat on the couch in the living room looking regal, as usual, in a pink chiffon sari and pearls.

'Arre, Rajmata.' I bowed low before her, my palms together, and received a fake slap on my shoulder from her.

'Ready?' she asked, smiling happily.

'Ready.'

Maya was waiting downstairs in the car with Dhruv as the three of us slid into the back seat. (Rhea and Dhruv were a thing now, by the way. Fina-fucking-lly. They refused to give us clear details of how they got over their nerves and managed to tell each other how they felt, but Maya and I suspected a drunken night of wild sex had something to do with it. They're cute together, I have to say, and we're thoroughly entertained, so it's all good.)

'Where is that strange boy ... Martin?' Aaji asked.

'He's meeting us there, Aaji,' Maya clarified. 'All aboard?' she asked as she put her car into drive.

'Yes!' we chimed in unison.

The drive was a quiet one and I stared out the window thinking of the past few weeks of late nights and early mornings. Of hard work and then some more. Of therapy and good food. And of finally coming to terms with my life and putting on my big-girl pants.

A lot had changed in the past 121 days ...

Here's what happened.

Three Months Ago

I landed in Pune that night, every wound that I had stapled shut split open like an all-you-can-eat buffet. Haemorrhaging emotionally like I probably should have a year ago or maybe twelve years ago. Feeling everything and nothing at the same time. Confused and lost because life had thrown me enough chances to make things better for myself, but I had taken none of them. Denial is a funny thing. It works like a charm, till it doesn't—and when being that way stops making sense, the waves come crashing down on you. You can swim or you can drown, baby.

I chose the obvious option and drowned. Hopelessly. With no mercy whatsoever. I didn't bother showing myself compassion. I didn't tell myself that it was going to get better. Hell, I refused to even let myself believe there was ever going to be a day when I'd leave my bed, take a shower and breathe fresh air. It was full and complete surrender. And the further I let myself sink into doom-thinking and night terrors, the better I felt when I woke up the next morning. The oppressive guilt of putting in absolutely no effort towards the betterment of my mental and physical health felt oddly liberating. I'd allowed old metal chains to be tied around my limbs for so long that they had now started digging into my skin. The pain was killing me, but I had also started enjoying it—liberation, laced with excruciating neglect.

Aaji had taken me in, again, and tended to me like I was a lost, homeless puppy. Every meal arrived at my bedside, my devices went missing for the first few days and were magically replaced by romance novels. And I was left alone to wallow in my little puddle of sadness.

And then, just at the right time, I wasn't. Aaji had given me nine days to stew in my emotional juices. Nine days is all it takes, she'd said. Not one day less, not one day more.

'Unpopular opinion, but okay,' I'd told her.

There was no proof for the theory that nine days were all I needed to get over everything plaguing my thoughts—my parents' broken marriage, with its baggage of abandonment issues, trauma and loss of trust, the shock of losing them both at the same time, the PTSD and guilt that had followed, and then the heartbreak of losing the man I had so deeply fallen in love with. But it was all I was given, and now I could say that it had worked, in whatever fucked-up way. Seems like a lot when I list it out like that. But something about Aaji's refusal to let me sink shone like a very, very, very, very, VERY faint silver lining around the dark-as-fuck cloud of my life's fuck-ups. Impeccable sentence formation, I know. I'm sorry, I went to therapy for mental wellness. Grammar lessons weren't included.

Two Months Ago

'That does feel better, doesn't it?' Dr Sneha Kumar, my Indian-American therapist, who also happens to be smoking-hot, in her mid-forties and gay, said as we took a stroll on the stretch of lawn behind her clinic.

I'd spent a whole session bawling my eyes out till I could feel every blood vessel from my brain to my eye sockets throb. I had started therapy again, after many months, on Maya's incessant nagging and self-driven initiative to locate a recommended therapist close to home in Pune, and now I wanted to hug her and tell her I couldn't thank her enough. She does make good recommendations, that girl.

It took us about a week to finally get the fucking dam inside me to burst. How predictable, isn't it? It took the poor little broken girl seven days and a good chunk of her savings to start getting normal-people feelings again.

By then, I'd given up my cute flat in Mumbai and moved in with Aaji again. Martin and Rhea had packed up my life and shipped most of my stuff to Pune by mid-October. I missed Mumbai, I missed Shanta Tai and the neighbour's obnoxious cat. I missed uni, I missed the bookstore and Meera Aunty and my friends, but Aaji's presence, and all the deliciousness she served up with so much love, Pune's relatively pollution-free air and my conversations with Dr Sneha had made me feel comfortable again. My department head at uni was kind enough to let me attend classes remotely, so there was that escape from my demon mind. I was grateful for it and I grabbed it with both hands.

It really is surprising how much we underestimate the connection between our mind and body. I'd started the month feeling like I was standing at hell's door with a bottle of champagne for Satan (never go empty-handed to anyone's house, Aaji had taught me), but ended it with only a partially numb mind and the renewed ability to sleep through the night without waking up to cry on my balcony.

Progress.

You're waiting to hear about what happened with Aman, aren't you? I can practically hear you violently nodding your head in agreement and egging me on to wrap up my sob story and tell you about the hot guy.

Ugh. Rude.

The last time I saw Aman he was in his impeccable blue suit, staring at me, shock, sympathy and regret written large in his gorgeous brown eyes even as I packed my stuff and walked out without one backward glance. If everything I'd read in the books were true, the only hope left for us was in that last look, but I couldn't get myself to face him. Much like everything that had hurt me till that point. Walking out seemed like such a well-rehearsed move, it came to me naturally, with no effort whatsoever.

Aman must have called his parents as soon as I walked out that door, because there was a helicopter waiting for me at the helipad when I exited the Raina home. The party had moved to the pool area by then, thankfully, and I'd been able to slip out of the service exit when Ramesh emerged from the side of the lawns to take my bags from me. I don't remember much after that, other than being strapped into the chopper seat and flown to Pune like express mail. I didn't cry a drop until I got out of the SUV, courtesy of what I should call the 'Raina Courier Service' that dropped me to Aaji's apartment. And then I felt a hand on the side of my face and Aaji's familiar scent that rushed to my brain as she pulled me into a hug. The tears came then.

Aman had evidently called Aaji as soon as I'd left and told her everything that had transpired in Mussoorie. He'd also texted Maya, who had texted Rhea and Martin, and they'd taken the bus out to Pune the following morning to be with me.

One evening as I sat on Aaji's balcony after a really helpful session with Dr Sneha, evaluating what I was hurting about the most, I tried to file my life events chronologically in my mind to identify which one was making my chest feel like a demonic child's rattle toy. Turns out, it didn't matter how recent or how old the trauma was, it kind of haunted you the same. Just at different times and places.

Like thinking of my parents' death always gave me a very distinct migraine. The kind that hampered your audio-visual settings and sent currents down your spine. Memories of their separation always gave me a panic attack or a nightmare that lasted a few minutes every few weeks. My abandonment issues surfaced when I had a high-achieving day, like the day I graduated from high school, or the day I cleared my law college entrance exam, or when I learnt how to drive a stick-shift, or when I opened my first bank account all by myself. It always hurt in some hidden nook of my chest to think that they would've been proud of how I'd turned out—if only I'd reached out to them in time.

But walking away from Aman—that hurt me right in the centre of my chest and in every nerve ending that began there and spread to the rest of my body. It hurt to blink. It hurt to think. It hurt to feel. It hurt to breathe. Every breath came in just fine but left very, very slowly, like the air was taking its time to ensure every inch of my being hurt before it left my body, only to return and repeat the whole process.

You'd think that death would hurt more, right? But there was a strange sting in knowing that the person you loved continued to live in the same world as you, but without you. I don't know if the two feelings are comparable. But I felt them in such quick succession every time that I couldn't help but wonder if I should feel guilty for comparing the two events. Death was so final. It didn't hold out any hope. I missed my parents, no matter how troubled our relationship was, but they left when they left. Their funeral was the last postage stamp on any hope I had of ever seeing them again. But Aman was very much here. Living, breathing, smiling, smelling great. The heavy weight of regret started settling in when the fog of unease started thinning with therapy.

'It was, after all, a ME problem, then,' I heard myself say at the end of a session. Both Dr Sneha and I raised our eyebrows in sync and let out a breath. It had cost me a lot of money to say that stupid sentence. I should have just listened to my friends.

I resumed living my life the best I could. My final term exams were coming up and the voice in my head commanded me to shut the fuck up and start paying attention in classes. Every minute I spent in my therapist's office, every chai I had with Aaji on her balcony, every new book I read, every class I started getting better at, every minute I slept longer and better began to make living a little easier.

My days started to go into a slow but steady routine—waking up at 8 a.m. to the scent of Aaji's milky masala chai brewing in the kitchen, freshening up to study for a few hours before my classes and, after they were done, spending the evenings with my books and then kitty-party gossip about everyone in Aaji's apartment complex. I spoke to Rhea and Martin often, but only when they called to check if I was still a functioning human being. Maya and I spoke every single day, though. She told me things that had nothing to do with my life—a much-needed respite from my very busy mind.

'How's the prep for the finals going, Ani?' she asked one night as I strolled in the green patch near Aaji's building after dinner, phone to my ear.

'It's going well, actually.'

'When's graduation?'

'29 January.'

'We're all coming, okay?'

'You don't need to. Aaji said she'll be there.'

'Are you crazy? Of course we'll be there. You have to come here a couple of days before that, so we can go together. Stay at mine!'

'Oh, okay. That might be good, actually.'

'So proud of you, Ani!'

Something about those words hit me at a spot that nothing but despair had touched in the past few weeks. My eyes welled up. It was a new feeling, and as emotional as it made me, I also felt strangely exhilarated.

'Thank you,' I replied, sniffling and smiling at the same time.

One Month Ago

December flew by.

As my finals inched closer, the focus tunnel in my mind started getting narrower and narrower. Days seemed shorter as I spent most of my time cooped up in my room with my books, only occasionally surfacing for air. The nights got shorter too, though I'd have to credit that to the luxury of real sleep brought on by the absence of nightmares and ugly thoughts that had been crowding my mind. I had begun to smile more at Aaji's taunts and laugh more at Martin's inappropriate jokes. I started going for walks in the evenings when I needed a change of scenery and on some days I surfed Instagram a little more without feeling much guilt.

I'd be lying if I said I didn't go to Aman's profile every time I opened the app, but the last photo was the one he'd taken of me after our coffee date in Mussoorie. The day life had flicked the finger in my face and fucked off.

At least he hadn't deleted it.

Every once in a while, I played that last conversation out in my mind and thought about everything I should have done. I should have given him the answers he had deserved to know the whole time. I should have heard him as much as he heard me. He heard me when I asked him to back off, he heard me when I pulled him closer again and he heard me when I needed the space and asked him to leave me alone. Would he hear me if I asked him to come hug me one last time?

I'd walked over a lot of good intentions to reach this golden peak of mental wellness in my very eventful life. I'd trampled on every last bit of hope I had, just so I could shelter myself in my little pity palace. I knew I'd burnt some very sturdy bridges, but at least I'd got here without losing any more than I already had. Just the most perfect man in the world. No big deal.

I'd walked away from him knowing that a part of my world was dying. A little voice in my head had let out a huge sigh, like I'd been waiting for this to happen only so I could move on to fixing everything else that was fucked up in my life. There was a finality in that last breath I took in the same room as him. Like God was telling me to breathe in as much of him as I could, because I would never breathe the same again.

Are twenty-three-year-olds allowed to feel heartbreak like this? This early in life? Don't we have to go through numerous smaller heartbreaks, so that by the time we're sixty we can tell the twenty-three-year-olds in our lives that heartbreaks weren't the end of the world?

I don't know. And I hate not knowing.

But, then again, you win some, you lose some, right? Dealing with trauma and getting better, but losing love in the process? Stiff deal. But I'll take it. Hell, I'm just twenty-three. I'm sure I'll meet a lot of great men.

Who are you even kidding, Avani?

Present Day: 29 January 2024

I drew in a long breath as Maya pulled into the convention centre behind the university building where the law department—my department—had its offices and classes. Rhea squeezed my hand as I slung my tote bag on my shoulder and unlocked the door to step out.

I hadn't been on campus since September last year, but I'd attended every class from home. Strangely, most of all, I'd missed the half-cooked, bland food the university canteen served.

I walked towards the auditorium, the venue for my convocation. I saw my classmates walking in with big smiles. Some of them came over to catch up with me. 'Where have you been!', 'It's been so long!', 'How are you?', 'Did you lose weight?' I politely shuffled between 'Good', 'Thank you', 'How are you?' and 'Yeah, long time', and exchanged a few awkward hugs. As the alarm rang for everyone to be seated, I turned to look at Aaji and the gang, when it hit me. Like a truck.

Aftershave.

My limbs froze. I turned to Maya, my eyes wide, expecting her to be able to give me no answers whatsoever. But she knew something I didn't. I saw the tiniest tear forming in the corner of her eye as she broke into a wide smile and nodded at me.

Was I supposed to know what that meant?

I looked at Rhea and Martin and Dhruv and Aaji, and realized they were all looking at me like I'd just won an Oscar. I held the strap of my tote bag in a death grip and blinked a few times before I let my eyes wander in the direction of the scent.

My heart beat faster than I knew it could as I scanned the crowd. Rows and rows of students and their families settling into their seats, ugly maroon carpet and drapes, emergency exit door signs glowing lazily, huge speakers hanging off the walls, the projector room, more rows of people, the door I had just walked through …

And Aman.

He stood a few feet away from the door, looking at me. Smile, dimples, eyes. I parted my lips to take in what felt like an actual breath, and, suddenly, nothing hurt. Seeing him there, in the flesh, made me feel like I'd been walking through life in a smoky haze of uncertainty and doubt these past few weeks, and now someone had finally opened a window.

I stared at him without moving a muscle. I don't think my brain could code any instructions in that moment and, even if it could, my body wouldn't follow. Aman must have picked up on that, because he took one tentative step towards me and then another and then another, and before I could really prepare myself, he was standing in front of me.

I stood rooted to my spot, scared that if I blinked, whatever this dream was would shatter.

'Hi, gorgeous.'

An instant urge to duck arose in me but my brain somehow registered how useless that would be.

'Hi,' I barely managed to say.

He was within touching distance. Up for grabs. Mine if I wanted. Speak, I told myself. But the words wouldn't form. There was too much to ask and yell about and apologize for.

'Can we talk?' he asked softly.

'Yes.'

He nodded politely at Aaji and the gang, and stepped back to let me lead. I walked towards the exit like I knew where I was going.

Then we were at the parking lot of the convention centre. I stopped when I reached a corner where the buzz of the convocation ceremony seemed like a distant hum. I turned to see Aman right behind me, looking at me with crystal-clear brown eyes and hands held together like he was the next up at his school's fifth-standard elocution competition. When he didn't break the silence and it started ringing in my ears, I said, 'Talk.'

'Hi.'

'You said that already.'

'I know.'

'Okay.'

'I know you're upset,' he said after an excruciatingly long pause.

'What gave *that* away?'

'Avani …'

'Say more and say quick, Aman.'

The reality of the situation was suddenly beginning to dawn on me and all the feelings that I had carefully folded and piled away in the deepest corners of my mind were springing up like the vacuum seal had finally snapped.

'I know I should have heard you out. I know I should have been a little more considerate before reacting the way I did about what went down between Gagan and—'

I cut him off. 'You think that's what I'm upset about?'

He blinked at me like I'd spoken in Dothraki.

'Sorry ... what?' he asked after a medium-long pause.

'What?' I almost shouted back. 'WHAT? I left your room with my suitcase in September and you walk up to me in your perfect fucking suit and tie in January asking "WHAT?" I'll ask you ... "What?" First, WHAT the fuck were you doing all this time? WHAT is the meaning of taking me to your home and into your life and then shoving me aside like last evening's newspaper and going MIA on me? WHAT is your reason for thinking that no matter how bad things got, giving up on us completely was an okay way of dealing with it? WHAT was going on in your mind when you decided to grace me with your presence on such an important day of my life? WHAT did you think was going to happen? And lastly, WHAT gave you the fuck-all idea of not being with me when I needed you the most?'

Anyone passing by must have thought: Oh, another lovers' quarrel. But only Aman and I knew of the quicksand we were both standing on at that moment. My temper was running wild and only when I shut up after the last sentence did I realize how loud and screechy my voice had got.

This, I thought, is why I can't believe this man. I'd just yelled at him in this smelly parking lot and he was looking at me like I'd just finished singing the most beautiful ballad.

'I've missed you too,' he said.

I swear to God if I hadn't taken all that therapy, my fist would have made contact with his perfectly pointy nose. I was sure to miss it by an inch or so, but it would be contact nonetheless. What was it with men and their audacity to constantly assume?

'Avani …'

'Aman. Answer the question before I turn and walk away.'

'Which one? You asked a fair few—'

'Why didn't you call?'

'Baby …'

'I gave you every reason not to. But why didn't you? You're supposed to be the mature, reasonable person in this relationship. The bigger person. I'm the one with issues, who doesn't see a good thing when it's staring her in the face. But you know better. And you went missing. I asked you to leave me alone and you did. Why didn't you come? Why didn't you come when I needed you?'

'Because you didn't need saving, Avani. You needed time.' He took a deep breath and held my shoulders to sit me down on the concrete ledge behind us. 'I wanted to go after you and ask you to stay that night when you packed your suitcase and left my room. But I knew that if I did that, I would lose you forever. There's so much I wish I'd done that night. I wish I'd taken a moment to process everything before letting rage take over and landsliding into becoming a complete dick.

I regret so much from that night. But the one thing I did know was that you needed to deal with a lot before you could even get to you and me. Life had pushed you around and given you no room to breathe. You needed space ... and time ... to breathe. People you loved and trusted had left you with no explanation and you needed time to learn how to trust again. You'd lost all faith in love and you needed time to know that it was there for you if you wanted it. I didn't leave you, Avani ... I only let you be with yourself. Nobody could teach you how to deal with life better than you. You didn't need a saviour, you needed someone who would get out of your way so you could go be who *you* are. So you would look in the mirror and see what I see. And you would know that you make me want to be everything that you deserve.'

He took my hands in his.

'I've counted every minute, every second, every breath until now. I've waited patiently for you to love yourself again, so you would let me love you. This morning, when Maya messaged, asking me to come see you at your convocation, I almost didn't believe it would happen. In the past few months, I've walked to the bookstore and had coffee with Martin every day on my way back from work so I could hear how your day had been. I've worn my aftershave every day only because it reminds me of you. You've been my first and last waking thought every single day. How could you even think that I wasn't going to be here when you were ready for me? I've been waiting, baby. And I'm yours if you'd like me to be. I loved you the day I first saw you at the bookstore and I love you today. I knew you would hate me if I hogged your attention immediately after you left. You know you would have. I didn't want to lose you any more than I already had. Even after you ignored all the e-mails I sent you in October, I kept writing, hoping that someday I would hear back. Whenever you were ready. And when your replies nev—'

'What e-mails?' I asked between sniffles.

'My e-mails.'

Wow. CEO of a company, and this is the answer he comes up with. 'What e-mails, Aman? I don't have any e-mails from you.'

'Of course you do. I mean … I sent …'

He opened the e-mail app on his phone and held the screen up for me to see. He scrolled through hundreds of e-mails starting with 'Avani…', followed by a bunch of words that blurred out as he scrolled up and down. I took the phone from him and opened the latest one.

Avani, I don't know when you'll read this, but …

I scrolled through it like it was spam and went up to the top of the page to check the receiver's details.

From: aman.raina@gmail.com

To: letmeluluyourlemons@gmail.com

I looked up from the screen with eyes as wide as I could stretch.

'Where did you get this e-mail?'

'From the feedback form you filled out at the restaurant from our first date.'

'The day you told me you wouldn't have added your actual number in the feedback register of a local bookstore?'

'Yeah.'

'And you believed I would give my actual e-mail id to a restaurant I would never be able to afford going back to? And, an even bigger question, you thought my actual e-mail id is LET ME LULU YOUR LEMONS AT GMAIL DOT COM? You have a business degree from fucking Oxford, Aman! What the actual fuck?'

I threw the phone at him. He quickly moved to catch it while I smacked him on the shoulder, then his chest and was violently about to grab his shirt so I could hulk-smash him, when he held both my wrists and pulled me towards him and picked me up in a bear hug.

I'm not sure if I was laughing or crying in that moment. I buried my head in the collar of his shirt and wrapped my arms tighter around his neck even as he tightened his grip around me like he'd never let me go. And I let myself fall. Hopelessly, tirelessly, mercilessly and endlessly in love—all over again—with this fine, fine specimen of a man.

Finally—yes, finally—the other shoe had dropped. For real this time. There WAS something wrong with him, after all.

letmeluluyourlemons@gmail.com

For fuck's sake.

ACKNOWLEDGEMENTS

Writing this book has been one of the most rewarding and challenging experiences of my life, and I couldn't have done it alone.

To Gurpreet and Sudeep, thank you for always believing in me—especially on the days when I wanted to run in the opposite direction screaming God's name. Your unwavering confidence in me is my greatest strength.

To my beta readers, Sourav and Mansi, who endured terrible drafts, questionable plot decisions and tooo many follow-up phone calls—and still managed to find kind words. Your feedback didn't just improve this story, it kept me from throwing it into the void.

To Mamma, Baba and Vrishank, who forgave me for forgetting important dates, bailing on plans and zoning out mid-conversation because I was mentally rewriting Chapter 27. Your love and blind support is the foundation of every ounce of courage it took me to see this through.

To Poulomi, my editor, who turned my messy drafts into something readable and reminded me (over and over again) that commas are not optional. Your patience is nothing short of heroic, and your guidance made this story shine in ways I never thought possible.

To Ujjaini and Gayatri, for your eagle-eyed editing and proofing magic—and for putting up with my tendency to include three typos every five words.

To ChatGPT, for helping me write this acknowledgements section, because, let's be honest, I had no idea how to do it—and I've never actually read the acknowledgements in any book I've picked up.

And, finally, to you, the reader. Without you, this book is just ink on paper. Thank you for picking it up, for giving these characters a place to live and for making this dream of mine a reality.

ABOUT THE AUTHOR

Prajakta Koli, also known as MostlySane, is one of the most successful digital content creators in India, with over 17 million followers across social media platforms. As an actor, Prajakta is known for her lead role in Netflix India's *Mismatched* and has starred in films such as *Jugjugg Jeeyo* and *Neeyat*, and the upcoming Amazon Prime series *Andhera*. A passionate advocate for social causes, Prajakta serves on the advisory group for Goalkeepers by the Gates Foundation and represents UNDP as its first Youth Climate Champion from India in global summits since 2021, advocating for climate action and sustainability, and representing young voices on global platforms, blending her entertainment success with social impact. She has also featured in Michelle Obama's Daytime Emmy-winning docuseries promoting girls' education. *Too Good to Be True* is her debut novel.

Prajakta lives in Thane, Maharashtra, and can be found on Instagram (@mostlysane), YouTube (MostlySane) and X (@iamMostlySane).

HarperCollins *Publishers* India

At HarperCollins India, we believe in telling the best stories and finding the widest readership for our books in every format possible. We started publishing in 1992; a great deal has changed since then, but what has remained constant is the passion with which our authors write their books, the love with which readers receive them, and the sheer joy and excitement that we as publishers feel in being a part of the publishing process.

Over the years, we've had the pleasure of publishing some of the finest writing from the subcontinent and around the world, including several award-winning titles and some of the biggest bestsellers in India's publishing history. But nothing has meant more to us than the fact that millions of people have read the books we published, and that somewhere, a book of ours might have made a difference.

As we look to the future, we go back to that one word— a word which has been a driving force for us all these years.

Read.